A Dream of Fair Women

'My Dreamer is John Ruskin…'

DONALD MEASHAM

'But whanne I woke al was ceste,
For there nas lady ne creature,
Sauf on the walles old portreiture.'

Chauceres Dreme from the old poem,
A Dream of Fair Women,
of uncertain authorship.

LULU

A Dream of Fair Women:
My Dreamer is John Ruskin

First published 2009

Copyright © Donald Measham

The right of Donald Measham to be identified as the author of this work has been asserted by him in accordance with the Copyright, Designs and Patents Act of 1988.

All rights reserved. No part of this publication may be reproduced, stored or transmitted in any form or by any means, electronic, mechanical or otherwise, without the prior written permission of the copyright owner.

Every effort has been made to trace the ownership of any copyright material used in *A Dream of Fair Women*.

ISBN

978-1-4452-1361-3

A Dream of Fair Women: My Dreamer is John Ruskin

Tennyson re-used the old poem's title, and Burne-Jones made a painting in which Chaucer (1340-1400) is shown dreaming the story. But his authorship is doubtful, the phrase-maker unknown.

For twenty-first century readers, **John Ruskin (1819-1900)** — a world-figure, who influenced Gandhi and Tolstoy, championed Turner and discovered Tintoretto, who taught us how to 'read' a building, whose voice was persuasive in the founding of the British welfare state — this great and odd man, sagacious and childish, the 'reddest of the red' and 'a Tory of the old school', who set up libraries and galleries for working men but never voted in an election, whom Wilde venerated as a stylist and a practical proponent of physical labour for the middle classes, may now seem a strange phenomenon. So much so, that it's quite possible those parts of my narrative which seem plausible are invented, and those things which seem unlikely are true.

One of the odder truths behind the book is the fact that **Ruskin's Fors Clavigera**, his monthly public letters to the workmen of Britain, were given their idiosyncratic collective title in 1871 — *before* his encounter with the working women (here called Betty and Ann), whom Ruskin actually did meet, in 1877. *Fors Clavigera* means, literally, 'Fortune with the Nail' or 'the nail-bearing Fate'…

But as the John Ruskin of the novel and some of my other characters had real-life equivalents, I supply a modicum of verification here and at the end of the book. All conversation and all interchanges with fictionalised characters are invented. However, Effie and Rose's letters and notes have a real basis; and everything which is referred to as having been written by Ruskin — bar letters involving fictitious characters — actually was written by him. That includes the last eleven words of the novel.

A Dream of Fair Women

After 1853	7
Summer 1877	23
Autumn 1877	159
Into Winter 1878	237
End Note	259
Mr Ruskin's Illness…	261
Principal Sources	262
Credits	264

After 1853

1

As they walked together, Ruskin was composing in his head a letter he would never write.

'...I cannot engage in the act of generation lovelessly,' came near the end of it.

Effie, the subject of his meditation, for once caught his attention by a little movement.

'You shiver,' he responded courteously. 'I think you are cold. Do you not have a wrap?'

'Don't put your arm round me like that,' she replied. '— you know I never feel the cold — just because you do. You shan't take away my warmth. You need so many clothes, so much protection' — it was a sort of question, but she did not wait for his answer — 'because you were spoilt and coddled so as a child.'

'You take every occasion to insult me through my parents,' he snarled in his beautiful voice.

2

The thumb and fingers of the figure's right hand are coming together as if to grasp an idea — or moving apart, so as to let something or somebody go. John Ruskin is depicted standing with his hat held low in the left hand, in greeting or valediction. The setting is wild Glenfinlas (not far from modern Gleneagles), the portrait is the famous one by John Everett Millais; begun collaboratively in 1853, finished in silence the year after.

*

Millais had been commissioned by Dr Henry Acland to make a pair of portraits of Mr and Mrs John Ruskin. But, though producing many striking likenesses of Effie — water-colour, pen, pencil, chalk — Millais could not get the design for her large canvas to take.

An ardent twenty-four, he laughed off the setback, made more and more little rapid studies of the mettlesome Effie without taking them further.

'It's just, I suppose,' he said, 'that I'm not cut out for this kind of thing.'

'Nonsense,' said Ruskin, coming over to look, and wiping his brow. He and Millais' elder brother William Henry were engaged in a bout of manual work, of the Ruskinian kind appropriate for the non-labouring classes. The two of them, in their bucket-and-spade way, were seeking to divert a stream to make it less prone to flood.

'Nonsense, Everett,' he repeated, 'you've managed the lady perfectly well before.'

'People thought so,' said Millais, 'but that was in an assumed character. Play-acting, with a backdrop of Highland bricabrac. Mrs Ruskin, in her own self, deserves better than that.'

Ruskin said nothing, but took up a pencil in his soiled hand, and, still standing, lightly added a tree or two and distant crags and turrets to one of Millais' set-aside figure studies.

'I wonder you don't undertake the commission yourself,' said Effie stiffly.

'Not at all, my dear,' replied Ruskin. 'If that kind of thing was ever before me, it's behind me now. I draw only to learn —'

'And to instruct,' said Millais dutifully. He admired both the eloquent critic who had championed his work and the critic's fine wife. He was not yet required to choose between them.

'Instruct? Well, I hope I do sometimes,' said Ruskin, and with a cheery wave went back to the attempt to cut a canal across a tight meander.

Finding occupation for Effie was rather like putting to work an idle part of his own capacity. After five years' cohabitation they were still not one flesh. That they should be of one mind (his own, not hers) was the essential thing. In this Millais was a godsend. He not only freed Ruskin from the possibility of wifely interruptions, but by using her as a model imbued her with usefulness.

Millais thought he had heard Effie utter the word 'insufferable', but kept his eyes down as if to evaluate Ruskin's touched-in background. She, too, kept the silence until Millais referred once more to the compositional problem — 'which your husband has resolved in his own way —'

'Oh, yes,' said Effie, 'my husband always resolves things in his own way.'

Millais, seeming to acknowledge the jibe at Ruskin as a compliment, gave a little nod, continued:

'But I'm not sure that I can work in the way your husband desires. I am finding it difficult to marry this miniaturist detail with, with the bold generalities of Mr Turner.'

Millais' phrasing, his difficulty in 'marrying', took Effie aback for a moment. He, for his part, was confused about what had caused her little confusion. He scratched his head, pen in hand, and spilt a little ink on his pre-Raphaelite curls. Effie, turning her eyes full on him, called him a black sheep and laughed.

'Where?' he replied, smiling like a schoolboy.

'There,' said Effie. 'No, there. Oh, let me!'

She got up and rubbed his head like a young mother. After which — her high colour a little higher than usual — she added, teasing him:

'I'm going to leave you now to your serious business of landscape study or we shall both be in hot water from John, shan't we?'

Millais wanted to demur, but Effie would have none of it, and went off in the direction of their accommodation. He could see her safely nearly all the way back there, and contented himself with watching till she was out of sight, for he knew she'd not want to be fussed.

*

Ruskin had kept his own gondola in Venice, but (being of Scottish stock) felt himself entitled, if not obliged, to live frugally in Caledonia. The lodgings which he had taken for himself, his wife and the painter consisted of a small anteroom and a single long bedroom; at each end of which was a box-bed.

connected. He had claimed from the beginning that the two modes, having truth in common, shared the same tradition; had wanted it to be so. Voices in opposition had asked for the evidence. They would have it — in the Glenfinlas portrait.

Millais had by now understood what Ruskin was after, and grew in confidence. He worked steadily, but, as the days went by, with a lessening of his personal regard for Ruskin— though rather the opposite for the skill of the man: whose finished study of gneiss rock turned out to be not only a fine exemplar, but an extraordinary painting in its own right. However, he could not but blame the husband for what little he had come to understand of Effie's marital situation.

Her breathing when asleep, which alternated with a sleepless rustling from her — this continuum of sound kept him awake; amplified as it was by the contraption, almost a little house, in which she slept. The box-bed acted like the sounding board of a stringed instrument. He and she seemed to be sending messages to one another, over or around the Ruskin bachelor couch: the sense of her body and his in the night in the same bed-contraptions.

Nevertheless the work on the figure of Ruskin, with its Turneresque rocks and tumbling waters continued to hold the interest of both the painter and the critic.

*

The weather broke and Millais' mind was in a turmoil not merely from his sympathetic observations, but from certain further thoughts which Effie had now – suddenly — trusted him with; so — vowing to return to Glenfinlas next year to complete the landscape part of the painting — he went, back to London. There he had more commissions than he could cope with, but continued to labour in his then painstaking manner in order to curb thoughts of Effie's dilemma — which had taken over that part of his mind where formerly fanciful plans for pictures had been projected.

3

Effie had not forgotten Millais' sympathy for her divulged 'unhappiness' — she had disclosed to him little more than that single word. Emboldened by the experience of his support, and miserable without his presence, she finally spoke to Elizabeth Eastlake — Lady Eastlake, wife of the Director of the National Gallery — who imputed the worst of motives to Ruskin, and put them in writing; which observations were enclosed in the letter which Effie sent to her father, George Gray, on 7th March 1854:

'...I have therefore simply to tell you that I do not think I am John Ruskin's wife at all — and I entreat you to get me released from the unnatural position in which I stand to him — To go back to the day of my marriage on 10th of April 1848. I went as you know away to the Highlands — I had never been told the duties of married persons to each other and knew little or nothing about their relations in the closest union on earth.'

*

For the last ten months things had been worse than before. Other husbands, she had begun to realise, either loved their wives or kept them quiet by giving them children. She had tackled John about it last May, on her birthday.

Ruskin had been unimpressed by Effie's anniversary. Yet she had now turned twenty five, the age at which he'd declared he would physically make her his wife.

Hard and brave as it was for her to do so, she asked him to make her happy.

'In what respect?' replied Ruskin, to gain time.

'As a bride,' she said.

'You have been — indeed, you still are — a bride,' he said, obtusely.

'Happy — as a mother,' she said.

He had his answer about the act of generation ready, pat. But he could not speak it. He had always thought of it as a letter. And he saw it was not the whole truth: he had learned from Rousseau how to take the edge off his desire – any desire that there was. There were things about her – though she looked well enough when she was dressed to go out.

Ruskin urged patience. He had his work, she had her beauty — both should be carried forward unimpaired to the edge of middle age:

'I am not myself vain about my person — you used to tease me about my lack of concern with fashion — yet there are still some who would call us as a handsome couple. How odd of them! But isn't that enough for you? You have a generous allowance — and you come and go as you please, un-chaperoned.'

Effie bit her lip, guessing the turn of his thoughts. He continued as expected:

'And you should remember all the jewels you had — more, it seemed to me, than any other woman in Venice! Until you let your fine Austrian friends, your fine Italian friends, your fine English military relieve you of them. No, no, I'm not going to upbraid you for keeping company with thieves — no, I'm not — not even in respect of those operatic threats directed at me (a scandal which brought my father and mother to the brink of distraction) when I tried to get your property back.'

Effie turned aside. He wanted the credit of a peace-maker, but hoped she would go away:

'Come, Effie,' he continued in a kindly tone and with a smile, 'at least, I've always looked after you — done my best to ensure that your hands aren't idle. You can't say I haven't. If you've completed the various projects I outlined for you, perhaps I might cast an eye over your diary or the accounts.'

Effie, knowing her paperwork would be imperfect, would have none of that: returned to the subject of children.

'Am I to understand,' said Ruskin, 'that you are incapable of exercising self-control?'

'Do I have the opportunity of doing otherwise?' said Effie.

'You'd betray me then, would you?' said Ruskin, seizing his opportunity. 'If I hadn't got better things to do, I'd engage to force some sense into you. I'll tell you what you need — you need a father confessor rather than a husband. That's what you need — to give you a spiritual hammering. I've a good mind to get us both converted to Romanism — that would be a way of teaching you.'

'Ah,' said Effie, seizing her opportunity too, 'But wouldn't such a conversion — a change of religion in that particular direction — prove to be the death of both your honoured father and your devoted mother?'

'How dare you, madam,' turning on her, 'speak lightly of my parents — even, to your shame, of their Protestantism!'

'I'll speak as I wish,' she said, not cringing. 'I'm sick of the whole batch of Ruskins, if you must know.'

*

After which neither she nor Ruskin, in their separate rooms, had recourse to tears, but sought calm — an uneasy calm — through re-working old gripes; adding new notes to old notes of the other's cruelty and silliness.

Ruskin recorded further examples of Effie's dereliction of her duties, both housewifely and secretarial, while Effie continued to pick over the evidence of John Ruskin's total lack of concern for her, or for anyone — except his wretched mother and father. It was Effie's misfortune to live with a milksop, a spoilt child.

'Poor Effie,' she said aloud. Then shushed herself like a little girl, though keeping up her quiet, intermittent, solitary chatter: 'Poor Effie…Look at this.' *This* consisted of scattered references (in a tiny private notebook) to the all-demanding mama, old Mrs Ruskin and her daily letters to her son; with the requirement that he respond to them in writing, all of them, at the time, at once. Write daily to an old woman who lived a few doors away!

'Her to the life,' she promised her notebook. 'Listen to this.' Then read quietly out loud in a special voice: *'Pray write us directly a long account of your health, your pulse, meals and sleep, perspiration etc.'*

After which, she added a note to her parody:
This kind of thing comes nearly every day interspersed with lines from Mrs R in a style almost of amatory tenderness, calling John her beloved and Heart's Treasure and a variety of other titles.

And then she started to pack an overnight bag. Only to unpack it again. She would wait until after Glenfinlas.

*

But after that, and with Lady Eastlake's written support, Effie packed her bag once more. This time she did not unpack it until she was safely home.

*

Ruskin said nothing in public about his wife's departure, but presented himself privately as the unfortunate victim of public injury; reacting angrily to Lady Eastlake's assertion that he had engineered a liaison between Effie and Millais. (He could not directly state, by way of refutation, that Millais' art was too precious for it to be constrained by such a burdensome woman as Effie.) If only that Italian scoundrel had taken the lady along with her jewels, both Millais and himself would have been free. Yet, instead of blackening the name of Effie who had deserted him, Ruskin took on himself all the public blame, and went off quietly on holiday with his mother and father.

*

Gathering what had occurred and something of what Effie had had to say, Millais wrote to Effie's mother, broke with Ruskin — but not with his commitment to the portrait. As he had promised, he returned to Glenfinlas and completed the work, though without the exchange of a single word between artist and sitter. The finished painting was swiftly despatched into the care of Dr Acland, as Ruskin's father had threatened to put a knife through it. That it bore the image of his adored son in his famousness might in any case have prevented him from doing so.

*

On 15 July 1855 John Everett Millais was married to Euphemia Chalders Gray; Effie Gray, 'still a Spinster but since falsely called Ruskin', having been granted a Decree of Nullity twelve months previously.

The decree was granted on account of Ruskin's 'incurable impotency'. His sworn statement to the effect that he had offered, and Effie had refused, sexual congress was withheld — possibly out of generosity, possibly to effect an escape.

4

Thereafter Millais' virility and Effie's fertility was as regularly demonstrated as human biology allowed. Seven healthy children were born in the first ten years of their marriage.

So Millais was in need of money. He painted hard – and, some would say, sloppily. He abandoned time-consuming Pre-Raphaelite principles. Working in a freer and more cost-effective manner he went on to claim annual earnings of around £200,000.

Ruskin, on the contrary, had set about dissipating a similar capital sum — the inheritance from his wine-merchant father — on quirky social schemes and utopian projects. He had also taken on a first female pupil, Miss Rose La Touche.

He was forty, she was ten. Eight years after they first met he proposed marriage. Effie heard of it and became alarmed.: if Ruskin were to marry, were fit to marry, the grounds of her own annulment, 'his incurable impotency', might be thrown into doubt. She took legal advice – probably not the best legal advice – fearing for the legitimacy of her offspring.

Word of that spread: Rose La Touche's mother wrote to Effie asking for her views on the suitability of Ruskin as a husband for her daughter. Unsurprisingly, Effie responded with a letter which was designed to damage Ruskin and protect Rose. The letter, which destroyed the pair of them, is lost — and even in a fiction had best remain lost.

On its receipt, Mrs La Touche, a good mother, advised her daughter to break with Ruskin and to effect a return of all correspondence. Both parties complied – more or less – with great suffering on her part, and anger and bitterness on his.

Six years later – six years of what we would guess to be anorexia, together with what Ruskin saw as religious mania – Rose was failing, fading. Mrs La Touche eased her prohibitions and embargoes; and there were possibilities of a meeting. Poor real Rose, suffering all the ill-fortune of a Hardy heroine, set out on a make-or-break rail journey to find him again. And not having read Mrs Gaskell[1], she had not even the idea of a last straw of technology to assist her in her attempt to visit Ruskin and his family.

…A starved Rose La Touche, almost a spirit presence already – is striving to write in a jolting train. She saw it as her final throw of the dice, her one chance to see and make peace with John Ruskin in Herne Hill, London – when, banally, there was no one home.

*

A little ghost of her sits alone in a first class compartment without a maid and with no luggage. It wishes it could lift up and let down the heavy strap which holds the carriage window open at the top.

The steam continues to drift in from the dark and the noise of the rails to redouble itself as the train slows and clanks towards Crewe, in whose abominable precincts (for she has missed the through-train) she will have to await her Holyhead connection; and so resume her interminable journeying to Ireland and then back again to Tunbridge Wells and London. There to miss not only Ruskin, but all his household too – they having just popped out, while he, the Professor, is at Oxford for his Michaelmas lectures.

---

[1] 'They… remembered his starting up and cursing himself for not having sooner thought of the electric telegraph', Ch. 34, *North and South*, 1854-5.

She is trying to write in the train[1] — because there she has privacy — through all the lurching of the motion. She has returned Ruskin's lovely letters in sadness and anger and required the return of hers — bar one. Has sent him no others — nothing else to occupy the rosewood box he may or may not have thrown away.

In or out of the world, she is alone. Knowing nothing or almost nothing. Understanding only that a blight has got at the stalk of her life that can never be outgrown.

She cannot tell whether anything has been said. There may or may not be permission one day for her to have a bit of a letter from him now and again. She cannot tell whether he has forgiven her.

For consolation she has only a rose in her jacket — or the scent of a rose — plucked, with everybody out, from the garden of his house at Herne Hill.

She lowers her head to the flower and — if that is all that is left for her — resolves not to let it go. The scent of her name.

---

[1] Rose's letter is reproduced in *Ruskin: the Last Chapter*, pp 30-31.

Summer 1877

1

The June sky was black and Ruskin could make no sense of his Turners. They had lost their looks — or he had lost his looking. That occurred, and recurred after Rose's death.

Yet there had, after all, been a reconciliation. She had somehow found her way to Herne Hill again; found him not at home once more – the difference being that this time she waited shyly and successfully for his return. Then she put up at hotels in Paddington and elsewhere and they talked of opening a teashop together.

But her health was broken. She was travelling backwards and forwards to Ireland and back again. He followed. She still insisted there were no marriages in Heaven. ('You'll know when you get there, Rosie,' he said, 'but that won't be yet awhile.' 'You know it will, St C' – the old pet name – 'let's talk some more about tea.')

Ruskin made a deathbed sketch of her, seen from above. Rose's hair, very long, stretches out upwards, flattened, bizarre – for whatever ease against the heat of it she could achieve. Two equilateral triangles of it, flat on the pillow behind her; faery ears, great eyes and a tiny unused mouth. He drew her drawn face, tried to draw her into him.

She looked, poor thing, like a stranded mermaid, but with no more flesh on her than a fish – one with many bones – a flat fish such as a skate.

She was interested only in what St Peter would have to say to her. On marriage and Heaven she and Ruskin achieved no accord.

He was agitated. Her mind was gone. Rose La Touche had slipped away from him. An unsuccessful teashop briefly opened.

*

Now he was fifty eight and had been on a pilgrimage — not to the La Touche mausoleum in Ireland where his dead love lay — but to the (as he saw it) Idea, spirit or form of her in Venice. There he had spent many weeks studying and meditating upon the image of a fourth-century saint, as depicted by a quattrocento painter; in making a scrupulous watercolour version of Carpaccio's *Dream of St Ursula*. According to legend, she and her eleven thousand virgins (though Carpaccio couldn't find room for them all) had been martyred by Diocletian.

Ruskin saw about-to-die Ursula as the picture of life, as a girl in a dream, a dreaming girl; dreaming in her simple chamber, with her sabots by her bed. He was taken, too, by her nose, a straight nose like Rose's. Rosie-posy's. And dead Rosie wasn't idle. It was Rosie herself who had sent him messages in Venice, by tricks of light, by the gift of a dianthus, by turning a page in the breeze. And all this strangeness he put to rational use, just as he had learnt about good health from his own illnesses.

The perceived blackness for example he knew to be a sign of heightened sanity. A glimpse of black truth and confirmation of blackness. Of destruction of all the old ways of life by steam-powered industry which had altered the weather. The mossy banks were cindered, the buttercups and nightingales at risk; and the sun was no longer to be had in Summer. If there *was* any sun he could no longer see it; neither that nor his magically luminous water-colours, his Turners. Which proved that the world was in a bad state and getting worse. How could the inhabitants of such a world be the judge of anything whatsoever?

He and the weather, he and the world, were best kept apart. Cousin Joan Severn was his dragon when callers came to the mouth of his London cave — the doorstep of his old parental house at Herne Hill where the Severns lived — leaving half-eaten heads and skeleton rib-cages on display, as in Carpaccio's picture of St George.

Joan coddled him and told him Scottish ghost stories.

Delight in their dark humour brought about a temporary equilibrium. Joan told him the one about the lowland carl changed by a witch into a cat and the scrapes he got into — before winning back his human shape, save for the one night of each year when he once more took on feline form.

'Miaow,' said Ruskin appreciatively, eyeing his cats. The wrong cat came: his favourite was two or three hundred miles away, at Brantwood. 'They say Tootles inspects the coach house every day to see if I've come back. Does she really?'[1] Joan confirmed that was so. After which, he tickled a couple of his other cats behind the ears, gave his cousin's elbow a squeeze and cheerfully retired to his childhood bedchamber in what had been his father's house.

*

The morning found everything spoilt again. His Turners had as usual (unlike the cat) been transported from the Lakes via Kendall to greet him in Herne Hill. Usually they brought him great joy. Yesterday morning they had abruptly ceased to be visionary. Today he feared that this double deprivation — in themselves and for the observer — might have become permanent.

Fearful alternatives for him, therefore. Either his capacity to perceive beauty had fled, or the pictures had never had any beauty in the first place — and, if so, all of his voluminous writings were

---

[1] The cat was female, according to Arthur Severn, op cit, p129.

25

based upon a falsehood. Ineffectual contemplation of this dilemma appeared to occupy an entire day. Yet several pieces of complicated correspondence were dashed off in a minute or two.

Simultaneously all sorts of business was taken on, and all sorts of business put off. Days flicked and lingered by — as days did that year.

*

By the 22nd June things had stabilised: his art collection was beginning — albeit slowly — to reassume its identity. He recorded in his journal 'Some broken sunshine' by noon. The observation was more than meteorological: other things were broken too. Ruskin patted his pocket, touched his broken heart, took out the gold plates which encased the emblem of it, as if he were an Aztec plucking the live organ from his breast or waistcoat and placing it like a repeater watch on his work table.

He did not open the letter which the plates of gold preserved, a precious letter returned to him only two years ago in consequence of a spiritualist experience. He sought to abstain from its perusal as much as possible in order to protect the fragile hinged thing that the folded paper had become. Instead, he pronounced each syllable it contained from heart, uttering each separate sound aloud as if each one were a poem. A heartbreaking poem, though not at all on the subject of heartbreak — a hymn to young happiness and delight. He carefully set the paper back in the plates, breathed upon them hard and close and watched the mist of his devotion fade away from edge to centre.

Her relics on earth — the early precious letters — retained the younger Rose's quirkiness and mischief, and the capacity for mortal love which had eluded them both. St Ursula, on the other hand, was Rosie transfigured — sainted Rose La Touche, yes; but also, stable, emblematic, and no longer the agent and patient of her own punitive fundamentalism.

He was suddenly angry with her. Whatever she'd supposed, she was waiting for him in Heaven. But what would happen if they weren't able to agree the basis of their reunion? Was it possible to quarrel in Heaven?

He continued in rather a rage at her for the rest of the day, but accomplished – as he always did – some business; and when it was time to retire he was at ease with her again. Or his idea of her. He kissed the gold plates and placed them beneath his pillow. He was up and down. Sometimes caught by spontaneous glee. Sometimes dependent on those disciplines and rituals which were the successors of the huge biblical recitations which his mother had required of him from infancy.

He had been down, in various senses. He was now up. A rapid water-colour sketch of the dawn's barred clouds went well and unthreateningly, and the daily memorisation of Plato without flaw and within the allotted time. Ruskin found a reassuring recognition of something familiar — not in the climate, for when there wasn't blackness there were disturbing summer flashes — but in his own identity. Nothing to do with fame, nothing to do with all that he had managed without noticing since his return from Europe — a little visiting, a little theatre, and all the fidgety detail of property law to safeguard St George's Guild — forgotten amongst the successive depressions and elations. It was as if he had been introduced to himself and discovered that the two persons had met before, had even known one another very well. He moved the gold plates from under his pillow to his pocket, ready for when he went out; shifted his tongue over his front teeth and was conscious, as always, of the ripple in the inner flesh where the family dog had bitten through his upper lip and spoiled his infant good looks.

Conscious of the child within him, unchanged from that child — coddled by the father, whipped by the mother — he stepped out, as if to preach the sermon 'people be good', which he had delivered as a four-year-old quasi-Jesus-in-the-Temple. His mother had dedicated him to God before he was born. His father had meant him for an eminent divine.

The father was dead, the son had undergone a religious de-conversion. He gave secular sermons now — the method impromptu, conversational — in secular temples. Such as the new Grosvenor Gallery in the West End, which had opened for the first time while Ruskin was still abroad. This was his first visit.

Some had wondered at the effrontery of Sir Coutts Lindsay in installing as the main entrance to his gallery a Palladian doorway removed from the Venetian church of Santa Lucia. Ruskin, on the other hand, thought Venice well rid of it.

He glanced up at the glum classical visage on the keystone as he entered:

'Poor Renaissance stuff,' he declared, 'it looks very much at home in New Bond Street.'

*

From the first, Sir Coutts Lindsay's gallery in New Bond Street was attractive to ladies. It was not merely that its owner was reckoned the handsomest man in London, there were other reasons beside his hooded eyes, his wings of hair, his velvet jackets. Nor even was it the possible presence of his antithesis, the flinchingly assertive Professor Ruskin — though when *he* was there, the buzz of young things about him was like that which emanated from the autumnal flowers of old ivy.

'Mrs Lavenham,' called out the professor, catching sight of Sir Coutts Lindsay leading the lady-artist into his gallery.

She looked about her rather wildly — Sir Coutts Lindsay still half in attendance.

'Mrs Lavenham,' Ruskin continued, 'I have the happiest recollection of our last conversation at the Water Colour Society.'

'I too,' she agreed with a smile — confounding the vanity which had allowed her to linger in the entrance hall until Sir Coutts himself could catch sight of her — when her needs were quite other than having a fine gentleman to take her arm; and she married barely a year.

'I shall die,' said Charlotte Lavenham to herself, as Sir Coutts Lindsay's handsome eye released her and Ruskin took her hand, 'I shall die.'

Ruskin looked at her with disappointment. So much so that Charlotte feared she might have upset the distinguished critic by a crazed or improper mutter.

In fact, her conditioning had held good in adversity. The words she feared might have passed her lips had remained unuttered. Those to which she had given voice were:

'I hope very much that we may resume our talk, Professor Ruskin. But for the moment, I must ask you to excuse me. There is something which I hope to show you.'

He would, she knew, think she meant a drawing.

'Delighted,' he said. And Charlotte Lavenham sped away and downstairs.

This was the other reason for the Grosvenor Gallery's popularity with well-to-do females, it was one of the few public places in London where they could use the lavatory without embarrassment. But not on this occasion. The pain within Mrs Lavenham's bladder had become keener from anticipation of its easement, and now she found the cubicle occupied, the door fastened. It could have been worse, for Lady Lindsay after the mishaps at the opening, had thoughtfully set several washstands against the wall, in each of which was a chamber pot. Charlotte took one thankfully behind one of the screens — with its Eastern figuring — and, her clothes being loose and light in lady-artist's fashion, was enabled with some expedition to relieve herself. She placed the coverlet supplied over the contents of the pot and took herself back to the washbasin where she poured a little cold water over her hands and reflected on the looking-glass.

The high collar and the puffed sleeves became her, though the apple cheeks of her girlhood were gone; a loss accompanied, she feared, by a certain gauntness about the jaw. She touched her lower cheek. Something helpful was happening here since her marriage. In another woman, she might have said there was a hint of sensuality in the face, for the eyes — the eyes of her craft — were quick to judge. They looked well, too — the heavy-lidded, observant half-moons. Not too dissatisfied with what self-scrutiny said to her, Mrs Lavenham rearranged her hat and wondered what she should say to Professor Ruskin. Perhaps he wouldn't recall that she was to return with something to delight his eye; perhaps he would respond well to a skittish, 'another time, dear Mr Ruskin, another time.'

Charlotte Lavenham remained irresolute. At which point great jangling and rushing from the water closet led to the presence by her of a pretty girl — curls escaping from her bonnet, a heart-shaped face and a straight nose — a little like (for Charlotte was aware of Ruskin's obsession), if not St Ursula herself, then a minor maiden out of Carpaccio.

'I am so sorry, madam, if I have seemed to monopolise the facility. I came out in a hurry and was in any case nervous. My mother was to have accompanied me, but being at the last minute indisposed, allowed me to come with just the maid.'

Mrs Lavenham smiled and gestured that she was quite finished with the wash basin and looking-glass, using which would allow the girl to compose herself.

Those who knew the girl — or young lady — and her family would not have said she took after her mother. But today she was anxious — about her mother's anxiety for her, though calming herself in the company of Mrs Lavenham. For a moment or two, she continued her explanation:

'She — Alice that is — was supposed to walk round the gallery with me, for I don't have sisters or anything like that. And then — though she's dressed so that no one would know she's the maid — she wouldn't come in. Insisted on staying outside — I should have guessed she would, I suppose. "No, miss, " she said, "don't ask me to go in there." And now I think I must go back to her and leave for home, since I'm afraid I, too, have lost my courage.'

She did not add, though Mrs Lavenham guessed, that the young lady had just endured great humiliation and awkwardness with her fashionable crinolette in the closet, which gave the apparently simple dress a front like the bow of a ship, a back like the brow of a dolphin.

'No, no,' said Mrs Lavenham, ' you must not think of it. I am used to these assemblies, do not be intimidated by them. Most of those present understand very little of what is displayed for their attention. My name is Charlotte Lavenham and —' she still felt a little breathless — 'just been talking to Professor Ruskin. And I promised to show him something. He thought I meant a painting, but haven't got one. But, you see, you're the very thing!'

'How do you mean, Mrs Lavenham, the very thing? My name, by the way, is Claire — Claire Stott.'

'Claire Stott. He'll like that too. Tell me, Miss Stott, do you draw?'

'Oh not really Mrs Lavenham. Well, ever so little.'

'Ever so little? Ever so little in quantity — or ever so little in quality?'

'Thank you for putting it in that way. The quantity is ample, but the quality is not such as would interest a lady — a practitioner, for I think I've seen your name — let alone someone like Professor Ruskin.'

'Don't worry,' said Charlotte, looking in the mirror again — at them both, ' it won't come to that. Not yet at least. Don't think of leaving — why should you? And Alice must wait — she'll be glad of having nothing to do, why shouldn't she? No, my dear, take my arm. As I say, I am in need of you to explain my absence.'

Claire, now that it was settled that she should meet Professor Ruskin, felt that haste was incumbent.

'No, my dear Miss Stott, you must learn to dawdle. A certain languor in a gallery doesn't look thoughtless, you know. On the contrary, for one should be on nodding terms with the principal exhibits.'

Claire took her time from Charlotte Lavenham as they ascended the spacious staircase.

'This, for instance, Miss Stott,' for they had reached the top and seen it looming, ' is the work of Professor Massim — of Rome, no less — *Cleopatra*. It's reckoned very fine, but I can't much care for it.'

Claire agreed that her own regard for the work was also limited. *Education Maternelle* by Eugene Delaplanche in the great West Gallery was better, but, Claire would have preferred a less prescriptive title.

'I like, you see, I expect it's naïve of me, to make up my own stories about a picture — but...and, oh yes, as you say, the qualities of the brushwork.'

Then, to the right, up to the East Gallery — and there was Ruskin (a slightly stooping unbearded figure, in an old-fashioned frock coat) disappointingly disregarding the Tissots ('vulgar photographs') which Claire had wished to inspect.

He seemed to recognise Charlotte's footsteps and drew himself up on legs long for his height, and away from a Watts portrait of a dwarfish woman. He had bright blue eyes and a loose tie to match them.

'Deplorable,' he said, 'as ugly as a Goya without the saving grace of Spanish malignity... But who,' he broke off, straightening up, and growing younger, 'might this young lady be? Please, Mrs Lavenham, do not keep her as a secret to yourself.'

The introductions effected — his eyes were his best feature, Claire decided — Ruskin became assiduous in his attention to Claire and rather more generous in his critical observations. He caught up in an indicative glance not only a prettier thing by Watts near at hand but the Lindsays themselves at the further end of the room:

'It has to be said that Sir Coutts Lindsay's own portrait of his wife offers more in the way of character than Watts' party-piece. A view which I shall make no secret of. But, I have further observations in reserve — reservations to observe, in fact — in case Sir Coutts should think I seek to ingratiate myself —'

Charlotte Lavenham smiled a sceptical smile.

'You are right, Mrs Lavenham. You know me too well. I'm not likely to set out to talk myself into anyone's good books — save (for I know myself even better) save in the presence of, forgive me Miss Stott, some young lady who is unusually charming.'

Claire was pleased that the duties of young ladies did not extend beyond the receiving of compliments to the giving of them. For she preferred to tell the truth. And the truth, as she saw it, was that there was something loose, almost unformed about the middle of Ruskin's face, though his brows were strong and craggy, a good setting for the flashing eyes.

The practised Mrs Lavenham had no such honest problem. She and Ruskin were conspirators in a harmless procurement. It did not matter that Miss Stott probably found him slightly unprepossessing. The Professor was sensitive to such things, and would put himself out to be entertaining.

That his eyesight — hitherto extraordinarily keen — was for the first time causing some trouble was evident to Mrs Lavenham, when she saw uncertainties in the posture of his head, in the way he positioned himself to view an exhibit. However, the beginnings of difficulty in this respect did not in the least inhibit his opinions:

'No,' said Ruskin, though there was nothing to controvert, 'Sir Coutts Lindsay has used his money to handsome purpose — too handsome. For, while (as I have said) his own painting shows taste, his notion of furnishing a gallery in which to present the work of others serves to draw attention, vulgarly, to the generosity of his patronage — that is to say, to his expenditure. Let me show you how his hideous crimson hangings detract from what is noble in noble work (though I grant they may serve to offset meanness in other exhibits).

Claire hoped Professor Ruskin was not referring unfavourably to the Tissots, but forbore to ask.

'See,' said Ruskin, moving to the wall where eight examples of Edward Burne-Jones' work were hung together, 'See how my poor Ned suffers. Though the hideous trappings may be thought by some to offset the crude display of Whistler (from whose abandoned daubs you were best advised to avert your eyes).'

He shielded his blue eyes stagily, then cupped his hands binocular-wise to encompass as little of the scarlet hangings and as much of the works of his friend Ned as possible.

Images of Maria Zambaco, Burne-Jones' Greek mistress, were not entirely absent from the banquet of art — Ruskin interposed his person between *The Beguiling Of Merlin* and the ladies, and made no comment on the snake-haired Nimuë's power to bewitch, even in paint. She had, fortunately, been overtaken as a model, and was here outnumbered by, the chaperoned English rose: Frances Graham. That is to say, Frances Grahams in the plural: standing, sitting, right-profile, left-profile, three-quarter-face, full-face, neck-to-nape.

Acceptable idolatry. As Michelangelo mythologised the Medici, as Rubens set James I on Inigo Jones' ceiling in Whitehall, so did Burne-Jones etherealise the healthy daughters of prosperous manufacturers.

Ruskin led them past a set of winged maidens bearing baubles to Burne-Jones's *Mirror Of Venus*, exhibited here for the first time. Frances Graham in seven persons balletically peering, seven to the right and two to the left of a Venus, re-touched so that the notorious Zambaco was effaced by the Uffizi Botticelli.

I had,' he said, 'the pleasure of seeing this work both in its earlier stages and its completed state in Mr Jones's studio. Its splendid muted colours — I still have Carpaccio's images imprinted on my retina (not merely my mind's eye) from my recent Venetian sojourn – where their subtleties could not be disfigured by Sir Coutts' raw red. It's as if he had meant to turn Ned's Venus into a scarlet woman…

'But, ladies, I would like, if we may, to undertake a small experiment. Nine maidens — yes? — Nine Miss Grahams, a friend of mine, under the instruction of a, shall we say, eclectic Venus. One of them is still attending to the goddess's words — so, eight maidens are peering into Venus's celestial lily-pond. You cannot see because of light from windows on the glass? I do not wonder. This is not so much Venus's Mirror as Venus's Fly-trap, a carnivorous looking-glass that eats fair creatures whole. Please, step forward.'

Mrs Lavenham a shade resignedly, and Claire Stott, by now full of smiles, did so:

'You will be able to discern from your new standpoint, eight — seven maidens peering (for the one on the far right seems indecisive); and, behind them, this landscape of great, mountainous dry valleys. Seven of them peering into this geologically unsound, though magically acceptable, lough or tarn. Of those seven maidens, four have cast their images full upon the waters, one partially — that of Venus herself being obscured by water-lilies...'

'Now,' said Ruskin, 'were these four ladies to walk away from their reflections, what do you feel would happen to those faces in the water?'

'Why,' said Claire, quite boldly, for she still liked this kind of fancy, 'why — they would remain there in place, in the water, on the canvas — as they are, I do believe.'

'Very good,' said Ruskin, 'very good, Miss Stott. Now, then for our experiment. A further step forward, please. You, too, Mrs Lavenham. I have in mind — yes, from my viewpoint you have it. Not quite? I wish to have, to the left, Miss Stott; to the right, Mrs Lavenham — to have both of your living faces superimposed on this wretched reflective glass. Yes, in the water. Just above the forget-me-nots on the margin of the little mere. Just so. What do you think of that now?'

Mrs Lavenham put into polite words that she thought the exercise might prove profitless.

'I grant,' said Ruskin, 'that the reflections of your faces (returned to you from a vertical plane unlike the maidens' horizontal mere) are right side up — in opposition to Ned's facing-upwards necks.'

He began to laugh, an immoderate laugh, and Mrs Lavenham recollected that he had been ill and was worried for him.

'But,' said Ruskin, 'that is the view of anatomical pedants only. For everyone else it is the animation of a dream, the realisation of a fairy-tale, and ' — he bowed — 'charmingly enacted. I wish you now, ladies, to move away from the painting, never looking back at it — though (as I said before) protecting your eyes from the adjacent daubs by the fraudster, Whistler.

'Beautifully done. Now, I will put a proposition to you: that (on condition that you keep to the instructions I have just given) that the fair faces of you, Mrs Lavenham, and of you, Miss Stott, will permanently replace those of two of Madame Venus's company.'

Claire Stott, won over by Ruskin, clapped her hands in pleasure as she was walking away; only to be caught looking back (checking the cut of her gown in the looking-glass pictures, rather than emulating Eurydice or Lot's wife) which — said the Professor soberly — proved the correctness of his story: the magic image had been broken. Claire, nevertheless, fancied that a touch of her gown still twinkled on the glass. She could see it, she really could.

*

Ruskin, his performance concluded, bade them good day. He settled to making a note about the eighth Burne-Jones, a study of St George — 'handling very free. Exhibited as "unfinished". Why so? Answer: St George's work is never complete!' Meaning that of his partly-established Guild of St George: with its wonderful and dotty, retrogressively radical, utopian notions.

After which Ruskin went in search of his host, Sir Coutts Lindsay to take his leave of him – and to apprise him that, while applauding Sir Coutts and Lady Lindsay's initiative in providing the new gallery, he, Professor Ruskin of the Oxford Drawing School, thought its pink hangings were unfortunate; as were (and far more so) the alleged paintings offered for sale by Mr Whistler – 'work' which was the close kin of idleness…And yet here they were, and with an asking price of 200 guineas!

*

Claire and Charlotte Lavenham were continuing to look and talk and over-hear. Claire, in her inexperience, began to be concerned that Alice might expect her to have emerged from the exhibition by now. Mrs Lavenham, however, took the view that she should be kept waiting in the interest of young ladies' freedom of action.

'I am coming to believe you are right,' said Claire, 'I must learn to be more assertive. But here — and I can see this is one of the intentions of such a place, I do feel more at home than in most public gatherings. Perhaps that is because — and this must please you, Mrs Lavenham? — lady-artists are well represented in the display. I should like to know whether Professor Ruskin approves or disapproves of that development. I felt too awkward to mention it when we were talking together.'

'You may well have other opportunities, my dear. But you will have need to frame your question with care. I do know, for instance, that Professor Ruskin believes oil colours are best avoided by ladies.'

'Oh, and why is that? Is it because he fears for our pretty clothes? If so, one — they — could always wear an apron.'

'Professor Ruskin would, I think, prefer them to be pretty aprons. And then the same objections would apply. But really I fear it goes deeper than that; and to be fair to him, for all the skill of his hand and the knowledge of his eye, he himself shows only water-colours — and then not for their own sake, but for some educative purpose. It is rather that he does not think of the profession of an artist (and to work in oils is to set out one's stall as a professional) as appropriate for a lady; the life of the *atelier*, that is — let alone the life-class!'

'But, Mrs Lavenham, you are an artist. A married artist. Do you share a studio with your husband? Mightn't that make the way of life more generally accepted?'

Charlotte laughed: 'Heaven forbid that married people should have no escape from one another,' she said. 'No, studio co-habitation wouldn't suit either of us. In any case, my husband is a writer — we do not compete, you see. He was known before I had made any appearance on the scene, but since our marriage he has ventured into other literary work with a view to my illustrating it. That is my principal occupation at present, though I do receive some regular small commissions.'

They exchanged cards.

'But,' said Claire thoughtfully, 'For a lady artist to be (please excuse me) at best an illustrator, or more likely only an illustration...?'

'Even to be Miss Frances Graham peering into Venus's mirror?'

'No, not even that. I'd rather be the artist than the model. (Though I do now feel I've met Miss Graham, and am glad to know her.) I am a fidget, you see. I couldn't sit still for long enough for Mr Jones or anyone else to do his work properly. It'd be better if the gentleman sat still while I wore my pencil away, ineffectual though my attempt would be...'

She had unconsciously lowered her voice as some conversation from the artistic world came upon their ears.

'Oh yes, she painted too,' a shaggy-looking gentleman was saying to a hollow-cheeked auditor. 'Had, she claimed, a better eye than her old man. And, talking of eyes, when they quarrelled' — Claire could see a nudge over the edge of her catalogue — 'she used to paint them out of his work in the studio, his portraits, whatever — like the ancient iconoclasts, you know. Poke their eyes out because she couldn't get at his. Fill the spaces where their eyes had been very neatly in black. Blind his society beauties…'

Claire and Charlotte shuddered and resumed their conversation. They moved on and around, and talked a little more to Professor Ruskin, who had lingered. He spoke now of false notes in painting — 'bogus "musical" titles, quantities of base coin', and 'paint-pots' — which Claire did not follow.

Seeing she was nonplussed by his rehearsal of what he intended to write about Whistler in the next issue of *Fors*,[1] Ruskin turned to the kind of homily at which he was very skilled, along with an affectionate but imprecise invitation. As he did so, the shadow of man with an eye-glass — a shadow with a glint — went over the threshold of the room and stopped short: whether to look again at his own work, or even to prepare to meet the Professor — who was about to perpetrate a famous libel.

*

Claire wanted to leave now while the memory of all this was fresh in her mind — though she had somehow managed to catch no more than a glimpse of the Tissots. Mrs Lavenham went with her

---

[1] *Fors Clavigera*. See page 3, above.

to the cloakroom, because she once again needed to visit the lavatory, though she had taken no liquid at the gallery.

Charlotte could only suppose it was something to do with being married, with the attentions of her husband. He, Herbert Lavenham, was twenty years her senior — not much younger than Ruskin — but had proved to be an energetic lover. She had been less surprised in principle than most ladies of her era by the vigorous exercise to which she had been inducted, for she came from an 'artistic' family. Nevertheless, in fact, and with specific reference to Herbert, she had been quite unprepared for her own response to his keen interest in her physicality. That there was no sign of a baby was a blessing: having said which, there were these visits to the lavatory, though they were probably attributable only to Herbert's energies. Perhaps, she thought, I am a late bloom, too — and when she looked in the glass again a little more of the gauntness seemed to have gone.

Herbert Lavenham had departed that morning for their seaside home in the town where he had been a full-time customs official, part-time writer, leaving her in their apartment the other side of the British Museum. He had given the maid an unexpected half-day off and called Charlotte back to the bedroom. She was happy for him that he had found the capacity to make her feel thus, fragile; happy also that they had the sense to work apart at intervals.

Claire Stott, too, was in something of a flutter as she left the building — from the purely verbal attentions of Ruskin — which symptoms were compounded by the fact that Alice was nowhere to be seen. Mrs Lavenham suggested that they forgot about maids and took a cab together, which would drop Claire in Russell Square. This they did. Claire was handed down by the driver onto the pavement outside her home, Charlotte staying in the cab for the short conclusion of her journey.

*

Claire's father was a barrister who had had a hard day. He had no wish to linger in his chambers that evening. Since Mrs Stott was unwell, it was Claire who rose to greet him first as he came in, early but tired.

Claire, though eighteen years old, was still his little girl. She had never been adept at any instrument, so after dinner he asked her to show him her sketch book.

Claire had spent the time since her return from the Grosvenor jotting down impressions of what had transpired. Her small-scale annotated drawings were not very skilful, but provided talking-points for Mr Stott and his daughter.

'Your mother was indisposed, I gather, so you went with Alice?'

'Yes,' said Claire,' and used to frankness with her father, explained that a misunderstanding with the maid had meant that she had been accompanied on her return journey by a new acquaintance.

Mr Stott expressed some irritation, tempered by hearing of Mrs Lavenham's kindness — Claire having instinctively minimised Ruskin's gallantry — and by Claire's expressed wish that Alice should not get into trouble.

'Nevertheless,' said Mr Stott, 'I shall speak to the girl.'

'But, please, papa,' said Claire, 'not on my account.'

'As you wish, my dear,' said her father, '— it shall be on my own.'

At that point Claire's mother, still with a headache, came in.

'How are you, my dear?' he asked, as she gave him a little kiss on the cheek and Claire a little squeeze of the shoulder. She was their only child.

'Improved, thank you,' his wife answered. 'I'm afraid I could not help overhearing the matter which you and Claire were discussing. Indeed, I have just returned from a visit to the kitchen where I learnt something which has quite put me out.'

'And what, pray, is that, my dear?' asked Mr Stott.

'Something which makes me feel that Claire should spend a little time with my sister in Worcestershire.'

'Really, mama,' said Claire, dutifully enough, 'it would be a change — London is becoming hot and crowded — but a trifle unexpected, when I am — it seems — making new friends here.'

Mrs Stott gave her husband a meaningful look:

'There is, dear both, a lot of illness around...'

Mr Stott was a mild man and his wife not one of those whom Ruskin took to task in *Sesame and Lilies* for failing to influence her husband. He knew that on his wife's lips, 'illness' embraced any general malaise or specific unease. He chose not to question her in front of their daughter. He would do so quietly later.

But after that conversation had taken place, he made no demur to the suggestion that his darling should spend some weeks in the country.

2

It was Sunday evening. Everyone except Ruskin was at church. He was sitting in the back parlour of Herne Hill, where he tried to catch some sense as he often did of that blissful point in his final reconciliation with Rose… after all, after all …when he returned from giving a lecture on Botticelli to find her waiting successfully and quietly for him in this very room. Rose, at her most Botticellian — unhealthily so. To do so, to remember her – the detail of her, caught up too many sick changes in her face and arms – and all that he could see or guess of her wasted flesh. Rose was living and Rose was dead, only two years and a month ago, no more than that. The symbolism reversed. Alive in the Winter and dead in the Spring.

He was doing what she would have wished, reading the Bible. Though – but she need not know – reading it for pleasure. Reading Ezekiel on the duties of a shepherd.

However, Ruskin's household flock having returned, he resumed work — retired to the study he had made in what had been his old nursery. His recent memories of Venice bright in a mind over-stimulated by intensive work. His observation and recording and transcription and interpretation carried out there: transferred, as in a kind of reliquary, into as much as his head and his heart could take; spilling over into his Gospel, into his catalogue of drawings for the 'Working Man's Bodleian', his Sheffield Museum. It was there, not in the parlour, nor in the Bible that he was going to find Rosie again.

Venice was the key. For St George's workmen in Sheffield, and of course, for himself. Carpaccio. St Ursula.

About Carpaccio's *St Ursula* (Fairfax Murray's copy of it, that is), which he had already assigned to the Sheffield Museum, he wrote:

'The black square behind the head is the mythic symbol that while she puts the marriage ring on her finger, the wedding is to death. Such another black space is put behind the head of the angel in her dream.'

…and his pleasant, aspirational melancholy was replaced by a black space; which was then re-filled with sad recollection of — a wildness about — all that he'd found, but all that he'd been unable to get his own hand and eye to render of St Ursula, to discover of Rosie.

On this empty space was projected – not an image, mercifully not an image – but a blank and pleasurable thought: that there had been in Venice not a single trace or vestige in Venice of his sham wife in either his mind or his eye. Nothing of Effie who had been his supposed companion and amanuensis when he'd made his five hundred drawings there to record a Venice that was crumbling away and was under threat of destruction — actually under bombardment from, bizarrely, aerial balloons. Not a trace. Not even of her bills. And when, in what seemed such a long-ago past, when she had supposedly been there with him, when he would climb down at the end of a hard morning's work, tracing, copying at eye level from a distant vault or a high capital, only to find her gone, or idle – having deciphered nothing for him from the lower monuments.

How he had climbed his high ladders into the vaults and recesses of churches and galleries – in that same Venice, where Rosie had never been – and found *her*, found Rosie everywhere! He'd persuaded the authorities in Venice to take down the great, if damaged, *St Ursula's Dream* from its dark place high up on the wall of the Galleria dell' Accademia. Had the picture placed beside him on the floor in good light for his water colours — was even locked in with it un-chaperoned; with *her*, the picture from which Rosie had emerged, the picture which Rosie had entered into. He had been disheartened by his lack of progress with it — until Christmas 1876. It was then that the gifts of St Ursula's dianthus and vervain had come to him — first in the picture; and, then, as it were, out of the picture. This was the first physical intervention of Rose, and quite distinct from what he now felt as the morbid foolery of spiritualism. He awaited her next move, her second sign — the third, counting the recovered 'star' letter.

*

Arthur Severn knocked (in what was now his own house, though of course it had been Ruskin's father's) and peered round the door. Ruskin intimated that he'd like him to come and stay a while. Arthur mimed that he'd fetch drawing material, and shortly returned with it.

For all that the Severns were parents and Ruskin childless — and that he slept in their house in what had been his nursery — they sometimes called him 'Papa': he had become a spendthrift simulacrum of his thrifty father, reading Scott aloud at the meal table as the dead man had, working while Arthur Severn drew.

Ruskin continued to a second full stop: 'For the teaching of these labourers, schools are to be erected, with museums and libraries in fitting places. The mountain home of the Sheffield Museum has been chosen, not to keep the collection out of the smoke, but expressly to beguile the artisan out of it.'

He looked over what he had written, then crossed out the second sentence for use elsewhere.

'We will have, Arthur,' declared Ruskin, 'nothing in our Sheffield Museum — or at Bewdley, for that matter — save what deserves respect in Art, or admiration in Nature.'

'Very good, Papa Coz,' said Arthur with his usual cheerful, deference to the Professor's crackbrained social schemes. If he thought about them at all, that is the way he thought about them. But he was too wily to give even a hint of an opinion, especially to Ruskin's blood cousin, his wife Joan.

Ruskin nodded, as if he had needed support, then drafted three broad heads:

'Large Sliding Frames: First compartment — Illustrations of Early Italian Religious Art / Second Compartment — Illustrations by Photograph of the Sculpture of Venice in Her Commercial Power and Religious Faith / Third Compartment — Treatment of Foliage in Sculpture.'

He lifted his pen and, with the scratching of it stopped, heard the fainter movement of Arthur Severn's pencil. Ruskin did not look up, resumed writing:

'List of Drawings Belonging to St George's Guild (On Screens) —'

Then grew weary at the thought of having to put all this in order even on paper. It irked him momentarily that he was unable to trust an in fact entirely trustable curator with these matters, but he knew it was not in him to do so. He stopped therefore, but not to give up. He would grumble in print if he had to — grumble at himself if no one else was at hand — but he would not give up. A moment's silence from Arthur, who began to work with brush and water.

Ruskin kept his eyes down as he spoke:

'You know, Arfie,' (Arthur Severn, after his marriage, had had the Ruskin family's baby talk thrust upon him), 'I can tell, Arfie, by the true tune your brush is playing against its water pot that you're putting on a wash and doing it exactly right. I believe someone newly-blind could tell as much. Don't you think, therefore, that if such an eyeless man had made use of previous sight, he would do a better job than some of our current critics?'

Arthur chuckled with a little obsequiousness, with a little boredom with his own work, but with now more attentiveness to what his dear coz, the professor had to say.

'I thought,' said Arthur, 'it might be useful for me to record you at your work, Papa Coz, this morning. So if it's to your liking, I'll just sit here until you've done.'

'You know me too well, dear Arfie, your brush will keep me to my duties a little longer than I should otherwise manage. Otherwise, I shall find myself writing to Miss Stott again. Did I tell you about Miss Stott? No. Perhaps I should not have written to Miss Stott. I have so many pets. It can be troublesome having to separate them. That is maybe why I have become such a wanderer — that and (let's make no bones about it) my broken heart. I shall make a visit or two and then be off to Oxford — and, after that, in pursuit of my Bewdley Museum, to Birmingham, to stay with a Mr Baker, a trustee of our St George's — and mayor of the town, he tells me.'

Ruskin put his hands under his work pile and picked out the Bewdley papers. He looked at them, he looked at them for a moment with other people's eyes. What had been fame had shaded into notoriety since his radical Economics in the 1860s; while his Christian usage of his father's entire fortune to endow the Guild of St George and other social schemes was widely regarded as the worst kind of profligacy. People, intending parody, correctly said that he intended to build marble halls for workers to sit in, with books in their hands and pictures on the walls.

Some of this was going on in Ruskin's head. Suddenly he declared: 'I'm good for nothing.' (Arthur was obliged to disagree.)

'No, Arfie,' Ruskin replied, 'I have to ask myself just what it is that I am. I am defined by my work. Yet what is there that I am able to concentrate on without — confusingly even to myself — switching to something else?' (Arthur made some helpful suggestions.)

'That's all very well,' said Ruskin, 'But if I could have settled at just one thing I might have been the top geologist in Europe. That would have been best, wouldn't it? Better than the job-lot I am — part of me doing one thing, part of me doing another. Drawing – as it were, drawing with one hand (and I'm thankful for you, Arthur, for taking that on now), with the other writing to the capitalist to tell him to forego his profit and the cobbler to stick to his last. My mind translating Plato, my eyes studying Carpaccio… As to my heart — well, you've become used to this — my heart can't tell whether it would be better off mended or more and more broken. You know me by now, Arthur, and the tricks my heart gets up to.'

'Not, Coz, with making you ill again, I hope. We can't have that. Though I'm sure you'll soon enough be away from the here-and-now, off to Italy. Stuck into times past. More's the pity there's not enough to keep you home.'

'No, not enough — not enough at all, save for you Arthur: save for the two of you, Arfie and Joanie – and,' said Ruskin, brightening, 'now I come to think about it, I do think there's a place for Miss Stott amongst them, my pets.'

Arthur smiled: 'I've never known anyone with so much time for young ladies and such — I hope they appreciate the attention, that's all. Never known such a man,' he concluded with a chuntered compliment — ' never known such a man for so many pets —'

'— Pets who have sought him out,' said Ruskin. 'It is they are the agents and instigators, not I (all save that one, once and wonderful) — and that's the way it's remained. Subjective and Objective mode, as against the perfection of the Complement.'

'Just so,' said Arthur, not following.

'I'm glad we're in agreement,' said Ruskin. 'I'm not sure I can manage much more of what's supposed to be my business for today — the thought of so much unanswered and unattempted since

Venice weighs heavily with me. You might do best to leave me to myself. Do feel free to join Jo'anie.'

'Best not,' said Arthur, 'she has things to do and I'll only be in the way. She'll fetch me out soon enough, then maybe she'll sing a little.'

Joan had always had a sweet voice. Ruskin listened to her when they were both children, then very often later when she'd been companion to his ailing mother. He nodded.

'So,' said Arthur, 'I'll just keep my head down and —'

He drew in his breath through his teeth and, rapidly rinsing his brush, plopped it on his drawing, gave the brush a squeeze, sucked up globules of water before they could blot, worked over a small area, tested it for dampness, counselled himself to let it dry.

'I think I see,' said Ruskin, 'why I have broken off my attempts at work. Usually I think best on paper — insofar as I'm still capable of thought, but tonight ...'

'Tonight,' said Arthur, 'why don't you just think aloud a bit if you wish? It'd suit me. I'd like to catch your different facial expressions at this time of day — just as you yourself like to get the dawn down on paper.'

'No dawn, worth looking at since Venice,' said Ruskin, 'just blackness shading into greyness. And on occasion it's been a grey sky at night and a black one passing for day.'

But he nodded at Arthur's suggestion.

' Let me tell you, then, of a discovery which lifted my spirits — the inscription, you remember, on the font of the oldest church in Venice - "Hoc circlum templum etcetera: Around this temple let the merchants' law be just, His weights true, and his agreements fair." That leaves nothing more to be said on the subject. Work from that, and everything else falls into place: the end of usury, the end of exploitation, the acceptance of just law.

'And, yes, these words must have a prominent place not only in the Sheffield Museum, but again, when St George raises his banner in Worcestershire — white with the red cross which was handed to him by St Ursula herself. Its import ought to be as plain as the nose upon an ordinary working man's face. But there are prettier noses. The idea of womankind must be there — the platonic idea, I mean: more than any particular maidenliness, Carpaccio's vision of St Ursula as Rose, of Rose as St Ursula. I want that there. I want that precious image there. Yet, though I am not unhappy in giving up to the Museum Fairfax Murray's fine water colour rendition of Carpaccio, I cannot bear to be parted from the version which I so painfully made during the last months in Venice.'

'You could have your drawing copied in photogravure and tinted,' said Arthur, 'for you shouldn't part with it — not after the hours you spent getting it down just right.'

'Yes,' said Ruskin, 'I think that's what I shall have to do — reluctantly – I dare not tinker any more with it — such a precious remembrance ' (he touched that other golden secret in his breast pocket). I shall have need of several, Arthur — copies — so I think, yes, I'd best have my drawing chromolithographed...In putting it in the Museum, though — showing my pain — am I seeking to emulate poor, dear Ursula, my poor deluded Rose —?'

'Not really,' said Arthur. 'You've not given up your life entirely to the painful past — nor, since you ask my opinion, Coz, should you do so. You've still got your pets.'

Arthur did not understand that Ruskin had still got his Rosie, too. Rosie had her emissaries. He needed her and them more than he needed his pets. True, he had sometimes felt in gazing upon the picture of St Ursula asleep in her Dream in the Galleria that the saint was beginning to stir, to breathe. But, knowing himself to be 'more Turk than Catholic', he did not expect anything of that kind to happen. He knew that St Ursula could not lift a finger of her own; that her substance was no more than a few old close fibres bound together by compounds of pigment; that her drawn hand could never do more than support her drawn chin, even though it did so in such a tangible and delightfully Rosie way.

All the more need, then, for his admirable friend Lady Castletown to be in Venice with her daughters at the same time as he, so that she could be the instrument of St Ursula. Rose and Ursula needed a mortal hand to do their work from time to time — in this instance, the innocent hand of Lady Castletown to bring the gift of dianthus to him. The dianthus which had come with the sweet Rosie note, 'from St Ursula out of her bedroom window, with love.'

The clear image of the dianthus — five-stemmed like the one on the window sill in Carpaccio's picture — gave way to a perception of Arthur's silence.

'I'm glad, Arfie,' said Ruskin, finally, 'that you don't see me just as a man of sorrows, a Werther. I've no intention of shooting myself because I covet my neighbour's wife like that repugnant Junker. When I place the St Ursula picture in the museum — Sheffield or Bewdley, or both — I shall do so, yes, as an example of Christian art in Venice. But I shall do so also (I am aware), so that anyone who has eyes and heart enough will see in my copy of that face something of what Rosie has been — what Rosie is still — to me.'

Joan Severn popped her head round the door:

'Arthur, I hope you are not bothering dear Coz.'

Ruskin replied: 'No, dear Joanie, Arfie has been quite behaving himself. Oh Joanie, it is I — yet again — who have been misapplying my diminishing energies. Instead of working upon my tiresome catalogue — or, rather, under the pretence of working on my tiresome catalogue — Now that I see you, Joanie, I realise that I have become melancholy.'

Joanie put her arms about his shoulders as he sat:

'It's two years or more, isn't it, Coz.'

'It is,' said Ruskin, pleased. 'I keep May 25th as Rose's Death Day — a date she shares with Saint Fermin of Pamplona, though that was long ago, and of interest, I gather, only to bulls. Rosie wouldn't keep that sort of company. Except it happened in Amiens – his beheading…And, yes, sometimes the dear girl still sends me a sign…

'But not tonight — unless the present thought of her interrupting my work (while yet being essential to my work) is her doing… Do show me your picture, Arfie — and then perhaps some music?'

Arthur looked at his little water colour through half-closed eyes, shrugged at it, passed it over.

'Good work, Arthur — but tell me,' looking close, 'what is this gleam — this little flash of gold — here beside me? Did you see it, Arthur?'

'Oh that,' said Arthur, 'why that's just where I made a small error and drew off the paint.'

Ruskin seemed not to have heard:

'But did you see it, Arthur? — I think your brush has caught a momentary something, the appearance of a something too quick for your conscious eye. It has happened before — and when it happens it turns me from a lump of flint into a firefly.'

Joan looked at Arthur meaningfully. The best he could manage was:

'Ah well, now, brushes do seem to go their own ways at times —'

But Ruskin's eye had had a vision of great benignity, his face still registering an inner excitement; excitement which did not on this occasion shade into perturbation. So the evening concluded pleasantly.

*

Ruskin continued his struggles with the Sheffield Catalogue; winced at unanswered correspondence; juggled proofs, corrections, final drafts, fresh ideas for the seven or eight works which he had in the press at one and the same time; dined pleasantly with Ned and Georgiana Burne-Jones.

He had been a day behind with his diary since visiting the Grosvenor Gallery. He caught up two days of it, penned a brief affectionate note to Mrs Lavenham and a contrary postscript for her to pass to Miss Stott, full of peremptory instruction.

By the next post, having crossed with his own, there came a letter from Mrs Lavenham with an enclosure (part of a letter) from Claire Stott. It asked for information about lady artists and then, in novelettish vein, told briefly how she was being whisked away to the country — to an aunt in Worcestershire, 'for her health'.

Mrs Lavenham had thought it best not to convey to Ruskin Claire's fuller account of what had transpired. It was as follows:

'...Alice was lucky not to lose her place — but it was cook's fault, if you ask me, for listening to her; and cook's someone that they can't do without. Mama has many household anxieties, and papa eats a good dinner — at the Inns of Court — though he tries to be at home as much as he can — and still reads (and even acts out!) the bard with me...

'What seems to have happened is that Alice, while waiting for us, got talking to the doorman at the Grosvenor — and he (and he's to blame in this), going off duty, sat with her in the square and told her "artistic" stories. Not able to fathom what this had to do with me, I insisted to papa that I be told something of its bearing on my sudden country holiday. He was obliged — mama was still reluctant — to give an instance of the overheard stories.

'One concerned the famous (infamous?) Mr Frith when he was working on his big painting of the Railway Station — his name wasn't mentioned, but I guessed — who was caught by his wife in Paddington posting a card to her, addressed as from Brighton.   I did not at first take the force of this example of what I was being protected from — until I was told that the artist had been disguising his whereabouts for a certain reason. Reward or punishment for my innocent slowness of comprehension? — I'm not sure how I'm to regard it, but I am to help aunt, I gather, through some instruction of her youngest children. Address me when you are able — please do — care of Mrs Melville at uncle's house.'

*

Innocent girls became in the fullness of time virtuous ladies; the dark age between the two being a shadowy period which Ruskin avoided as unsafe. But, since Charlotte Lavenham was known for her discretion, and he had much enjoyed the prettinesses of Miss Stott at the Grosvenor, he saw no harm in giving the latter a provisional age four years short of what he guessed it really was. In order to accomplish this fancy — or to fail to carry it off — he needed a mould or measure of her eligibility as a 'pet'.

He had brought back from the Grosvenor Gallery more of the image of Claire Stott on his mind's eye than he had intended. Naturally it was juxtaposed with the painted likenesses of Frances Graham made by Edward Burne-Jones.

He had gone from the gallery to Ned and Georgie's; stayed for a charming dinner and taken a turn round Ned's studio: much new work there, commissioned by Miss Graham's father, the Liberal Member of Parliament for Glasgow. Everything from bedroom slippers to a grand piano... Ruskin decided to call at Miss Graham's house, hoping she would prove to be at home and her parents out.

His luck was in; and he was particularly pleased to be shown again a small Burne-Jones of theirs, *The Wedding of King René*. The family normally kept it at their Perthshire house.

Frances mentioned some verses — William Morris's, of course — which were either the source of the picture or derived from it. Between them, they remembered the whole poem. Frances Graham took it on almost to the end:

'"And this day draw a veil over all deeds pass'd over,
Yet their hands shall not tremble, their feet shall not falter;
The void shall not weary the fear shall not alter —"'

When she paused to impel Ruskin to complete the quatrain:

'"These lips and these eyes of the loved and the lover"' — which he did with the sense of pleasure and modest accomplishment that might have come from singing a duet.

He gently clapped his hands — for she had done most of the work:

'Well done, Miss Graham. I continue to wonder at Morris's soulfulness — such a John Bull of a man.'

'Maybe he has some medieval secret, that we don't know about — I mean, we wot not of,' said Frances Graham.

'Maybe he has,' Ruskin said, smiling, while touching with a disguised movement the gold-plates at his own breast.

*

Seeing Frances Graham – a shade too School of Michelangelo to be one of his pets – and thinking some more about Claire Stott, had brought Ruskin's mind back to the Grosvenor Gallery. He must hustle. Most of the type was set. He had only a few lines to spare, and little time to compose even the little that was still needed. Yet he meant to have his monthly *Fors* ready for June despatch, with a note about the merits and demerits of Sir Coutts' enterprise in it.

Accordingly, he called on his printer, looked at the *Fors* proof, provided a light remark à propos Sir Coutts' role as either artist or 'shop keeper'; leading into a few words of advice for him at the Grosvenor as to its future policy and standards:

'Sir Coutts Lindsay ought not to have admitted work into the Gallery in which the ill-educated conceit of the artist so nearly approached the aspect of wilful imposture. I have seen and heard much of Cockney impudence before now, but never expected to hear a coxcomb ask 200 guineas for flinging a pot of paint in the public's face.'

Ruskin was pleased to have made his distribution deadline, and with finding exactly the right number of words required for the vacant space. He was satisfied, too, with his phrasing of the reproof he had administered. He knew that Sir Coutts would take his remarks in good part. As to Whistler, the Professor gave him no further thought, felt no uneasiness, arrived home in good spirits.

3

Ruskin slept well most nights now. The Surrey hills about Herne Hill, soft and nightingaled, reassured him that the great convex leafiness he'd missed in Venice was still to be found at home. It was that which had brought him back. But his ideas and impressions from Europe — the observations, notebooks, sketches collected there — rose on the good days to swirl around in his mind like a shoal of minnows — and then on the bad to sink dead to the bottom of the tank in his head.

The night before he was due in Oxford was not one of his best. The prospect of travelling by train had put him in a grump, but he had the satisfaction of taking a cab as far as Paddington and finding a sympathetic bias in its driver against 'the subterranean puff-puff'. He happily tipped the man a little more generously than usual; and a porter was quickly got: which was as well, for he'd cut things fine; partly because there'd been many things to gather together for three nights away, but also because he disliked being seen in the precincts of a railway station.

Arrived at the School of Art, he was annoyed to discover that the master, Alexander MacDonald (whose post he had endowed) was not to be found. He seized upon the assistant Crawley and countermanded previous revisions to the contents of the Educational Series display cabinets.

There were things here which he needed for the impending Bewdley Museum: a little drawing by Burne-Jones which he wished to offer to Mr Baker (who was putting up the money for the project) as an earnest — it could be brought back from the mount-cutter! Another was an instructive image obscured by a wrong alignment – he ripped off the back – and yet another ruined by false juxtaposition. Everywhere things misrecorded (because of a misreading of his scribbled annotations), and a failure to reserve prime space for chromolithographs after Carpaccio — in the service of Rose La Touche and St George. The Carpaccio must show in detail the dianthus, flower of Zeus, and vervain, the ancient symbol of domestic purity…

His thoughts turned again to Lady Castletown and her gift of dianthus. As the lady did not know — or even pretend to know — that the flowers were (through her) being sent by Rose, there could be no deception. Lady Castletown had simply sent him a pot of pinks with a hand-written note. Sent 'with St Ursula's love', recorded Ruskin. That is to say, Rose had put the action into Lady Castletown's head, without divulging its significance. A precious gift, indeed — yes from St Ursula, but also from Rose.

A precious gift, more than one precious gift, was brought to him by the artless Lady. For she also had caused a botanist to send him an example of vervain (which he now knew to be verbena).

There would be more signs and portents. Every so often (the latest through Arthur) an unexplained rosy glow. Another would arrive between now and the next sacred February 2nd. He sent for the mount-cutter, was high and mighty with the frame-maker — and then sweetness itself, when he saw the fellow was upset. He was arbitrary and brilliant, exhausting and silly.

He sorted some manuscripts, broke up an early Book of Hours and despatched pages from it to Ned and Georgie and others, felt better, went to his rooms and slept badly. He would have expected to sleep badly on the eve of a visit to Birmingham, though he'd had the foresight and interest to procure directories and yearbooks so that he'd arrive with some understanding of the place.

A leather case, a wicker one containing books, a heavy bag about which he was protective, and several packages were got safely to the railway station for him and onto the train. The locomotive made good progress until the outskirts of Leamington Spa, where the brakes were applied, leaving it steaming steadily and emitting an occasional clank in the middle of a very dull field. Ruskin could not be annoyed single-mindedly when a steam engine proved inept: it bore out his pre-formed opinion; and, in this case, provided an opportunity to leaf through the local reference books he'd brought, now that the steamy process of getting there was (in theory) nearing its end.

*

The train stood stock-still for half an hour, then, after some trucks had rattled by, moved forward in a series of lurches accompanied by noisy gouts of steam. The journey had recommenced, and was completed without further interruption.

Awaiting the train at Snow Hill Station — earlier than necessary even if the train had been on time — was George Baker, mayor of Birmingham. He had decided that it would be unhandsome to his native town not to wear his chain of office, though the visit was by his personal invitation rather than from the corporation. But he was, therefore, accompanied only by his eldest son, his housekeeper (an unmarried cousin), and his youngest daughter. His wife had died bringing into the world this twelve-year-old who carried a posy for the Professor.

Baker, a rich Quaker, who had consistently supported Ruskin's social schemes, regretted not being able to entertain their instigator at his new house in Bewdley — a country retreat adjoining Ruskinland, those sylvan acres he was making over to the Guild of St George. He might then — for he had learned to overcome traditional Quaker antipathies to the plastic arts — might then have had Ruskin cast an eye over the carving and ironwork made by Benjamin Creswick which was almost in place, and even the projected fresco by his son-in-law Joseph Southall. The craftsmen had rushed the work at his first instruction, held back on his second — then swung from one job to the other. As a result, the under-plaster in the area reserved for Southall's design had cracked, and

Creswick who had a point to prove to Ruskin and would rather be cautious than sorry had grown fussy about his raw materials.

Benjamin Creswick had been a grinder in Sheffield and made his own way. He still worked the same long hours now that he received a fee for sculpting as he had when he was paid coppers for finely-finished cutlery. He made demands on himself and on his material; had, in fact, learned to be exacting and intolerant of slackness from his reading of Ruskin and from his work with a Ruskinian stone-mason. Creswick himself had acquired a follower, a man who could be trusted with rough shaping and fitting; a man who had walked from Worcestershire to Sheffield when the nailers were on strike to look for work in the edge-tool trade.

Happening to go back one day to the firm where he had once been employed himself, Creswick had seen this fellow, whose name was Will Manning, disconsolate; taken him on to care for his tools and as a general labourer for shifting stone and timber. He was at present in Bewdley at the new Baker residence, Beaucastle, seeing that everything was tidy and ship-shape in case the mayor and the Professor should call there against expectation: Creswick had reluctantly agreed that an inch had to be cut from a piece of his dressed stone, because of an error by the bricklayers and carpenters. Will was to see to that; and stay there as watchman over the weekend; after which he hoped to beg a ride from a carter to see his wife and family.

Beaucastle, Bellefield — these were the names of George Baker's two houses. The latter was at Heath Green, a village surrounded by town; no longer pretty. But, as mayor, it was more suitable that he entertained the distinguished visitor in Birmingham rather than seeming to escape from it. Besides, having arrived by the Great Western Railway at Snow Hill station, Ruskin would have only a short carriage journey before him — rather than having to change trains or jolt immediately along country roads. Furthermore, George Baker wished Ruskin to meet his colleagues and associates; men of Birmingham all.

A steam-whistle (a sound Ruskin hated) excited the waiting crowd. Ruskin was anxious not so much to be amongst them as away from the steam-monster: he had the window down and the carriage door ajar before the train came to a halt. Baker knew Ruskin, of course, from portraits, though he looked frailer than they had suggested.

Ruskin was not familiar with Baker's appearance, but he saw with his one good eye (there was a cinder in the other) a little girl in her best frock approach. Taking the proffered posy, he said something gracious and popped a flower from it straightaway into his button hole in a way which made her laugh. He nodded his way through the introductions and shook hands with Baker, a sensitive-looking middle-aged man plainly dressed; his concessions to vanity or self-consciousness being beautifully spread whiskers and a careful layer of hair on a broad and enlarging forehead. Ruskin's face was fresh and his head of hair full beside the mayor's.

Soon they were at Bellefield in Heath Green where the bags of the 'Master' – of the Guild of St George – whom Baker had corresponded with were unpacked. Baker noted that Ruskin appeared to prefer the style of 'Professor' face to face. After tea, Ruskin and Baker looked at maps and papers. Each put to the other what should be seen and determined during the visit. Ruskin had particularly asked that there should be no company at dinner that evening; shortly after which, begging to be excused, he retired to his room (where, of course, he worked).

*

The next day got off to a good start. Ruskin had slept well; had had pleasant dreams of Rosie who brought him a (chromolithographed) banner of St George on a great pole, and told him to pierce with it the turf of Ruskinland to hasten the growth of the great central avenue, where noble trees would be rationally managed. A heartening and encouraging dream and one in accord with the purposes of the day. A communication, though, rather than an intervention. He looked forward with pleasure and pain to the anniversary of his proposal of marriage to Rose on 2nd February 1866, and — from that day — the beginning of his three years' wait (each day separately numbered and marked off) for her refusal. Dear dead Rose, who had gone where the hawthorn blossoms go, but also dear un-dead Rose living in St Ursula. His reflections, and the prospect of a day combining both interest and business, sharpened his appetite for an early breakfast. He and Baker were on the road to Bewdley before seven.

*

Ten miles down the road and three hours earlier, there had been just enough light in a dark coalhole for a little lad, no longer frightened of bogeys, to see his way to the hearth. Not that he needed any light, being so inured to the work, nor that his eyes were open at first.

Some of the clinker was giving little cooling tinks as he fetched it out. He relied on sounds a great deal in what he was doing — and the feel of cold and hot, mainly cold, on his skin. Sensing that one tiny residuum from the furnace was still not dead, he thrust in a little splinter of wood and smelt smoke; touched it with another and — suddenly — there was a sputter of light enough to see what he was simultaneously doing. He scraped more clinker away to give it air.

He began to cough, threw the clinker into the yard, clambered over the bottom half of the stable-door, got some of the dust out of his lungs, trod some of the clinker into the floor, replenished the bucket with 'breeze' from the gasworks — out of the pram in the yard; carried it back into the hovel. Awake now, he made a pile of the breeze, breaking the first lump into pieces with a small hammer which he set upon a little cage of stick and straw (for there were chickens in here with him, hence the lower door) a little cage or bivouac, inside which was — if there had been time to think of play — what might have been a little campfire.

The boy, whose name was Thomas, drew out a small piece of smoking stick and blew on it until his lips felt the heat from its glow. Then he thrust it under the cage.

The chancy part of the work done, he leant upon the great bellows — until there was a strong flame, cracks from the sticks, a settling of the coke, and a roar in the flue.

Above the roar he heard his mother cry out in the cottage, as she always did at this moment, 'First down, best dressed!' He could make out the thumps and creaks as the five younger children set upon the heap of clothes at the foot of the stairs — but they would go about it in an orderly enough fashion: were not well-nourished enough to have energy to expend on family bickering.

The fire in the forge was drawing well and there would be a cup of tea for him within. He liked the responsibility now that his father had to be away. Tomorrow would be Sunday where he helped out with teaching the little ones their book. He got more schooling than most and meant to make a show of things: he got some at the beginning of the week, because his mam, who'd been a scholar put extra hours in for him here — so he did some for her there; some bookwork she'd 've liked to have had chance of.

*

The sun was rising behind Mr Baker's carriage — a fine, red-and-gold flecked dawn had not been allowed to go to waste: water-colour touches of it on Ruskin's favoured smooth white paper were spread on the window sill of the guest bedroom at Bellefield.

But the mayor and his guest were by now on the Kidderminster road.

The tract of neglected parkland towards which they were making their way was, Baker was saying, in some ways a precedent for their own project. He stopped, recollecting Ruskin's insistence on de-personalising the endeavour):

'For, that is to say, St George's project. — Though, I hope, my dear professor, you will savour its aspiration rather than its decay.'

He'd had a sudden unease that seeing it now, as the ruin of itself, might bring about one of those mood swings of Ruskin's into blackness, which he had heard about — and had some evidence of in their correspondence.

'All things decay,' replied Ruskin — and the truism gained in weight from his speaking it, 'as for the aspiration, I doubt whether when Shenstone laid out Leasowes, he had St George's purposes much in mind. But I am willing to be surprised — and it is not likely that I shall be going this way again...'

Baker wished Ruskin not to suppose he might be coming to Worcestershire for the last time, but repressed any rejoinder, saying to himself that when Ruskin — unto a ripe old age — should come direct to Bewdley and stay at Beaucastle, he would see the Ruskinland community productive and equitable, without needing to repeat this part of the journey.

They were drawing near Halesowen — for which Baker had no responsibility either as mayor or as instigator of this part of the visit. As an adviser to the School Board, though, he was often in the area, and had seen the landscape – particularly that part near the canal – become overgrown and encroached upon in recent years.

Baker was apologising for it in advance, but Ruskin was already out of the coach. He wished to see what there was left to see of the place before onlookers — onlookers of Ruskin, that is — were out and about. Leasowes had been the home — and, more significantly — the pleasure grounds and model farm of William Shenstone, eighteenth-century poet and landscape gardener.

Baker hurried to follow him because he felt the need to say something of his own about this experiment in land management which Ruskin would have come across only in a book, probably Johnson's *Lives of the Poets*. Having caught up with him, Baker began to brief Ruskin (as tactfully as he could, but rather as if he were a committee) about the little that remained of Shenstone's ferme ornée. Which was not easy to do, as the party addressed would not stand still so that things could be pointed out. For instance, 'Evidence there, professor, of a gardener's seasonal landscape through a farmer's crop rotation' —

'My dear Sir,' said Ruskin, running out of patience, 'let me make my own mind up about such things if I may.' Relenting, he continued: "Though, to be sure — present company excepted — when I do make my mind up, there's precious little notice taken nowadays. Indeed, I often have small regard for or recognition of what other people present to me as my own views. I make my mind up and unmake it several times a day. Otherwise what's the point of forming an opinion? To be unable to change one's mind is like being unable to see a scene in another light or another angle. That's my way. I cannot help it.'

He smiled to take away any sense of rebuke and Baker was smiling too, because this was the Ruskin he had been led to expect. The voice was beautifully modulated, but more Scottish in character (it seemed to him) than others had said.

Ruskin now set out in earnest; with a good spring in his step for a man of fifty eight who was in fits and starts overwhelmed by personal sorrow, and was as usual overworking.

But very soon there was a need to stop and orientate themselves. Ruskin was looking at a chart of the place as it had once been, and struggled to relate where they were and the little that there was to see to what had undoubtedly been an ambitious design.

At his back was the canal — cut through the estate at the end of the previous century — its horse-drawn barges laden with bars and strips of iron for the hundreds of small workshops round about. To his right were the Clent Hills sparkling above intervening smoke; before him the plantation which Shenstone had called Virgil's Grove.

Ruskin strode up the hill towards it, passing the ruins of the poet's Cascade.

'Better in decay than in good order,' said Ruskin of it, shortly. 'If I want regularity, I'll read heroic couplets, not look at water. What there is that remains, in its little unplanned irregularities, has more about it, than the shifting sheet of water intended by its author.' He touched his gold plates, as the meagre trickles reminded him — not unpleasingly — of the little waterfall he had made for Rosie before his parents' death, in the garden of his then house in Denmark Hill.

He smiled, it seemed as if to linger, but caught himself up in his habitual fear of wasting time; and quickly arrived at Virgil's Grove.

'Designed,' said he after some pacing about and peering, 'to produce, as you have said, melancholy thoughts in Shenstone. Or, rather, angry ones in me — the alleged ruined priory appears to be a gardener's shed, the house a plain Jane that I'd rather not catch better sight of. And as for the canal! Yes, angry thoughts are in order here, Mr Baker.'

'But do you not feel,' said Baker, 'some sense still that this is a place which was the product of a vision?'

'Vision? A poet-farmer, who foresaw so little? One who took no care to make legal or familial provision to secure what he had set up. It is his neglect and its consequences that are useful to us. They reassure me that I was right to spend precious time on the constitution of the St George's Guild — some of my followers were much irritated that I did — thus enabling it to hold property in perpetuity through its trustees' (he nodded to Mr Baker who was one of them). ' That, in fact, is the best, tedious work I've had to do. Shenstone was building only for himself, or so it has transpired. Nothing here, as you warned me, but a neglected pleasure ground — no sight of country work or country workers — only the industrialism on the sky line and down below us — no trace of agricultural innovation; the unity of labour and a speaking rural picture all lost.'

Baker was impressed, and correctly saw that keeping silent was the best way to convey that. He essayed some nods, which Ruskin noticed and appeared to appreciate.

'It's just as well,' continued Ruskin affably, 'that Shenstone left us his poems. Poems, thank God, don't require the same maintenance as a field system and timber.'

They returned to Baker's carriage.

'Master,' said Baker, 'I should like to propose a short detour.'

Ruskin appeared happy to be 'Master' when he was on St George's business; waited courteously to hear the suggestion.

'It seemed to me, sir,' Baker continued, 'that our visit to the idyllic site which I propose for the St George settlement — I trust you will find it so — would be enhanced, and its sense of purpose made more purposeful with a foil to set it off. I like to give myself such a reminder, to look on this picture and on that, as it were, but I am in your hands.'

'On the contrary,' said Ruskin, 'I am in yours.'

So he made no demur. Quite soon they were in sight of a place of nightmare sky, noise and incandescence.

They stopped half a mile off and looked down through black, blue, yellow and flame-coloured smoke. The black came principally from a great round stack in the foreground. Behind that an older square chimney sprayed globules of sulphurous spume. There were no mansions in this Hades: only monstrous, makeshift square constructions of blackened brick; parodies of mountain crags peeping out of mist — surrounded by sounding steam and flame and lit before by a giant brazier. Twelve, thirteen, fourteen, fifteen or more subsidiary chimneys they counted — each with a shooting flame, serpentine and intermingling, augmenting the clouds until you could not say whether the sky was dark or bright.

And all around windlasses and trucks and spoil heaps and cinders and poisoned waters — 'where,' said Ruskin, 'though saying so again and again is almost as wearisome to me who cannot refrain from repeating myself — where men are made ugly by making ugly things' — and (Ruskin would have added, if he'd known) heaved and coughed and had no spittle left to spit.

'Industry prospers here,' said Baker, ' as you see — or some of it does — with terrible consequences.'

'Anger,' said Ruskin, 'which used to drive me on — can still do so at times — is not what I am here for today. Let us see no more of this smoke.'

They drove and were silent for a little while. 'But,' said Baker after reflecting upon Ruskin's previous deferral to him, 'take away smoke and you take away lives. Here now on the edge of Halesowen all seems quiet and pretty. A touch of Wordsworth's Westminster Bridge about the place. But the lack of smoke in the little workshops means poverty and ruin at present...'

Ruskin did not reply: rather, out of his own train of thought, he, so it seemed to his companion, hit out:

'Tell me, Mr Baker, do you see yourself as a squire?'

The roots of Mr Baker's whiskers took on a pink tinge:

'As you know, Professor, I am mayor and — for that matter senior magistrate. I did not have the advantage of a university education, being obliged to enter my father's business at the age of fifteen because of his failing health. I built up... But I have no need to account for myself. After twenty years of public work in the town, that I should seek to live in a decently-designed house in the country and do good with my money — is that an unseemly aspiration?'

'Not at all, Mr Baker. Not at all. My late father was — as you yourself have been, I am sure — was a truly honest merchant (and these words are those which have pride of place in the inscription which I have made upon his memorial stone), though he had little sympathy with my wish to give labourers back their dignity, together with a tithe for them of what has been stolen by the rich. But, then, he aspired (for me, not for himself) for an eminent position in the ranks of things as they are, things which – as he saw it — always have been and always will be. But I should let his spirit rest — not drag the upright old gentleman into the argument — discourse, rather, for you and I are not at odds with one another. I ask simply whether you see yourself as a squire.'

Baker, reassured by Ruskin's first private confidence to him, ceased to flush, but was torn between guessing which answer Ruskin sought from him and finding one for himself — for he had not thought of his relationship with the new Bewdley community in terms of squiredom.

'I am happy, Master,' he said at length, 'to think aloud with you on the lines you suggest — and find myself a shade perplexed as to what to say, but if you are willing to hear my unordered thoughts on the subject...'

'Nothing would please me more,' said Ruskin, ' truth is best spoken extempore.'

'Very well,' said Baker, shifting his posture on the carriage cushions, 'I find myself reluctant to admit that I am what Carlyle calls a Gigman — feel myself the object of scorn through such an appellation — yet I undoubtedly keep my own carriage.'

'But, my dear sir,' said Ruskin, 'I can come to your assistance, being a Gigman is not simply a case of keeping a carriage nor are either of these attributes sufficient to identify you as a squire or one who has any aspiration to become one.'

'Thank you, sir,' said Baker, emboldened, 'and as to owning a carriage, what is the alternative? Consider our present journey. Were we not presently jogging along (I admit some jolting too) in my Gigman's gig, we would need to wait and sit upon a train. We would have been strung out behind one of your smelly iron monsters — with predetermined route and prospect and a climate of perpetual drizzle — instead of trotting along quiet country roads, free to turn or return as we wish.'

'And,' said Ruskin, 'in so doing we play our small part to ensure the persistence of traditional crafts, of the wheelwright, of the coachmaker — of the man who works with his own material for his own customer — though you seemed to imply that we will soon find ourselves again in the land of forges, flues, barges and pig-iron.'

'Though not, as it happens' said Baker, 'of smoke — or not at present. And, though that may be good for our lungs as we pass on our way, it spells disaster (as I have said) for those who are unable to work, or in some cases, choose not to do so. There's been a strike in these parts, and some of the people have sold off all their raw material and not had the foresight (or the wherewithal) to replace it.

'But if and when I do see some indications of work going on, and I catch sight of a little smoke, there's something I'd like you to see, if I may be so bold.'

Suddenly he tapped on the inside front of the carriage and the driver stopped.

'Are we there?' asked Ruskin.

'Not quite, Master,' said Baker. 'Will you excuse me for a moment? I've spotted someone who can advise us.'

Baker was swiftly gone and soon back. He had a word with the driver who moved on, slowly now.

'That's a bit of luck,' he said. 'I caught sight of the young man that we helped put in as headmaster at the Board School. Hill. I needed to check with him we'd be likely to find someone working who's, well, more or less comprehensible. The trouble with many of them round here, you see Professor, is it's only the other worker people can follow them. It's their way of talking, and they are happy enough with it, but it's hard on the ears of even a local chap like me. Now this one, the one we're making for, can "speak like a book" as Hill puts it — that's the young man, did I say? — when needs must. He tells me that's where the "foreigners" tend to go, when they come — and there are a few besides ourselves. So, Master, I think you should be able to get proper answers to any questions you care to put.'

'So,' said Ruskin, we're going to see some handicraft, are we?'

'That's right,' said Baker, 'and I think my driver has a good idea where to stop. He won't be able to take the carriage to the door, though — there'd be no room to turn.'

'I look forward to stretching my legs,' said Ruskin, 'as I look forward likewise to resuming our discussion of the role of a squire in St George's scheme of things — you'll note the different nuance in a knightly context.'

*

In the lanes behind the church, neat enough, but soon becoming uneven and broken-bricked (and at first there was some green), Ruskin against all his usual practice and precept was in search of smoke. They could see the low brick chimney — a live one, surrounded by many dead — whose fumes and occasional sparks (even in daylight) would usually have been lost among others. There was a musical sound of hammers.

'The men hereabouts,' said Baker, 'are still off work, though they've gained their point — or think they have.'

Ruskin made a slight and rather feudal comment about the old bond between worker and master. Adding, 'but I suppose the workmen are up against forces, which are neither understood nor understand themselves?'

'There's certainly no kind of bond any more,' said Baker. 'The men are paid in kind and have no control over supplies. So all they can do is put in longer and longer hours, or clear out altogether, or pass over what used to be their work to their...to their kin. In here, sir. In here, you'll see what's happened, what's happening.'

Baker had stepped ahead and put his head round the top of a stable-door. He gestured to Ruskin, who stepped inside the low brick workshop. Whereupon, as promised by Baker, he saw — two workers.

*

Two slim workers, dressed in aprons and sacking; with their heads caught round with cloth — their hammering suspended for a moment; slim, muscled right arms fixed and ready. Androgynous:

thin-faced the one, fresh-complexioned (as Ruskin's eyes became accustomed to the strange light of this place) the other. Their clothes seemed to have skimped their shoulders and to have built out their upper torsos, as they stood slightly stooped for a moment's respite or in deference to their visitors.

A young boy was working the bellows with one hand and passing over iron rods with the other. Young and undernourished as he was, he seemed more robust than the two labourers. Two little girls were prodding some washing with a dolly peg, others — younger — were on the floor of the workshop. And then Ruskin realised what he was seeing.

At a signal from Baker they resumed their work: with a rapidity and precision that was breathtaking, but mechanistic. An elaborate dance — heel and toe, arm and elbow: yes, as measured as the Fairground figures of kings and queens striking the bell of the great painted clock in Birmingham town.

Ruskin and Baker had got just space enough to stand — chickens and children around their ankles — in the doorplace. But it was the involuntary twitching of their own limbs which almost fetched them off their feet, as they watched the predetermined convulsions of the workers. Intent only on output; feverishly and soberly so. Their eyes never deflected from their work: their hands busily shifting and clutching — first at the bellows or the fire. But then the boy set down the baby he had been attending to, to man the bellows, and the nailers had only to deal with their irons in the fire, their irons onto the block, their irons under the pincers, their irons under the hammer: perpetual motion, workers as machines.
Mechanical worker-women.

It was the light hoarse voice — the one who could 'speak like a book' answering for them — which revealed their femininity. The coarseness of their dress, the harshness of their work had made them seem otherwise — taken away, not only their sex, but their humanity. Far removed from Kate Greenaway's drawings, quite unlike anything in the Grosvenor Gallery, these were women: whose occupation it was to wield a heavy hammer.

And so this was Venus's Forge: would Ned — could Ned? — transform it: place Frances Graham to the right of the bellows in classical draperies; pose, say, Mrs Lavenham and Miss Stott with jewelled implements, engaged in slow unhurried craftsmanship — while the boy, though on the skinny side for a Botticelli page, would do as he was — though he would be directing the bellows to cool the ladies' cheeks. Venus's fire with its flowerets of flame would have no need of his labours, as it would be eternal, inextinguishable by mortal means.

The two labouring women were of an age with the two ladies from the Grosvenor Gallery; of similar stature, too — and, bar the sweat on their brow, the smudge on their face, the uncouthness of their garb — the worn look, of them (not of the clothes, which were hideously unwearable) — they might have been no less comely. The younger of the two, if one ignored the figure she cut, might have been pretty; while the older — a woman in her thirties — had an alert look.

Mr Baker had withdrawn briefly to cast an eye over some building work at the Board School — and to allow Ruskin more elbow room, which enabled him to make notes. Four strokes with the hand hammer to give the nail its wedge shape (the ancient cuneiform); a touch of treadle to release a massive blow from the heavy hammer to put a head on it, more treadle to cut the nail off and flick it out...

Women even women of the lower classes, Ruskin believed, liked to be identified in the way which flowers (Ruskin was equally sure) liked to be given a name — the basis of his botanical classification was to name the flowers after his 'pets', the young females who told him fairy stories, sat on his knee, ran through orchards with him — until they were too old for such pursuits; whereupon they were put out to grass; married to someone suitable if they were the marrying kind, put in charge of out-of-favour pets if they had become matron-ish. And very occasionally, they were kept on as adults to break his heart, and his health anew.

The older of the two women before him now — she'd look younger if her life were easier — reminded him of some flower, or plant rather. Not rose, not dianthus, not vervain — though that was nearer. An honest dock, such as was used in the foreground of many paintings by Turner. But he knew that even she would not choose this as her name. So he picked a girl's name out of his own past writing — from *Ethics Of The Dust*, which was in need of a new edition: Violet.

'Tell me,' he began, 'Violet, is it?'

'No, sir, Betty.'

'I beg your pardon,' said Ruskin, 'but tell me, Betty, does the great treadle hammer which you apply so dextrously also have a name?'

'I can't be sure of your meaning, sir,' said Betty, without the least deflection of eye or hand from her work.

'What's it called? You may not think of it as a name.'

She looked at her young companion whose mouth remained part open showing surprisingly good teeth, but whose lips did not move while she worked away.

'Well, it's the big Ommer, most of the time. But it's, like, a nolliver, sir.'

'Nolliver,' said Ruskin writing on a pad — 'Ah, an oliver. A noble name, most probably dating back to the English Civil War — to Cromwell, the Hammer.'

No reply being expected from Betty, she worked rhythmically, skilfully — her economy of movement emphasised rather than hindered by the fact that the third finger of her left hand had been lost in the service of her trade.

Ruskin with a certain delicacy took his eyes from her hand and addressed the other younger woman.

'Tell me,' he began, 'do you, too...?'

But Betty intervened before he could ask what he had in mind.

'Yes, sir?'

Ruskin, surprised at this boldness, took a half pace to his right, found himself a shade close to the central heat of the forge, drew back, stepped on a long handled rake or scoop which he had earlier been examining. This swivelled on itself and touched the base of a detached upright rod of iron which leant against the wall — which, in turn, brought a stack of the raw iron rods crashing down behind the unnamed girl, who — with, it seemed, unnatural discipline — continued working, undisturbed.

Ruskin looked at her — her eyes still on her business— and then back to Betty.

'No, sir,' said Betty, sensing, but still not looking, 'her hasn't got no hearing. Nor do she speak neither.'

Ruskin nodded. 'Let me help,' he said.

'Let 'em lie, sir, them rods. They'll do no mischief.'

'Nonsense,' said Ruskin. 'Not I. I was never afraid to get my hands dirty. I advise all my correspondents to keep a set of workmen's clothes in their offices, so that they may do some physical work daily. For this I need only my own hands — they're not workman's hands, but the best I have at my disposal.'

So first he stacked the rods neatly enough, then (transferring a little rust to his notebook) wrote, 'The other one... "Nor do she speak neither", and yet so comely.'

'Betty,' said Ruskin, 'it does you credit that you try to protect your companion, but if your great hammer has a name surely this nimble young woman merits one?'

'Yes,' said Betty, 'she's Ann. She can tell that you mean her when you say that, if her's looking at you like.'

Ruskin nodded. And wrote in his notebook again:

'But she doesn't look.' His pencil moved. He traced the words of his thoughts, but did not write them: 'Should I try to persuade her to turn to me? Has she any idea that she is beautiful? Presumably not, with her affliction and unwomanly sackcloth. And as to Betty: does a missing finger matter to a woman of her class?'

It did he decided. It was curiously misleading. It was almost as if she were a creature of great wealth whose jewels had been stolen by brigands by severance of her finger. Then he wrote: 'It is a hard trade for women. And yet theirs is a job well done.'

He put away his notebook, dusted his hands.

'No, Betty, I don't mind a little rust. Besides,' he said, 'don't you think that rusty iron is nobler that the polished variety? Iron calls to the elements for drink. If there were no rust —no iron — how pale a landscape we would have! Where would be the redness of soil, the redness of good brick, though hidden in soot thereabouts. Do you not, Betty...?'

But then he broke off, assuming he had lost her and that he should get that look of perplexity (if she were able to look up from her work), which well-bred ladies had learned to conceal, but not women of Betty's kind.

On the contrary, Betty responded firmly without needing to raise her eyes:

'Yes, sir,' she said levelly. 'I do know what you mean. That there old iron hulk in the canal, like. It's come alive in its own way, grown like. And all red rust has come creeping up its hawser to the banks — from the water to the barge and down agen — and the grass has grown up kind of gold. It's a picture I sometimes think — like the fire of the forge gone cold, but with the look of heat on't.'

Ruskin's stock in trade was to be misunderstood, so he was taken aback by her apt reply. But he soon recovered himself to thank Betty for her thoughts Whereupon Mr Baker came for him at the door, thoughtfully discouraging the chickens' egress as he did so.

*

As Baker and Ruskin left — the latter talking of Leonardo's master Verrochio ('the great iron-worker, his very name a tribute to those who labour in forges') and thinking of Venus's Forge and Venus's Mirror — a mirror of mercury, of molten iron?) — they noticed a tidy-looking workman step aside as they left the court. He seemed undecided whether he wanted to be seen, but in the end gave a shuffle forward and touched his cap. Ruskin nodded slightly, but continued on his way, with just the thought that if the fellow had more confidence he might be worth talking to. He needed some hard figures about the hours and wages of these people.

*

The workman went into the nail shop. The two women, though they knew his step did not look up from their work (for all the chickens' squawks); but a small girl ran to him and the schoolboy, Thomas, worked the bellows harder to catch his father's eye.

Betty's face crinkled at her husband, but still she kept at her work. Will was home for the night and she knew exactly what he'd be after: best that she gave it him because in a place like Sheffield he'd have no problem in finding someone who'd oblige him — and pick his pocket for it — or so she'd heard.

He wasn't a bad husband, Will Manning. He'd have a few shillings for her and the children, but the immediate problem was to get some of the children bedded down elsewhere for the night, if possible — Ann would take herself off and a couple of them to Gran's for this once.

But Will's mind wasn't dwelling only on what Betty supposed.

'Him as just left. That was that there Mr Ruskin. Professor, wa'nt it? I seen him with Ben Creswick. Perfessor. What he want wi' yow? Mind, he keeps some funny company.'

'He was interested in nailing. People is as has never seen it afore.'

'And yow answered him what he asked?'

'I didn't stop work if that's what you mean. Just gave him me opinion.'

'And day he gie yow owt fer yo opinion?'

'Don't know that he did.'

But there was a silver tinkle on the brick floor lighter than the sound of the lightest hammer. The baby-girl had fortunately not swallowed the coin the Professor had popped into her fist.

4

During the increasingly beautiful journey into the Severn Valley, Ruskin plied his host with questions about the economics of working class life. Because of his office as Overseer and Guardian and his membership of many committees, Baker was able to give complete and satisfactory answers which Ruskin put into his notebook.

'So much,' said Ruskin, 'for the economics of the present age. I am indebted to you for your information, as well as on the Guild's behalf — there's so much to do — for our latest St George's settlement.'

Baker was happy to be of assistance, so the quixotic pair (though each with a touch of Sancho Panza in his disposition) drew steadily further from the smoke of Venus's Forge.

The location of the twenty acres that were being made over to St George's uses was, as Baker had promised, delightful.

They went on foot up St John's Lane ('I have no objection to a rival saint or two,' said Ruskin cheerfully, 'though St George is our man'); to a grove of ancient oaks — where the new Bewdley museum was to be planted (Joseph Southall, architect); up and down into Ruskinland, into St George's Farm, as the orchards were now re-named); through the proposed avenues of renewable timber — there was to be self-sufficiency from the smallest stake to the greatest beam; down again (avoiding the brickworks) to the rear of Beaucastle (which they were unable to enter, though Ruskin had a glimpse of Ben Creswick and Will Manning's exterior work), George Baker expressing a hope of Ruskin's future entertainment there. Leasowes was to be quite outdone in their joint vision of beauty through utility.

Ruskin was talkative during the return journey: 'Your best woodland bower, my dear Baker, shall stand as the only necessary guard about our new museum of St George' — his enthusiasm falling into place, a vacant space, because he was out of patience with the rate of progress of his original Museum in Sheffield, which he had founded as the working man's Bodleian. He felt Bewdley would be right from the start:

'Here we shall house treasures for all to see and use and learn from; safe from the smoke and noise of whirling belts and steam-hammers. The building will be a plain one but made from the finest marble — unadorned, undecorated, primeval. As a token of my intention, impelled by your own generosity, I have already chosen certain items for its galleries. And you must promise me, Mr Baker, that they will be put to immediate use. You will have all that is needful on my departure.'

Mr Baker was, of course, warmed by Ruskin's enthusiasm, particularly as he had received reports that the great man was in decline. No, his prodigious energy was still in evidence, for much of the time.

Arrived back at Bellefield in the late afternoon, Baker noticed a change in his guest. Solicitously, he suggested rest. Ruskin bowed slightly but took himself to the library, where he surrounded himself with Baker's best dictionaries.

'Fors[1] might have told me,' he mused, ' — *An oliver, an olive, a holliper, a holly* ... of all the trees that are in the wood. Ann has beauty, Betty has intelligence: had I had the humility to ask her further, she has wit enough to come nearer the mark than my notion of Cromwell!'

---

[1] In the novel 'Fors' refers to Ruskin's strangely-defined Fate or Fortune itself, as it goes about its work, while '*Fors*' indicates Ruskin's monthly bulletin.

Ruskin was beginning to have difficulty with very small print, but on this occasion — for the light was good — he was able to make out the whole entry including the citations, without the humiliation of a reading glass:

'An oliver, an olive, a holliper, a holly: A large sledgehammer set in an axis of wood from whence goes a rod of iron fastened to a pallet that reaches out a little beyond the anvil, which being drawn by the foot of the smith is returned again by three springs of holly that clasp the axis the contrary way. ...*a little beyond the anvil, which being drawn by the foot of the smith is returned again by three springs of holly that clasp the axis the contrary way.*'

Ruskin was familiar with ash pole lathes, still in use for making chair legs near Coniston; was delighted to find that the terminology of nailing showed its dependence, too, on a living thing, a tree, the crown of the woods:

'We shall, with the help of good St George see that those whose lives depend on that heavy hammer powered by, sprung by, sprung from holly, holliper or oliver are given back their grove — are enabled to work and study with delight.'

Cheerful, enlightened, but put out that his speculative etymology had been faulty (embarrassed, indeed, that he had spoken his guess at the meaning of 'oliver' to a woman — no matter how ignorant she was — whose *intelligence* he had felt), he went to his room and made the very few adjustments to his person which eating dinner, in his view, required.

The meal was a plain affair, attended by plain, earnest people. Baker had assembled all those who were progressive in the town's affairs: fellow members of the boards of guardians, overseers, committee men from the art gallery and museum, from water supply, from sewerage, from the King Edward's grammar school.

It was after dinner. There had been, a pleasant thought of Baker's, sherry from the Ruskin, Telfer and Domecq company, but the son of its late senior partner had made no comment. Some of the guests, whose Quakerism clung to them more closely than it did to Baker, took only water.

They had been warned that Ruskin abhorred tobacco. So those who wished to smoke were obliged to step out onto the terrace. The dinner had been hard work and the atmosphere — now that the ladies had gone — refused to become convivial (perhaps it was the moderation in liquor and the absence of smoke). Baker did not mind that. Conviviality was not an end in itself: rather than being sought, it would best grow out of a serious exchange of views among people with similar purposes.

Ruskin had remained quiet, tracing patterns upon the cloth at table, then fidgeting in an armchair as Baker orchestrated the discourse about him. The Professor would have preferred some parlour game with the ladies.

'Tell me,' he said to Baker in his quietest voice (but as he did so the voices about him deferentially dropped), 'tell me. What is it that all these gentlemen do? They seem busy enough, but what is the purpose of their activity?'

Baker, not knowing whether to draw others into the conversation (for they were clearly listening hard), mentioned the sewerage committee, the Board of Guardians, the lunatic asylum planning group... At which last Ruskin broke into a meaningful chuckle.

'I know all this,' said Ruskin, 'this kind of thing. And my amusement casts no aspersion upon the sanity of the citizens engaged in it. They see themselves as in the service of others. But by what right do they so see themselves? What have they done for themselves? How is it that they have become philanthropists, art collectors, committee people, councillors, politicians? How is it that they are able to take up these positions?'

'Sir,' said Baker, offended. 'As you imply, my colleagues did not acquire their positions of influence from the accidents of birth — there are few traditional aristocrats in this neck of the woods (few squires, even, to return to our earlier discussion). On the contrary, those in this town who hold public office have by their assiduity and integrity built up businesses, whereby they have not only furnished the means for our townspeople to earn their bread, but have also —'

'Yes, yes,' said Ruskin, 'have also enabled themselves to become art collectors, philanthropists, politicians and the like. Would it not be better if they had stuck to their brewing, banking, merchandising? Why put manufactories in the hands of others and take up the careers abandoned by the idle rich? Is this a case of *noblesse oblige*?'

'I was going to use no such expression, sir,' said Baker, angry now. 'Would you have us closely engaged in grinding out money for our own purposes when we have a sufficiency? Should there not be public work for those who have made their own way in the world?'

'No,' said Ruskin, 'no, on two counts. First, working one's way up — working oneself away from one's business is often associated with, and achieved by means of, the selling on of concessions, the taking of a dividend, the lessening of personal control in the quality of the goods, and the manufactory becoming — yes — no more than a false-promissory bank, whose concern is the issuing and redemption of paper promises — and reneging on them. You have read your Carlyle, sir, I refer to the market nexus. Second, I do not hold with the abstraction "public life": a man's a man. People had best perfect their craft and stick to it; to take an honest wage for their labours — not a percentage, not a tax on the poor — ; and when what they amass amounts to more than they can consume, let them not tell themselves that the large income with which they reward their diminishing labours is their just reward for gratuitous council deliberations; no, if they have more money than they earn directly, or know what to do with, let them give away their money, give it back!'

'And, sir,' said Baker, 'forgive my indelicacy, but have I (for one) not done something of this kind?'

'Indeed, sir,' replied Ruskin, 'and you must not think me impertinent in upbraiding you in your own house, indeed you have. But, equally, you must not suppose that you have purchased my silence on subjects which — on any subject under the sun — by your gift to the Guild of St George of a tract of land — yea, a splendid tract of land. The Guild, as you know, is but a mechanism for returning to the people what was theirs in the first place. As to my own work for the Guild, I do it — I thought I had made this clear — not instead of my work, not as better than my work, not as guilt for what remains of my former fortune — but as an unwelcome divergence from my work, and something I cannot help. St George hinders my work, destroys my time — in unsought, but inevitable activity. Excuse me this *ad hominem* approach — of bringing not only yourself but — which is worse — myself into the argument —'

Ruskin was out of his chair, half standing.

'— this *ad hominem* approach...'

He seemed about to let go of what he'd been saying; but continued, eccentrically eloquent:

'You may be surprised, gentlemen, to learn that I entertained myself during my journey in the usual abominable spark and smut dispenser by perusing certain Birmingham directories for the current year. They did not tell me what I wished to know so I left them in the carriage when I alighted. I find, gentlemen, from your own entries in these useless publications that you are aldermen, councillors and justices. Have you taken up your present work to buy off Mammon? Mightn't the camel of the sewerage committee go through the eye of a needle? You, sir,' surveying the room, 'you, sir, and you. What is it that you do? What is it that you make? You, Mr Baker (my honestly dear Mr Baker to whom frankness is owing), my father had a sherry importing company which was his business, what is yours?'

'I entered the manufactory about which you inquire, sir,' said Baker, calmly enough, for there were things which he would not choose to say, but being obliged to do so, stood in his favour, 'at the age of fifteen, as I believe I have mentioned before. My father was ill —'

'My father,' said Ruskin, 'was never ill; and rightly or wrongly, he never put me to learn his business — so there was no question of my continuing it; nor of my keeping the bulk of his capital. Had he done so, I trust I should have showed myself a true son in following his honest example. As it is, I have found an occupation of my own... of which, to tell the truth, I at times despair —'

'To be sure, Professor Ruskin; No, no, Professor Ruskin,' came the voices, hoping he was not moving into one of those black moods of which they heard.

'Thank you, gentlemen,' said Ruskin, whose despair, in this instance, had been rhetorical — though his own mood often was affected by tropes directed at an audience, 'but I stray from my point. You, sir, or you, sir — I must ask you about these companies of which you had the making, and which have been the making of you: what do they consist of and to what are their profits put? Walter Scott left an exact record of his financial dealings. Byron made no secret of his. My recent writings make it absolutely clear what I earn from setting down my thoughts on paper; that I take for myself — far more than a working man with six children (to my shame, more than six times as much) — but I take for myself no more in my honest belief than that which enables me to do my work, and that work in turn provides the required sum. So, sirs, answer for answer: What is the work which you might still be doing, if you were willing to turn your hands to it? The Trades

Directories are coy, Mr Baker. What are the products made by the company called E Baker and Sons shown as operating from Bellefield Birmingham, from this very address? I see no busy workers on these premises other than domestic servants. Is it — for this is all I can find, all that comes near — is it a blacking factory, or are you a manufacturer of gilded knickknacks? Or is it some nobler enterprise? Or even a worse one? No — after all — do not tell me. If it is one of which you are proud you had best to have stuck with it. If it is one of which you are ashamed, then you should find better work for your employees. Let us none of us turn our backs on labour.'

There was, in spite of everything, a little applause and no great hostility. This was the Ruskin their consciences had been awaiting.

'Thank you,' said Ruskin, 'for your tolerance — but these are my opinions arising from this visit, not a species of entertainment. You will see them, albeit briefly and circumspectly, set out in my monthly *Fors* letter.'

They wished him good night. He smiled his sweet smile, climbed the staircase, carried out the reading he had prescribed for himself, withdrew Rosie's letter from its gold plates and read it in devotional fashion, replacing it with more care than he accorded to any of the precious things which he had purchased for the Guild of St George — let alone his own dismembered Book of Hours — thinking of which, he placed some material he'd brought for Mr Baker in a prominent position on the floor below his water colours (which were on the window sill ready for dawn).

That accomplished, he sat down to record for his monthly *Fors*, as he had promised Baker and his guests, his impressions of the weekend. He tried out several titles. At first, he thought of leading with his present location — Bellefield, Birmingham — crossed that through as banal and with having little bearing on what he had seen in the Severn Valley. 'Worcestershire', he wrote and added the word 'Clavigerae'. *Fors Clavigera*, the title of his strange cumulative work, meant to him the nail-bearing Fate, or avenging angel — or happenstance, or even involuntary associations or tricks of circumstance. *Clavigerae*. How curious that the two women were literally nail-bearing. That he should have chosen the image for his work, *Clavigerae* — nail-bearing in the sense of a studded club, a retributory weapon. Thus *Fors Clavigera* (through Fors) — like a fateful, fanciful trick of Rosie's, and — yes — a hint of Rosie in this — had chosen its own title, without until now telling him the full meaning or compass of the work. Were these two nailers to be in any sense part of his destiny? Unlikely that he would have any thing more to do with women of this class, whatever they might have managed if their circumstances had been different. Born earlier, or born later into the era of St George — into pre-industrial or into post-industrial Britain — their situation would have been different.

But he would give them their moment of freedom — or catch them as specimens — preserve them in a title: 'The Two *Clavigerae*' — Betty and Ann, weren't they? But that didn't matter. They were two women phantoms — like those who crewed the ghost ship in *The Ancient Mariner* — phantasms of Mrs Lavenham and Miss Stott. 'The Two Clavigerae', that should be the title. And whose fault was all this — that two coarsely garbed women, so strangely employed, should bear a phantom resemblance to two ladies, the younger in the height of youthful fashion — and reminding him just a little (though not so slim nor quite so tall) of Rose in her high-necked walking dress and fetching little hat? He saw Rosie clearly holding the paws of her great dog Bruno, as tall as she was when he stood up. He had sometimes wished he was Bruno, believed he could have been content to be so. The recollection changed to that of Miss Stott, and then to poor Ann, and then to Betty in sackcloth, the counterpart of Mrs Lavenham in her sensibly-adapted (simple and expensive) pre-Raphaelite gown.

He meant to retire to bed, but found the notes of nailers' earnings which Baker had given him; and began to write up their poor worldly reward for:

'...labour from morning to evening — seven to seven...The wages of the matron, I found, were eight shillings a week (sixteen pence a day, or, for four days' work, the price of a lawyer's letter); her husband, otherwise and variously employed, could make sixteen. Three shillings a week for rent and taxes left fifty-five pounds a year to feed and clothe themselves and their six children.'

How far would three shillings a week go, with even an unaffected girl like Miss Stott — let alone a stylish woman such as Mrs Lavenham? He thought of bringing their dress allowance into the published equation; but took a decision to refer only to his own income — against disparaging something which, after all, was very delightful in ladies. Like lilies of the field, they out-adorned Solomon, and, as vehicles for condescension, added to the concupiscent monarch's wisdom: which Veronese had truly shown in his great Turin picture of the Queen of Sheba's visit.

Beauty and virtue, through such living exemplars, could work upon men, achieve whatever they wanted; unto re-making the world. The pity was that ladies, not realising their power and purpose (though Ruskin reminded them of it frequently in his writings), sought to exert little effort beyond the betterment of their immediate families.

There followed a disturbing thought. Could it be that Rosie had not worked upon him himself strongly enough? She had fought with all her might and perversity for, as she saw it, his soul. He had to believe that she was mistaken in so doing. He had to believe that, as a man and an older man, he knew best. In this he had the authority of the Bible — her Bible — behind him. It had to be the case that she was mistaken in insisting that he must think of her no more — 'in that way' — as a precondition of her accepting him in some other way. But there was no other way. Love of another human being — as man to wife — far from entailing a diminution of the love for God — was to His greater glory. Ruskin was angry at the thought of her, angry that he couldn't argue her out of her obstinacy. Almost glad to have seen the back of her, though he thought of her constantly, waited for her sweet messages.

He slept well again, but woke to a rainy dawn of continuing grey. No depiction of that possible, he straightaway wrote in more or less finished form the opening of his August *Fors* Letter, incorporating the promised, gentler rebukes for his company of the previous night:

'I must say to my Birmingham friends a few things which I could not, while I was bent on listening and learning... All they showed me, and told me, of good, involved yet the main British modern idea that the master and his men should belong to two entirely different classes; perhaps loyally related to and assisting each other; but yet, — the one, on the whole, living in hardship — the other in ease; — the one uncomfortable — the other in comfort...'

This passage — and some graceful thank-you paragraphs (for he knew the possession of relics was important to his followers) — he would copy to Mr Baker addressed as from 'Bellefield, Birmingham', which location would be included in the published version, as soon as he was safely back in Herne Hill.

*

'Goodbye, my dear sir,' said Ruskin at the station. 'And as to Squires — they are all that England has. Yes, the land-owner will have come by his land unjustly, but he has it in his possession — and sometimes, even, cares for it — and therein resides a social order which does not depend upon smoke. So, Mr Baker,' taking him by the hand, 'I wish you well in your squiredom — a squiredom of St George. Let your sons be active manufacturers in Birmingham, while you cultivate your Bewdley — your St George's garden. You have taught me — all of you — a good deal, and if at any time I seemed to suggest otherwise, that is only my way. Those who love me have to get used to that.'

Baker fumbled for an answer and used the word 'admire'.

'I think I am too far gone to hear such things,' said Ruskin —' but saying so is only my mischief. I thank you again. And, on behalf of St George, for Bewdley. You will find, sir — we are suddenly short of time, that is the iniquity of these railroads (and by the by did you notice that the nailers we observed were turning out spikes for the securing of rails to sleepers? Another nail in my coffin — and of the railway-less countryside between Ambleside and Keswick — and of all those, including some of our colonial friends, who are no lovers of steam travel) — but, as I was going on to say, sir, you will find in the room I have just vacated at Bellefield a package and a labelled bag addressed to you. Open them both and see what you think. I shall be writing to you shortly, with — as I said I would — the first scratch of the next *Fors*, composed during my instructive stay with you.'

The train was on time and he had to scurry; as did Baker thereafter, for he wished to see what Ruskin had left for him, before returning to the town centre for one of his many municipal meetings. The package could have — should have waited — but he wanted to be able to tell any of his fellow-councillors who might have felt Ruskin impolite, how graciously the Professor had responded after all.

So he hurried to his carriage, and the driver got through the traffic as best he could. Baker was about to rush upstairs when his housekeeper cousin apprised him that the items he sought had been taken to the library. The package turned out to be a portfolio (at first the maid had been upset that the professor had departed without some of his belongings, but closer inspection showed these items carefully marked 'for the attention of Geo Baker Esq').

The bag contained a carved boss from St Mark's, cast in plaster; the portfolio, two images of St George — one an engraving by Dürer, with the note 'purchased October 1875 for £3-10s of my own money, kept at Oxford, though intended for the Sheffield Museum — now offered to Bewdley for immediate use'; the other, a photogravure version of Burne-Jones' St George ('as Jones noted, in unfinished state — like our project, but yes — with your generosity and sympathy, we move forward. JR'). There was also behind it a folded piece of foolscap, which had 'Study for Alcestis' written on the back in Ruskin's hand and a small EBJ, front right — a vigorously drawn three inch head and naked shoulder, at which Baker caught his breath: largely, because — there being no accompanying note — he might have thrown it away as part of the packing, which he now re-checked. Though there were two or three other pieces of torn paper; they bore neither image nor message. Still, Baker carefully put them back. Then, though time was short, he took the Burne-Jones drawing gently to the light.

In soft pencil, on thin unsympathetic paper, her nose and left eyebrow no more than a pot-hooked S, her eyes little outlined fishes (she's almost full face), her lips, two broken horizontal lines — yet he could tell her teeth; sense her hair brushed and falling forward from the crown of her head, with the back of it – the bulk of it – some of it, showing, flung behind her left shoulder. This was a real face. And a body moving in a real way. He could tell that she's just turned her head to the right. Herself still facing just a little left, yet her eyes further right. She's been caught. Would her hair have swung beyond her left shoulder if she had completed the turn? Her right shoulder would probably prevent that…

There was some perfunctory veiling and draping. She was naked – but could pass for propriety's sake as clothed. A rapid study. Instructive because imperfect, Ruskin might have thought. And Baker, no expert, could see that the artist had had trouble with her left forearm and rubbed a hole in the paper. A warm-blooded man himself, Baker recognised another such here in Burne-Jones, whom he had assumed would be a cold fish.

*

A different image, but the same time. Thomas was getting his hours of schooling at the beginning of the week. A hard-edged dunce's cap of a drawing, though not made by a dunce. Thomas, told to reproduce the conical plane set before him, had got to the stage where it was best to let stand what he had got down on paper: he was industrious — and he needed to keep working at his drawing to keep himself awake — but he was also judicious for his age. His partner at the desk had rubbed his own paper tearfully into rags and covered the hole which he had dug for himself with a crooked forearm, working ashamedly with his nose touching the paper. The erasers were of poor quality, so — though there was still time available to finish the task — Thomas turned his paper over, so that he would not be tempted to re-touch what he had done. He held the paper flat with his hardworking left hand — he'd have written and drawn with that one, if that had not been forbidden.

He looked at his right, with its chapped and wizened quality and its black-ended broken nails. Then, turning that right hand over, he laid it on the paper. With the pencil in his left hand, he started quickly to record what he saw...and first his open right hand.

The teacher — the young man appointed by Baker — was obliged to give Thomas several cuts for disobedience on that same hand as well as on the back of the left one (which seemed to the punisher and the punished appropriate). Both as products of the same system were stoical. Thomas's palm was too callused to feel much, but the back of the hand, with little flesh to it, pained him.

The teacher, whose name was Joseph Hill, conceded that the drawing was well done, though a strange topic and not one set for the standard. Still — for Mr Hill had taken, albeit in sedulous ape-fashion, his South Kensington certificate — he resolved to try to find paper for the boy for more compositions of this kind.

Neither bore the other any malice — indeed, both were well-pleased on reflection with the encounter: 'Tell me, Thomas Manning,' said Hill, 'what made you take your hands as a subject?'

The open-ended question produced an unpremeditated answer:

'Because, sir, they chose themselves like. But I intend to do summat — mek things with 'em, something of myself like. Not nails if I can help it.'

*

'But we cannot all be physicians, artists, or soldiers. How are we to live?' Ruskin was back in his old home at Herne Hill, well into the writing of his August *Fors*. He could answer his own question and answer it confidently, with St George's (and maybe St Ursula's aid):

So, 'How are we to live?' he wrote, wrote rapidly. 'Assuredly not in multitudinous misery. Do you think that the Maker of the world intended all but one in a thousand of His creatures to live in these dark streets; and the one, triumphant over the rest, to go forth alone into these green fields?'

Such had been his thoughts as he had driven with Baker to Leasowes and into the vale of Severn. He wrote two paragraphs to this effect. Then the women; coming across the strange women — androgynous at first sight — like weird sisters, like Macbeth's witches – though without their beards. Doing men's work, doing rough men's work, dressed in rough weave like men, doing heavy work. They could hardly be women, hardly remain women, hardly be expected to be women. Yet, yet. And he continued his writing:

'One about seventeen or eighteen, the other perhaps four or five and thirty; this last intelligent of feature as well could be; and both, gentle and kind, — each with hammer in right hand, pincers in left (heavier hammer poised over her anvil, and let fall at need by the touch of her foot on the treadle...)'

He described with due exactness their working processes and, in the following paragraph, set down indignantly the miserable sum of their earnings for their strenuous repetitive work. But then the image of Charlotte Lavenham and Claire Stott in their pretty gowns came before him once more, and – as it were – tried to interrupt him. Postponing any reference to them, he wrote on:

'Yet it was not chiefly their labour in which I pitied them.'

For he admired their skill. Had he not urged the Miss Stotts and the Mrs Lavenhams of his acquaintance to go in for handicraft, so where did the difference lie? Were idle ladies to be made to work and working women stopped from doing so? Could women who hadn't leisure and money enough to attire themselves beautifully have nothing of the function of their privileged sisters – their propensity to mould and fashion men?

No, working women's business was to be mothers and educators of children – for their men were mostly too far gone in their toil, and therefore unresponsive to and unfit for female influence. And yet – for all the squalor of their dress and the rigour of their employment – he had seen and sensed a capability in the two female nailers; and so, not to demean or separate Betty and Ann, he wrote of them as women – along with the two gallery-going ladies. Women too. Four of them. Four Englishwomen:

'Yet it was not chiefly their labour in which I pitied them, but rather that their forge-dress did not well set off their English beauty; nay, that the beauty itself was marred by the labour... And all the while as I watched them, I was thinking of two other Englishwomen, of about the same relative ages, with whom... I had been standing a little while before Edward Burne-Jones's picture of Venus's Mirror.'

And he added a word or two about his trick with the reflections of the ladies' faces. Mrs Lavenham, he suddenly thought, with a certain discomfiture, just might have experienced some such looking-glass play of his on a previous occasion. But certainly not Claire Stott. Hadn't she clapped her (pretty) hands? There had been something odd about the hand of one of the working women.

Also something odd about Ned's work. The sketch. He, John Ruskin, had brought together the ladies and the women – the Idea of them; like painting and reflected reality. Like the sketch which he had sent and, confusingly, also delivered. Something strange about the sketch – the sketch of Ned's that he'd sent to Baker. He himself had with his own hands left it with him. If he had not left it somewhere else. Had he, or hadn't he, had a package of that sort in the train? Or had he – the worst of all things – sent or left Baker something else, some other drawing? He thought he had left it to for him. Or sent the right one. He needed to have sent it to him. Or left it for him in the guest bedroom.

He *hoped* he had left it or sent it to him. He needed to have left it or sent it to him. There was a pressing reason why he ought to be sure he had. The alternative – he tried not to be melodramatic, and shoved the horror of the alternative to the side of his mind, in the same way that he now was now fumbling and shifting the papers and portfolios in the arm's length around him, and about his feet – and on a chair by his knees.

Then he forgot about the drawing — the two drawings? — for a little while, repressing the problem. It soon recurred, though to a calmer mind – the same mind, Ruskin's mind, but a mind which seemed not to have thought the thought, formulated the thought, faced the thought before.

…There was some other anxiety here about this, about this drawing. He had sent *something*. He thought he had *left* something. If he hadn't — as perhaps he hadn't — if he hadn't sent or left Alcestis, then had he left or sent something else in its stead? Something else in error. One piece of paper was much like another. Whether or no, what did it matter?

Ruskin knew that it did matter. A blackness came over him, and he felt his mind clench like a leg with a cramp. He put a hand to his head and caused the pressure to lessen until he was able to insist to himself convincingly — for the time being — that it had been the

Alcestis. And that he had, indeed, left it for Baker. Or had he merely thought of doing so? Visualised himself doing so — and then gone on to do something else?

Not so, not at all, that was it. He would certainly have left a precious reminder of the lady Alcestis, who had chosen to die in her husband's stead. Much in the end, as you could argue Rose had done. For here he was alive and working, and Rose was his wife in heaven, whatever she might think.

The ghost of Rose looked on. (Though small consolation to him, her quasi-widower on earth.)

So it might have been he who had died instead of her. But, yes, he had to believe that his own earthly work was truer than Rose's had been or would have been — her insistence that the Seventh Day was the seventh day, that Saturday was the Sabbath, that Sunday was Monday, that black was white, that life was death, that death was life, that marriage could be avoided by dying, and that in Heaven they would be no more than nodding neighbours. And that she knew all this and he didn't.

The ghost of Rose hadn't the strength to argue, or even the urge. Why should she contest this muddled travesty, not even properly addressed to her, and expressed so crossly, so rhetorically?

Ruskin, as if taking note of that, turned on himself. Was his life and work to be preserved at all costs? And could he have continued that work, if the strength he had gained in accepting the death of Rose, the collapse of his hopes, hadn't come to his aid?

He proceeded as if the answer to his first question was 'Yes'; accepted that the answer to his second question was probably 'No'. If put to the test, he would in some moods concede that Rose had died for him; not, in spite of him. (In other black ones, she had died to spite him.)

He struggled now to continue the *Fors* bulletin, that had been begun so easily. The theme was women's occupation. The image of the two women-nailers superimposed itself upon that of Miss Stott and Mrs Lavenham as he intended. But when he tried to see the four women side by side, he failed. He could neither visualise the first pair in a gallery nor the second in a forge.

*

He dipped his pen in the ink and wrote a sentence, which if his readers got beyond his question-mark, would show them — male and female — where they stood:

'Shall I say now whose fault it is?'

And the writing came alive. Beautifully, once again, he blamed the failings of gentlemen — and the lot of working women — not on Adam, but on Eve. On the propensity of ladies to make too few demands on the ruling, managing, guiding, male principle; of looking in Venus's mirror and seeing only themselves. As Ruskin's pen crossed the paper, it recreated pleasant little encounters, and flirtatious strategies, which took him away from recriminations:

'Shall I say now whose fault it is?

'First, those two lovely ladies who were studying the *Myosotis palustris* [forget-me-nots] with me;' — writing fluently now, with the parenthetical thoughts slotting easily into place' — and then, that charming — (I didn't say she was charming but she was, and is) — lady whom I had charge of at Furness Abbey, and her two daughters; and those three beautiful girls who tormented me so on the 23rd May, 1875, and another who greatly disturbed my mind at church, only a Sunday or two ago…, with the sweetest little white straw bonnet I had ever seen, only letting a lock or two escape of the curliest hair, so that I was fain to make a present of a Prayer-book afterwards, advising her that her tiny ivory one was too coquettish...'

He was losing the thread. The point ought to have been that he, John Ruskin, realised he should not have become quite so readily a man beguiled by ladies; rather, he should have striven — should strive — even now to become a man who put himself to the test of the bright minds and fresh perceptions – rather than complexions — of able young ladies. Women could re-make men for the better. Ergo, they should be more insistent, more pressing. But, no, no, not strident. A young woman's wisdom – a woman not enslaved by structured – strictured — theology like Rose's.

He'd murmured the name in its possessive form (how appropriate), but he heard it as 'Rosie', which was more pleasant. Was she back, was Rosie back, was the ghost of Rosie looking over his shoulder, as he sat pen in hand, but no longer writing? No, she'd let him be.

Likewise Claire Stott. Neither she nor he had written after she'd gone to her uncle's house in the country. Perhaps Claire was one of the ones who could hold her own. Write? She would, he guessed. She would respond in some way: when she saw the latest *Fors* and fancied that she saw images of 'two other Englishwomen', herself and Mrs Lavenham, projected onto the smoke of that forge; Vulcan's Forge — as they had been upon Venus's Mirror.

5

Worcestershire with its country air and helping out in the schoolroom had been proposed for Claire. But once installed with her Midland aunt and uncle, Mr and Mrs Melville, the former declared it would be better for her to read Shakespeare in the conservatory with twelve-year old Sarah or sit on the garden grass with her older cousin Mary and talk about other indoor things.

Mary had reservations about Claire's prettiness and her success with young Sarah, while Claire wished that the Melville's recently-built villa could have passed more plausibly for a country cottage, as depicted by Charlotte Lavenham; after seeing whose work her own pencil and colour studies seemed too rudimentary to persevere with. In any case, since meeting Ruskin, she had temporarily reverted to the kind of late childhood she sensed he seemed to favour.

Thus, to the irritation of Mary, Claire was making daisy-chains, which she now draped about the other young lady's neck. An insect came with the decoration. Mary, in brushing it away from the weekly paper she was reading, broke the chain.

'I'm sorry,' said Mary, 'after all your work.'

'Work!' said Claire, 'I can't call that work. There must be something — well, I know there's something...'

'Yes,' said Mary, absently, 'well, yes,' she continued with a little malice, 'there's always something. This, for instance, might amuse you.'

And she read out from her paper:

'"The Scriptural names — Where are they gone
   And the Echo answers 'Where?'
Mary and Sarah and Ruth give place
   To Beatrice, Ethel and Claire —"
— Now isn't that the two of us in a nutshell? Our respective households I mean?'

Claire thought this rude, as she had not brought either a Beatrice or an Ethel with her. However, she felt herself in no position to quarrel with her cousin:

'It is, I suppose,' she replied, levelly enough, 'a question largely of the difference between town and country.'

'Shouldn't you, then,' said Mary, 'consider being Ruth amongst our alien corn?'

'Only,' said Claire, 'if you are Ethel in Bloomsbury.'

'I'm not sure,' replied Mary, 'that I could — pick up the ways of the town or would even like to for more than a *short* visit.'

'I expect mama can arrange that for you,' said Claire ambiguously.

Mary, silenced, decided it would be politic not to squabble with Claire. She did want a proper stay with the Stotts in Bloomsbury.

'So, Claire,' she was saying, as she brushed daisies destructively, 'for the moment, you seek a rural pursuit. You still have' — with a semblance of good-humour — '*As You Like It* to finish with Sarah.'

'Yes,' said Claire, 'but Sarah has other studies which cannot conveniently be carried out in the garden, and Uncle does not wish me to work in the schoolroom.'

'Or,' said Mary, again mischief-making, 'it might be that Missy-the-Governess would rather her charge were not too much in the hands of pretty Miss Stott.'

'Oh,' said Claire, confusedly, 'do you think so? Not the supposed prettiness, I mean —'

'Supposed nothing,' said Mary, 'your prettiness is real enough.'

The idea that she was pretty, presented in a way which seemed to preclude all other desirable qualities, left Claire in mid air. It was as if she had clouds at her feet, without having climbed a mountain or having any mountain to climb. Out of the air, out of the *Tempest*-like island sounds about her, out of the fragments of the writings of John Ruskin and poetry in her head, trying to give form to her vagueness, she cried out, though quietly enough:

'I have immortal longings in me...'

Mary was turning over a page. She looked up:

'Cleopatra, Act V Scene ii before her suicide. A rather silly thing to say, don't you think? On her part, my dear cousin, I hasten to add.'

'Perhaps,' said Claire. 'And best not ask me what I mean. No, nothing self-destructive. But had I been an Egyptian Queen with the responsibilities of a third of an empire, I dare say I shouldn't have felt myself answerable to such an irresponsible paramour.'

'And there's no one of that kind. I am not unaware of your regard for the no doubt admirable and certainly elderly Professor Ruskin, but accept that that is the meeting of true minds only.'

'Thus far, yes — the true minds, I mean. Yet he would have young ladies so very educated in an antique fashion — reading dead tongues and conversant with the niceties of Florentine legal systems, with — still — our function as inspirational underlings.'

'To honour and obey you mean,' said Mary tartly.

'That goes without saying,' said Claire, 'even before or even instead of marriage — and after having done all that reading — to stand and smile. Standing and smiling and being angular looks very good in Mr Jones' paintings. But, no, I wish sometimes I were a working woman.'

'You'd like to be poor, diseased, and dirty?'

'Of course I wouldn't like to be poor, diseased, and dirty, but I have strong hands and would like to use them to better effect than opening walnuts at Christmastime. A working woman can benefit from the strength in her fingers, but one born a lady (albeit not a very grand lady), how can she use this, her best attribute?'

'Embroidery,' said Mary with an air of settling the matter.

'I thrust my needle through the stiffest stuff with great success but dislike the end product, not to mention the slavishness of the process.'

'In that case,' said Mary, with more interest than hitherto, 'mightn't you be better employed in reading Clementia Doughty or Reverend Maurice?'

'Thank you, but I don't think so. I'm no radical. But if you'll excuse me I think I'll go down to the potting shed and set up shop as a labourer since I can't be a workman.'

'But won't Giles object and tell father?'

'Not if I tell him of the beauty of his borders and smile very sweetly.'

'But are these feminine wiles the forte of a labourer?'

'They're the means to an end,' said Claire, the way before her suddenly, momentarily clear.

*

Claire's uncle in fact had to be taken into her confidence, so disapprobation from Giles didn't come into it. Both the gentleman and his servant became objects of her pretty behaviour. In due course she had what she wanted: a well-poised little hammer from Sheffield, three sharp-pointed little chisels procured locally, a handsome piece of porphyry delivered by post from Mr Tennant of the Strand. All this in accordance with the instructions of Mr Ruskin as set out in Letter 64 of *Fors Clavigera*.

This pamphlet was open at her left elbow. After her meeting with Ruskin, Claire had learned how to get some back issues and now was a subscriber. She had written to tell him so; and then sent a copy of the same letter, in case it had miscarried. She had attached the copy to a brief, even brusque covering note, for fear he might think her a toady for writing twice and to punish him for not yet replying if had already received the first version.

So *Fors* was to her left, and before her the porphyry (carving of which was deemed essential to anyone seeking to understand either art or history), fixed firm by Giles in plaster of Paris and rubble in a small millstone water-trough.

('Thank you, Giles, so much,' she had said. 'No, the height will do admirably — as you say, it is safest to have the trough on the floor — and I prefer to kneel, so that I can lean over the work.'

'Do be sure, miss, that you cut in the direction away from you like.'

'Thank you, Giles. I have full instructions which I shall not depart from.'

'As you say, Miss.')

In spite of her confident words she was nervous about the hard, hard material and spent a little while (as Ruskin had advised) on prefatory studies, in gouging out trenches from composition candles. The point, it seemed, was to observe how tiny spiral-staircases of wax spun upwards, 'like the most lovely little crimped or gathered frill,' and then to try to draw this phenomenon. The frill-effect reminded Claire of needlework, which was (if she had her way) a thing of the past — with, too, something of the frivolity of daisy-chains. Producing the curls of wax was too easy, and she did not share the Professor's aesthetic, childish pleasure in their production. As for drawing them, that, on the other hand, sounded too hard since the Professor himself said he hadn't achieved a satisfactory result.

No, she wanted what he had promised, to 'know more about Egypt than nine hundred and ninety-nine people in a thousand' — and all this from cutting out a cuneiform asterisk in a piece of stone. The porphyry was evidently unyielding, but then her tools were sharp and hard, and presumably fashioned with the task in mind. Who knows what success in this field would lead to? The Egyptological insights seemed tenuous, but no doubt future visits to the British Museum would come to seem quite different — if only for the sense that what was there in a glass case had once been a piece of stone: yes, a rough piece of stone, then a shaped piece of stone and then an incised piece of stone.

So much learnt already without even starting! The asterisk which would shortly be cut on her porphyry would be convertible to a floral flourish, beside which she would copy some fine saying of the Professor's that could be presented to him, and which he would treasure. And, later, she would be able cut gems of poetry, lines from Shakespeare: in the first instance as presents for family and friends; thereafter, by commission. She would have her own small studio, which Mrs Lavenham would visit and they would show their work together. Two successful working ladies.

A cushion under her knee, Claire took a chisel in fingers that shook a little. Supporting her right wrist with the raised thumb of her left hand (the other fingers of which were pressing down on a heavy steel rule), she managed to make a faint, straight scratch on the shiny surface.

'At least it's not crooked,' she thought. 'But yet so very faint a mark, such a little superficial one — how far short of a vast stone screen of hieroglyphs...'

Seeking to clarify the incision, she reversed motion and exerted more pressure. The chisel slid off course, and just missing her pale left arm (the sleeve pushed back) with its pretty veins, its alabaster look (but not substance), the vee of steel caught the rucked fabric at her elbow.

Claire came over faint but determined. Finding a small piece of light sacking, she bound it about her left arm to protect it against further slips.

She persevered. The scored short line (with a spreading spider's web of skids about it) was clearer now, but the point of the chisel already less keen than it had been. Soon she could no longer work with it — the edge had gone.

Two chisels left: how to convert the line into a firm asterisk? Had Mr Ruskin managed it better, she wondered. (Had he even tried? a disloyal voice added, retracted.) Perhaps he had stouter tools. But no, she would not have recourse to the bad workman's practice of attributing failure to everything — bar lack of skill.

As she made her attempt and mused and pondered on the difficulty — irritated that her strong fingers did not seem able to transmit their force and precision to this, their extension — the second chisel turned its edge and the third broke off short.

Claire went to brush the fragments of metal away; stopped herself — realising that if she did that they would pierce and work into the flesh at the edge of her soft hand (albeit a strong one for what it usually had to do); instead, blew the slight dust of porphyry from the block; and, augmenting the action with her protected left forearm, looked at what she now had. A small and tentative cross was all there was to be seen, like a three-year-old's drawing of a ship on a slate. No better than that.

Worse, the porphyry was impaired rather than enhanced and all the shining chisels spoilt. Most shaming of all was the consideration that everything that was solid and accomplished — the gritstone trough, its packing, the plaster of Paris setting, the polished porphyry as it had been, the chisels formerly sharp — had been fashioned by hands other than her own. Hers had undone what had been previously well done.

*

With Ruskinian determination she resolved to start again; elicited from Giles the opinion that the tools needed hardening in a forge.

'No,' said Claire to an offer that was only half made, 'I'll see to it myself.'

She put the tools in a bag and walked to the High Street.

A horse was waiting to be shod outside the forge. She walked round it onto the threshold.

'Let me come to you, missy,' said the blacksmith, 'you'll not like the smoke in here.'

The heat hit her face, the sounds — the bellows, the clank of pincers — hurt her ears.

'That's all right,' she said. 'No, as a matter of fact I like it in here well enough.'

A piece of red-hot metal showed and she did not flinch.

'That's as maybe, young lady,' said the blacksmith, 'but we must be sure you keep well away from the work. Come this way.'

'But I shan't be able to see. Mayn't I stay and watch?'

'I should be answerable to your uncle, ma'am,' said the smith.

But Claire stood there as long as she dared with the fire on her face. And when she finally took herself into the cool air she realised that she'd said nothing about the chisels.

She walked on in a dream and found herself in a narrow street on the edge of the little town. She was about to turn back, when the smokiness of the neighbourhood suggested to her that there must be a blacksmith's shop hereabouts.

From a back gate, she could hear a clanging of hammers on an anvil. No sign of horses, just a few hens in the smoke.

*

'You were so kind, sir, to ask after my own progress in post,' Joseph Hill was writing to Mr Baker, 'when you called to see the Board School building work during Professor Ruskin's visit…' This was a passage which Hill found difficult: he wanted to say he was sensible of the honour and how pleased he was etc (and was glad to have been observed at the weekend carefully preparing his Monday lessons), but was anxious not to lose Baker's good opinion, which he thought he might, by seeming obsequious, so in this, his third draft, he passed straight on to: 'I am taking the liberty of enclosing a drawing produced by Thomas the son of Betty Manning (whom I understand was the person favoured by Professor Ruskin's observations). It has to be admitted that what he has produced has no bearing on the curriculum for his standard.

Indeed, I had no option but to discipline him for the circumstances in which it was drawn: which may be easily ascertained by glancing at the obverse. Though I am certificated as proficient in the instruction of drawing, I have little claim to specialist knowledge nor do I have the advantage of acquaintance with any connoisseur of the visual arts. Forgive me, sir, but you are more likely to have both of these qualities than I. Perhaps there is someone on, for example, the Art School Board who could offer a word of encouragement or advice to a lad who gives of his very best but has not the best of prospects — though, to his credit, he seems not without ambition.'

After some respectful words of conclusion, he re-read what he had written; rolled Thomas's drawing, as he had learned to do at South Kensington, into a cardboard tube, which he sealed and put in the post for Mr Baker.

*

Claire felt foolish because the gate on to the alley from which she had heard the sound of hammers proved to be broken and jammed. And she hadn't wanted to dirty her walking-out dress by leaning upon the obstruction to try to force it open. Keeping the general sense of the direction of the place in mind (and at first the sound and smell of it gave a clear indication), she retraced her steps. The sounds had faded by the time she had got back to the High Street. From there she walked a little way to her left and turned up the first lane that she came across.

She was by herself, dressed like a lady and carrying artisan's tools, though broken-ended ones; but she was not going to be bullied and condescended to by some smith who knew her uncle. She headed towards work smells. There would be a friendly artisan in a forge who would surely not be too proud or busy to earn — what? — twopence, sixpence, a shilling for sharpening her tools…

Intermingled with the work smells, there were now other smells which she tried not to attend to, and broken bricks under her feet; dirt now and, even in summer, little pools with the contents of slop pails about them. She held her breath against infection and counted twenty rapid strides towards the (she assumed) safer part where the workers were. The lane had appeared picturesque seen from the High Street. Claire let out her breath. She hoped that the fiery particles which she now perceived in the smoke would fumigate and sterilise the spores and chances of disease. A rhyme came into her head: 'Ladybird, ladybird, fly away home; Your house is on fire and your children are gone.'

It was not just the smoke that had put the verse into her head, Claire realised, as she held up her skirts a little higher. The trouble she was having with her dress put her in mind of the sometimes protruding wings of the little beetle as it went its way amongst the daisy-chain material and maybe onto Cousin Mary's lap. (Claire had divested herself of the crinolette which had been so bothersome at the Grosvenor Gallery — in deference both to country ways and to Mrs Lavenham's evident sympathy with Dress Reform — but her gown still had all its fullness at the back; trailing and catching at the unevenness over which she was making her way.)

The noise of the hammers grew louder, the rhythm stayed constant. A gust of summer wind blew dust about her skirts; sending, she could see, the smoke of the forge back down the chimney and into the hovel. The place filled with smoke that came out of the top of the stable door. There was some coughing, but the sound of the hammers went on.

A boy whose lungs were evidently not in the best of condition stuck his head outside to gasp for air.

'A young lady,' he called, turning inside again — 'a young lady, to be seen to.'

The hammering continued. Then, to Claire's surprise, it was a woman's voice that answered:

'Ask what her wants, if you please.'

Claire wondered why the woman did not come herself and then, as the smoke blew back up the flue, saw the red hot rod she was working upon. Claire felt the heat of it from a distance of twelve feet. Beyond the woman (the boy's mother, she assumed) was another slight figure similarly engaged.

'I wanted, boy,' she said, 'someone to sharpen my tools.'

'Certainly, miss,' said the boy, after looking at the chisels. 'They'll be tekkin' a mouthful of tea in a moment and we can soon do summat for you. They need hardening like. Me on the bellows and mam with the big Ommer and this here grindstone can do that a treat.'

'Give 'em ovver, Thomas,' said his mother, ' I can fix you that, miss. You shun't keep a young lady waiting. It'll only cost you the price of a few nails, miss, if that's all right. No more than twopence.'

And proficiently and dextrously she did her job, and Claire returned to rudimentary chiselling feeling she was good for not much.

*

George Baker opened up the tube and took out Hill's letter and Thomas's drawing. At first he was disappointed because he'd assumed it to be something else from Ruskin, but he spread the drawing out by weighting its corners and inspected it. He was impressed. The right hand (palm up) was more strongly delineated than the left, because the left (palm down) had largely been drawn in the act of drawing — though some precise, but less vigorous details had been supplied by the right hand, with the left one at rest, as a model. Though Baker did not draw himself, he could see there was something to it — ambidexterity, maybe.

The fingers of the right hand were drawn like the spokes of a sturdy wheel and the base of the fingers had the solidity and form of wood worked with a spokeshave. But the fingers were not rigid, they grasped at the observer's gaze and conveyed strength — strength out of their depth on the paper, which came from Thomas's intuitive depiction of foreshortening.

Baker could see what Hill had in mind in sending him this work. As to his own response, there would be risk in it, but Ruskin was due an acknowledgement for the souvenir draft of the August *Fors*. So Baker decided to chance his arm. Before putting pen to paper — for he wanted to say something about the Professor's gifts of artwork — of, especially, the original drawing — he looked up 'Alcestis' in an encyclopaedia and found an entry which said, 'when the time came for her husband to die, she consented to give her life for his.'

It was natural that these words should remind him of his own dead wife; though the direct cause of her sacrifice had been the coming into the world of Lilian. Yes, Lilian was a blessing and his treasure (but needed still a mother). It was as if Ruskin had understood his position — before they had met — because these things (unlike the draft of *Fors*) had been brought with him from Oxford.

Perhaps Ruskin's Fors was behind it — the classical Fate which worked, so it seemed, towards Christian ends for the Master. Baker resolved to say nothing of his widowing in the letter, not wishing to obtrude upon someone so weighed down with care and the unconsidered consequences of his thousand enthusiasms.

Baker's note to Ruskin was friendly and concise, though making special mention of the Burne-Jones drawing — almost as if *Fors* had told him the Master feared it was lost. It accompanied both Hill's letter and Thomas's drawing to Herne Hill.

6

Ruskin had gone to Brantwood; and though Joan and Arthur were remaining at Herne Hill for a while, they had been instructed to forward nothing. No more correspondence, no more little gifts. He had more than enough to deal with.

The hexagonal table-top bore witness to that. Not an inch was visible. But Ruskin felt quite happy today in a shifting world; one where work rose and moved on of its own accord (as in his current geological experiments with dough). Work, that yesterday, like the glaciers he had been modelling, had appeared solid and immoveable...

He was writing and annotating — sometimes working on several letters or documents at once; sometimes finishing a task, sometimes switching to another; sometimes having to remove Tootles, his best Brantwood cat, from the overlapping papers. Ruskin did that only slowly and reluctantly – save in the dark evenings when he would swiftly, tactfully rescue her tail from the flame of his candles.

The bulk of the material set out before him consisted of unsolicited correspondence. Some of it had been waiting for him on this table since his departure for Italy in the Autumn of the previous year. Only anticipated replies to letters of his own or envelopes in familiar handwriting had been redirected to his rooms at Oxford. Consequently, what remained was almost exclusively from young ladies who made botanical observations, wished to become actresses, wanted to disobey their parents, were promising artists, longed to proof-read for him, intended to start schools, to revive folk dancing, enclosed manuscript fairy tales, sympathised with the poor, misunderstood things that he had said. Many of the correspondents were unknown to him, some turned out to be existing pets of his or former pets ('Are you jealous Tootles?) — some he scolded, some he encouraged, some he fended off.

Sometimes he judged that the person who had written was not best fitted to conduct the correspondence. So sometimes he replied to the young ladies, sometimes to their mothers, sometimes to both – and sometimes he wrote letters which were not replies, but on quite different topics which happened to interest him. He answered them in the following fashion, seldom repeating himself.

'This is a modest, star-like gleam of a little flower & may lack green leaves. Fix it in your mind that they are succulent and thick, like little juicy grains of corn; no, my dear, you cannot please me by painting plates for me, but only by doing something which will put food on them for others...'

(That was, maybe, to Juliet.)

'Never, never touch a billiard cue...'

(This solemn admonition was to Rosalind – somewhat later.)

'Peggy is an utter mystery to me! – but she took delightfully to her drawing — and I hope — in that direction, to be useful to her drawing and Ethel...'

(That was to their mother.)

'… I can't row you over the lake any more…'

(That a stock disengagement.)

'I should like you to write to the writer of enclosed, a sailor's sister, keeping a day school for poor children, about 200 I believe & show a little interest in her, saying I had told you to do so...'

(That, to a worthy young friend, a hand-over; and the following, a reminder that is time to grow up.)

' I will suppose that you are a girl of rank, and a Christian; and that you have been doing, hitherto, a more or less embarrassed and doubtful duty, partly to your relations and your own class, only through the poor. Your superiority to them consists in your power of helping them; to that end, and to that end only, you are rich, titled, or lovely, and in none of these powers have you any right to rest, while this suffering of others is around you.'

He rooted around for something from Claire Stott, but could not find anything. It was to her credit that she did not pester him – but a little hard of her to be neglectful. But wasn't that what he had been asking of a young woman? No fawning, not too much unthinking agreement. Yes, but not in the case of his pets. Miss Stott had, he thought sent to him twice – and he had probably answered – what? Maybe once. It would turn up. Perhaps this? Too odd and juvenile for Claire.

He found an odd-shaped package which he had neglected to open. Inside it was dried moss.

'What's this, Tootles?' he said to his cat, and with a touch of melody, ' You're to go no more a-bird-nesting, go no more a-bird-nesting — by the light of the moon, you know.'

But it was not a bird's nest. The moss — a sort of envelope of it — had been posted moist and within it, according to an accompanying note, was — or had been — a morning posy with the dew still upon it. The tiny dead stems and shrivelled but unripe seedheads hung in his hand. It wasn't the girl's fault, but his for letting it lie. He resolved to put the best face he could on it, and penned (with a pretty little drawing):

    'Only you, of all my pets,
     Sent me living violets,

> Only you, from Druid grove
> Sent the sign of noble love.
> Consequently, 'pon my soul,
> Here's part of my heart —
> My art, the whole.'

Ruskin trod a fine line between exhaustion and exhilaration, but was not unhappy in testing again and again his capacity for repartee, for eccentric observation, for affectionate plain-speaking, for accurate rudeness. More taxing to him than epistolary agility were the occasions when young ladies — or no longer quite so young ladies — would present themselves at Brantwood to pay a call or to stay with him: he would whisk them off to Kate, an old retainer on the other side of Coniston Water; and enjoy (it has to be said) the comical cruelty, when — as in a French farce — more than one young lady had to be lodged at a time, and to suppose herself (though fobbed off) uniquely interesting to this busy man; or be enlisted as a monitor to supervise the concerns of a social inferior or 'a fright'.

He moved his thoughts around much as he stage-managed his acolytes, turned from his table-top to a dozen copies of *Unto This Last* in dark-coloured roan, edges cut and gilt, on a low shelf to his right. It had a new Preface, though otherwise he had left well alone — former friends would have said 'ill alone', while unknown socialists and pacifists rejoiced that it would be in print again. These were complimentary copies of the reissued work which needed to be sent out before the 2,000 imprint became generally available on 13th August — shortly. But for the moment they could wait. He'd send Baker a copy — it was unlikely that Quakers could be involved even indirectly in Birmingham's small arms manufacture. Nevertheless, because such commerce was far from being as disreputable as it deserved, some of Baker's associates would need to have a care with their sub-contractors; and therefore they had urgent need to attend to the economics of *Unto This Last*.

A propos of which — and the current incursions by the Russian army into Turkey — he scribbled:

'The day will certainly come when workmen, conscious of their own power and probity, draw together in action. They ought in all Christian countries to abolish, not yet WAR — which must yet be made sometimes in just causes — but the Armaments for it, of which the real root cause is simply the gain of manufacturers of instruments of death.'

He put the scrap of paper which bore these words aside for possible use in *Fors*, then turned back to *Unto This Last* again, with approval of its sentiments and habitual anguish over the stupidity of the world in praising the worst of his work and ignoring or reviling, this — his best.

*

Another gentleman — almost a gentleman — still in London was simultaneously studying the works of Professor John Ruskin. This was James Abbot McNeill ('Jimmy') Whistler, the American painter and adoptive Cockney, whom Ruskin had characterised as fraud, extortioner, and coxcomb.

Papers from Whistler's lawyers relating to this affront, and prefatory to the famous libel action lay, amongst a heap of correspondence in Herne Hill, awaiting Ruskin's return. North of the river, in Chelsea, Whistler sat. Casually elegant in a smoking jacket with a dandy's eye-glass in place — and in self-parody — favourite parrot at hand and cigarette fuming in a dish. He was making a thorough, and profitable search of Ruskin's *Modern Painters*, for examples of pomposity, verbosity, hypocrisy, banality and error.

These early Ruskin lapses were being collated by Jimmy Whistler for use in written riposte, spontaneous gossip, and for the libel case. He was sidelining, annotating, and committing to memory such off-guard passages as the following disclaimer, written by Ruskin twenty years earlier, with a nod to his father's clerical ambitions for him:

It seems to me, and seemed always probable, that I might have done much more good in some other way.

'Art Teacher,' wrote Whistler sardonically in the margin alongside the sentence, adding aloud 'some art teacher — a Jack of no Trades!' He picked up the cigarette, sucked in its smoke, then — exhaling — made a note of the source — *Modern Painters*, vol V.

'And,' said Whistler puffing his reaction to some other early opinions of the Professor's, 'a gentleman of taste — a Daniel come to judgement, I'd reckon,' blowing smoke and copying out:

Now it is evident that in Rembrandt's system, while the contrasts are not more right than with Veronese, the colours are all wrong from beginning to end.

Beside which Whistler made the capitalised attribution: 'JOHN RUSKIN', adding with a jeer, 'Art Authority. Know-all Ignoramus.'

Seeking further sticks with which to lambaste the myopes, Whistler came across a paragraph where Ruskin noted that he had got particular pleasure from*: a little unpretending modern picture in Düsseldorf, representing a boy carving a model of his sheep dog in wood.*

Whistler drew in his breath and too much smoke, then guffawed and choked at the incongruities within this stolid piece of nonsense. After which he settled in an easier chair and took a glass of something to enhance his one-sided battle with the celebrated pedlar of eyewash.

*

Meanwhile Ruskin had become suddenly inactive. He stroked the peaceful cat and moved weary eyes over the table top. He had done enough work for one day. So much so that it was as if he had used up the whole of his diurnal brightness and was left with the awful despondency of that night 'when no man can work.'

Over the table top, avoiding the papers — he saw that it was not yet dark, in fact — lifted his eyes to the view through the window over Coniston. He saw a mile off Yewdale Crag, which gave energy briefly back to him. His thoughts began to whirl about like starlings in the evening sky, and settled upon his projected talk on Yewdale and its Streamlets.

'How did I come here?' he noted. And, 'Is Coniston Water filling up with stones? Answer, evidently so. In which case, how long? How short.'

His life – his gut – was full of stones; and of course papers. Dust in his nose, motes in his eyes; but never a golden hint of a glimpse of Rosie…; and St Ursula and Venice becoming distant realities.

'Poor St Crumpet. It works both ways,' said the ghost of Rose. 'You've kept me away lately. I don't suppose you know you can do that? You remember that spiritualist lady at Broadlands — at Mrs Cowper-Temple's as she then was? You were impressed by her at first. The one with tame butterflies. I don't believe that she really spotted the ghost of me leaning over your shoulder, but she guessed I wanted to tell you something (which isn't difficult). It was to not blame my mother. And you are beginning to make up with her aren't you, St C?'

Ruskin looked up, saw nothing, heard nothing:

Hadn't Fors, he mused, brought to him the beautiful lost letter two years ago after the medium had seen the dead Rose leaning over him at Broadlands?

'Rosie,' he called, then diffidently, 'Rosie Posie.'

120

'St C,' she answered unheard.

It was a gift. She'd have been at home in the Garden of Eden naming the animals: Lion, Rabbit, Bruno (her dog), Maude and Tootles (his best dog and cat). As for himself, who had been diminished from St Chrysostom to St Crumpet; and finally St C … He couldn't compete. His nursery-rhyming Rosie Posies were heartfelt, but uninventive.

He still had in the front of his mind the precious images of his recent experiences in Venice, which were taking written shape — in *St Mark's Rest* and the *Guide to the Principal Pictures in the Academy at Venice*. Places where Rosie had never been, and pictures which she would never see.

Resolve to pick fewer quarrels. Minimise differences. Even about *Ethics of the Dust*. Best to be sweet-tempered about its reception, about its lack of dramatic flair — to admit its shortcomings in a new Preface.

He sensed Rosie would not like it. So much the better — if she wanted to argue, she would perhaps send a sign. But, now he thought of it, such signs as he had received had been sweet signs, so (if girls such as Rosie thought at all in Heaven) she had possibly come round to his way of thinking. He turned the pages of the book steadily.

The dialogue is not as bad as they suppose, thought Ruskin, dipping into the work. He said as much to Tootles. Maybe Rosie, too, would not think it so bad, if she read it with him over his shoulder. Maybe she was putting that thought into his head.

It seemed to him no worse than any other neo-platonic dialogue. And his example of the genre had a modicum of self-mockery to commend it — and young ladies (dressed by Kate Greenaway?) to sugar the sermonising.

'Poor St Crumpet,' said Rosie. 'What a collection of stilted little creatures you've assembled.'

The Personae of the dialogue comprised girls aged from 9 to 16, together with their big sisters, from 17 to 20. The attributes of this second group were noted as key-holding, possessing dark eyes, knowing Latin, brightening a room; with the head girl having all of the others in awe of her, including their interlocutor, an OLD LECTURER, 'of incalculable age.'

'I'd not reprint it, if I were you,' said Rose.

Ruskin touched the gold plates, side-lined the sections of the work which he was going to draw to the attention of any new readers in the preface he was composing:

'...pages 303-310,' he noted for the quick and the dead, 'were written especially to check the dangerous impulses natural to the minds of many amiable young women, in the direction of narrow and selfish religious sentiments...'

'Your point being, St C,' said Rose, 'that I, if transfigured out of myself (and therefore no longer myself!!), would have no scruple about marrying you. But a contradictory, metaphysical little thing such as I had to be, could not marry anyone who would take me, my dear. Anyone who would not have had me would have been a more eligible suitor, for such a one would not be offering me the first place in his life; that first place which belongs to our Saviour, Jesus Christ. I think you did understand that.'

An old man now, arguing old scores, he called out loud: 'Rosie, you had no right to leave me!'

A maidservant outside his door, hand poised to knock, hurried away.

*

He awoke next day unable to put any thoughts in focus — a prefiguring of the last eleven years of his life, the years of silence. None of the servants knew that he had entered into the state which he recognised as 'dangerous dreamland'. Without a word he had withdrawn into his study and fastened the door — an indication, it was assumed, that he was engaged in undisturbable work. The day was spent in a mute and disconnected frenzy.

All the trees of Brantwood began to moan as the sun drew their sap away from the roots, causing them to creak and crack. This was no impairment to upward growth: bark stretched or, lacking elasticity, broke into platelets. Colliding and conflating overhead, branches arched into gothic gloom; leaves into cusps and pendants.

He was south of Edinburgh, aged nineteen and making a drawing inside the Rosslyn Chapel — chilled by the tale of the spiralled pillar carved by the 'prentice, who was foully killed by his own master mason — for envy of his preternatural skill and for the strange pagan tale he had told in stone.

All about him that diversity of gothic: a central tenet of Ruskin's teaching. He ran his fingers into the sandstone eye-sockets of the chapel's hundred 'green men' — into the smiles and pudenda of the grotesques; felt his feet slide upon stalagmites of hardened grease.

The hump of his old age began to fix itself upon his back, the beard of his later life to sprout. His torso grew in bulk and muscularity, thrusting itself (unwieldy) out of the confines of the ladder which bore him up to study the ceiling, out of the arms of the wooden chair which held him down; his backbone simultaneously sprouting, his knees shooting up into the pelvis, his stirring penis (though long and flaccid) strapping itself onto his belly.

Ruskin clapped his hand to his mouth. He looked at his palm expecting blood. Nothing – nothing of that for forty years — but all about him anecdotal horrors. He seemed to be sitting — lying? — in a painted shrine or chantry chapel, surrounded by some Germanic master's depicted cruelties. Little acts of torture and unfinished amputation going on in the background. Someone being flayed, someone else being consumed by a spiked machine, and a bound calf lying helpless for the sacrifice. It was the same animal which he had tried to comfort only a few weeks ago, falling to his knees on the platform of a hateful railway station, forgetting his business of the day, his luggage, his packages.

He had left behind for Baker an engraving by a finer Germanic master — the St George of Albert Dürer or was it the Dance of Death of Holbein? He glimpsed again the blackened vault. The vault lightened into open sky, then flattened itself into the headache of his room.

He feared the Dance of Death. The Dance of Death in the vault; and the paper Dance of Death, engraved by Holbein. This is what had concerned him earlier, he realised — though his mind had clenched at the thought. Clenched and unclenched again. And he knew Rose had left him for now, because of dreadful images which might unfold — as the paper in its literalness might unfold.

It mattered suddenly very much to him which of the two drawings he had rapidly, too rapidly, pulled out of some folder to give to Baker. That part of his mind, working so horridly that night, suddenly permitted a clear recollection of two other very different pieces of paper. And two possibilities. If he had left the St George for Baker, then maybe it was (after all) something such as an unaccounted-for little Alcestis that had accompanied it. But, if it had been the Dance of Death that he had left in his room at Belleville as his gift — with the thing that was secreted away in it — then he would be disgraced for ever.

Ruskin got to his feet, recalled, re-entered a richer and more haphazard archive than the ruins of his mind. A second Pompeii; from which he had shovelled away ash and found everything mercifully intact, wonderfully preserved. He had been afraid that

Turner might have lost his wits, and could have begun to destroy some part of his vast life-work. Nothing further from the truth. It appeared that the artist had kept everything, disposed of nothing.

This would be twenty years ago. When he, John Ruskin — Turner's executor and the authority selected by the trustees of the National Gallery to catalogue the hundreds of paintings and thousands of drawings found in the painter's house at his death — was…in the name of public decency — was said to be doing the right thing, avoiding prosecution under the new Obscenity Act: overseeing the official destruction by burning quantities of Turner's drawings.

Erotic drawings. Burning, or – by intent or accident — squirreling the filthy stuff away, selecting items for destruction, reprieving them by means of obfuscation, muddle, re-classification, declassification, calculation and miscalculation. Losing himself over the years in what he'd done, or not done: hardly knowing, hardly choosing to know, where things were — or where they no longer were. No smoke without fire. No fire without smoke.

Smoke rose from drawings, or waste paper, into the blackened vault of the Dance of Death. But just enough light for Ruskin to see that what he held in his hand was after all — Heaven be praised — the Holbein engraving. By luck, by Fors, he had found it: It was still there, not elsewhere,. So it couldn't be that which he'd left for George Baker at Belleville!

Where? Whence? It must have been on the other chair under his desk all the time. And if that was where it was, it couldn't have gone elsewhere — that and the other culpable thing, tucked in the back of the Holbein mount for disguise. Yes, Fors had been his protector, had ensured Baker received the intended pairing of print and drawing — the acceptable images.

He lifted the fly-sheet from the Holbein engraving, recalling its familiar economy — counted forty five lines, forty five cuts (this was an artist who drew directly onto the woodblock) which comprised the entire face and flowing hair of the preacher — an entirely truthful depiction of a sincere preacher; but a preacher of untruths.

This caught at his heart. An enemy had, or so he had heard, called him a hyena. Was there anything in that? He took up a glass and in it, saw darkly, yes, a hyena or a hypocrite before him. For he had to acknowledge, and be thankful for, his possession of the second culpable piece of paper behind the Holbein.

This paper, a drawing, had been brought from the Turner archive, amongst the huge quantity of torn sheets and pages from notebooks, to Ruskin's ex-marital home in Denmark Hill. There, dirty piles of Turner's sketches were sorted, dusted, annotated. Mounts were then cut for what Ruskin deemed the better ones. This example had remained un-mounted — unlike the woman, its subject (a gross thought) — but not returned to its archive; irresponsibly kept at home. Then — so the thing went beyond an accident — hidden away, amongst papers which travelled about with him. Hidden – half-hidden away. He opened up the folded sheet of outer paper which concealed the inner thing and looked at it closely, first this way up and then that.

*

Something has carried over. Something comforting? The curtain is going up as if at one of Ruskin's favourite pantomimes at Hengler's Circus or Drury Lane. He settles in his seat expectantly. The backdrop is lit. Instead of Cinderella's kitchen or Titania's bower or a woodland glade, it shows a kneeling man with elfin ears, seen from the back.

He is kneeling by a reclining naked women — her legs parted, her labia exposed. He is fondling the genitalia, but in such a fashion — careful observation here — that her sexual parts are not obscured. The detailed drawing to Ruskin's eye suggests the interior of a bivalve, within which the amorous investigator appears to have discovered a seed-pearl – before the legs open wider, to bear to the right: her arms winding to the left about his head and shoulder to swing him over to take her.

As Ruskin watches, horrifiedly excited, an actress, naked except for her shoes, enters, falls on her back, couples in the missionary position with a comedian partly-clothed in a sailor-suit; after which she turns her rump over to the gods and for the sailor, whose swelling member is lit by limelight prior to re-insertion.

They exit, sated, and Ruskin tries to will away the elf-eared man and his woman in the backdrop, but they persist. There is a darkness about the female pubes, which on inspection seems to be hirsute.

He asks himself again whether this condition — one of the several unfortunate things about Effie — was not, after all, the entirely rare affliction he had supposed. Possibly, it was normal enough in a more primeval order, of women.

To take another tack, might not the bizarre conjoining depicted by Turner be, to the participants (and in the eyes of God), of a piece with all the pretty pollinations of the vegetable kingdom? — If the eyes of the observer were not – as Turner's were — too sharp? (In his own part-published Botany, Ruskin has declared microscopic images of plant sexuality to be 'vicious'.)

He could perhaps have dimmed his own eyes, stuffed his nose, kept gloves on his hands and successfully honeymooned with Effie. But he had not, and it was well that he had not. And that was that. It was of no moment. He had loved — loved still — Rose La Touche. And knew that all was not finished between them.

'Rosie,' he called out. 'You're no use to me in Heaven. I want you, Rosie, on earth. In heaven I mean to talk to Socrates and Pythagoras — but perhaps not, after all, with Turner...'

The bravery, the bravado tailed away. Rosie was not going to answer, not even as she would have done in her life, with some affectionate name-calling. He was glad she hadn't — with the obscene drawing exposing itself and itself exposed.

He first concealed, then put the offensive, instructive drawing back with the Holbein in the folder. After which he forced himself from dreamland into acuity, and settled sanely and purposefully to work; breaking off only to give the staff instructions to make the beds ready for the return of Joan, Arthur, and their children.

*

They were back without mishap by tea time of the next day, and spent a merry evening together. The piles of correspondence they had brought from Herne Hill — including the letter from Baker, which might have been so crucial? It could all wait!

The following morning, with so much additional material to open, Ruskin asked Joan to send out the copies of *Unto This Last* on his behalf. So he did not after all pen a particular note for Baker, assuming that he would soon have some other reason to correspond further. As, indeed he had, when he began to examine the post bag they had brought from Herne Hill.

Once Ruskin had taken Thomas Manning's drawing out of one of several similar tubes sent for his attention and examined it, his reaction was an unpleasant one: the image called to mind a dream of extreme ghastliness which he had experienced months before and had put out of his mind (though into his diaries): that holes opened in his hand — caused by frost or illness — through which he could see the light, from one edge of the hand across to the other...that other hand being his left.

The recollection of the dream was so vivid that it seemed to him that Thomas's hands could be seen through the holes in his own - and his own through holes in Thomas's. A conflation of the story of the Doubter and his crucified Master? He put the drawing down in disgust and walked across the room for prettier matter, a competent imitation of a Kate Greenaway maid by another correspondent. Then something made him think of Mantegna's Dead Christ in the Brera Gallery and he returned to Thomas's ugly, striking drawing. For some time he was indecisive. Then, he popped it rapidly back in its tube, added a covering note and addressed it to Alexander MacDonald, at the Oxford Drawing School.

*

'Thomas Manning,' said Joseph Hill before class, 'tell your mam she's famous.' This was not because of any answer Ruskin had made to Thomas's drawing, because — though Hill was a little disappointed to have heard nothing from Baker (and a little apprehensive in case his letter had been too forward) — he had no expectation that the Professor himself would have taken any action in its regard.

'Tell her I'll try to call in later today. It's about those gentlemen visitors she had.'

Thomas accepted the teacher's friendly order with a thank you and got down to his school work — it was the beginning of a week and his cough easier. He could recollect the name of the one gentleman, the one called the Professor, because of what his father had said — but his father had had to go back to his work in far away Sheffield. The money that he brought over every so often had meant they were less hard-pressed, so maybe he, Thomas, might eventually break free from nailing.

*

Claire Stott, too, had read the August *Fors* — her copy having been efficiently delivered to her uncle's, where she saw herself described as one of the 'two other Englishwomen, of about the same relative ages, with whom [Ruskin] had been standing a little while before Edward Burne-Jones's picture of Venus's Mirror...'; with a brief description of the by-play between image and reality which he had set in train. This latter was thrilling to her, and she immediately copied it out into her journal.

Then, re-reading what Ruskin had written, she saw that they — she and Mrs Lavenham — were described as the 'other', and the gilt of her gingerbread was a little tarnished. Other than whom? Why to these forge women; these forge women in Worcestershire. So the centre stage was occupied, was it, by the kind of women who sharpened her tools?

Properly so, since the Professor was writing about working women, Claire admitted to herself wryly. And that they were better at their work than she was at hers.

She accepted all that. Nevertheless, in a switch of mood, she wrote Ruskin a letter whose rapidity of composition and its special pleading gave it an unfair eloquence. Its subject was the strength of porphyry and (by implication) the weakness of Ruskin's teaching.

*

By the following morning's post Hill received back the tube which he had sent. In it was a note which read only 'By instruction of Professor Ruskin the two enclosures. Alexander McDonald'; one of which was Thomas's drawing, and the other a sheet of photogravure, with explanation at its base: 'by Albert Dürer'.

'What do you make of that, then, Thomas?' said Hill, after school when the other pupils were dismissed.

'It's most indulgent of the gentleman, sir,' said Thomas cautiously.

'Indeed,' said Hill, 'but what do you think of this old drawing? — for I think it's hundreds of years old, but reproduced here by some skilful modern means. I'm not sure I fully understand the process. But what do you think of it — of them, of this set of hands?'

'They're very carefully drawn, sir' said Thomas, looking at it closely, 'with many tiny lines. The man who drew them — scratched them almost — had good eyes. Dug them out, like. I can feel the pieces under my nails. I could never do anything of this sort, sir.'

'But what lesson — for I'm sure there's some lesson we are intended to draw — what lesson is there in this picture? Say exactly what you think, we are not in school now, and I shall not hold it against you.'

'Well, sir, I should not care to have such hands. And because I would not care to have such hands I would not care to draw them.'

'And why not?' said Hill.

'Because,' said Thomas, 'they're not working hands, sir — they've come through to the bone, but not been worked to the bone.'

'And yet,' said Hill, 'as you say, they're through to the bone — and in a position of prayer. Maybe they've been prayed to the bone. Or perhaps they're an old man's hands at the end of his working life and who's thinking now of other things, of the other life?'

'There's little enough time for that, in lives such as ours,' said Thomas.

'You shouldn't answer like that, my lad,' said Hill, 'even out of school, but I know you're only repeating what you've heard others say... Just leave these two sets of hands with me, so that I can give some thought to what to do — for, as you said — and you said well then — we have been shown indulgence by a famous gentleman.'

7

Claire kissed her uncle on the cheek and immediately despatched a brief excited note to Charlotte Lavenham, who was invited to stay! But she did not yet divulge, even in writing to Charlotte, all that she had in mind.

Any observer of Claire — and there was only sometimes Sarah — might have come to a wrong conclusion: that she had become re-enthused with cuneiform carving; was resolved to get the better of her block of porphyry. She was managing better than before, now that she was not afraid of spoiling her chisels.

But spoiling the chisels was the whole point. Once they were spoilt, she could return to the forge and ask for them to be sharpened. That would enable her to compare the women working there with those whom the Professor had described in *Fors*. Then she would have many things, exciting things, to tell Charlotte. So Claire put on her hat and set out for the forge.

Barely out of her uncle's gate, Claire was handed a letter — Charlotte's reply — which Claire was about to open when she saw Thomas Manning. He had noticed her little bag containing the tools, and was asking politely whether he could save her the walk up their rough lane, if the lady purposed to have them sharpened.

Forgetting for a moment that the sharpening was a stratagem, Claire thanked Thomas very much, saying — in the confusion of handing the bag over and the simultaneous realisation that her prime purpose of inspecting the workers had been forestalled — saying, repeating involuntarily phrases she had been rehearsing, 'I'm sorry, I'm not getting on very well: it's work which Professor Ruskin has recommended for...'

She stopped in mid-sentence. There was no point. She had wanted to see whether the boy's mother could be of an age with Mrs Lavenham. Or if Ruskin might have thought her to be like the younger woman. Was there another woman in this forge? — and there had been no mention of a boy.

Thanking her for her twopence and the employment, Thomas continued on his way with the assurance that the chisels would be re-sharpened very soon, and that he would deliver them himself to Giles at the house.

*

Claire's disappointment in her failed ruse was mitigated by having obtained permission to go into town by train so that she might purchase some new things for Mrs Lavenham's visit: she wished not to appear either too much the country girl or conventionally fashionable.

So that same afternoon Claire and Mary took the train to Birmingham, where Claire's funds ran only to a long, light scarf and a sash that was almost a cummerbund. While in the town centre (in spite of her recent problems with artistic gossip), she asked Mary if they might step inside the premises of the Birmingham Society of Arts in New Street.

Mary acceded to the request, for it looked a sober, formal place. And, indeed it was. Under the portico — all heavy and no lightness — they passed, through a tunnel to the rotunda, where at a round table a custodian (no handsome receiving gentleman here like Sir Coutts Lindsay and certainly no Lady Lindsay), a functionary in a frock coat, put on his glasses and thrust a catalogue into Claire's hand in exchange for a sixpence. Still no lightness.

A gasolier depended from a grubby dome, then a heavy frieze gave way to cliffs of pictures; heavy frames containing heavy paintings leaning dangerously out and down; faces of heavy ladies stuck out from the chiaroscuro; pictures three deep like giant building-bricks — like a side of a ship, of a house.

The Grosvenor Gallery, for all its despised hangings had uplifted her, this place crushed her beneath its heaviness: a bespectacled gentleman in a tail-coat across the room was crouched as if to take refuge from the poised avalanche of art.

Claire shuddered at Mary who grimaced back — and they left, regretting their lost sixpences.

*

While Thomas was sharpening the tools — his natural left-handedness obvious while at this work — he was turning over in his mind the name which the young lady had mentioned. He was almost certain it was that of the man, the Professor — the only time he'd heard the word — who had paid them that visit, given the baby sixpence, written those pages which his mother had read out to him — though after following them once with her he could read most of it quickly enough to make sense on his own. He could read all of it well now, with good expression, even if some of the sentences wandered about within themselves. In learning to read it, he had got most of it by heart: some passages came now into his head:

'One about seventeen or eighteen' — that's our auntie — 'the other perhaps four or five and thirty; this last intelligent of feature as well could be' — that's me mam, which she is — 'and both, gentle and kind' — you spoke the truth there, old professor, all things considering.'

'And all the while as I watched them, I was thinking of two other Englishwomen, of about the same relative ages...'

Even before he'd heard this and learned to read it, it had occurred to Thomas that some people might think poor auntie Annie and the young lady with the broken chisels, barring their circumstances, both had a certain look to them. But he'd got into trouble earlier with Mr Hill for answering, so he decided not to speak out of turn about a lady even to his mam. And he did understand that the Professor was taken by the differences between them. But mightn't that be because the gentleman was put in mind to say what he did because had their situations in life not been so different, there wouldn't have been much to choose between them? But he didn't know enough about the world to judge whether it was likely or impossible that the young lady who'd come to the forge was the one written about. Just that she wasn't local, and he — the professor — wasn't local. So then…Suppose they were both staying hereabouts? Any road, she knew him – had spoken the name, that was for sure: Ruskin.

He showed the sharpened tools to his mother, who said he'd made a good job, and that being 'caggy-handed' was his own business, save when it came to penmanship, she reckoned:

'Any road, she may want 'em directly, so you could pop them in at the house — but don't you trouble nobody, mind.'

'No,' he said, 'I shan't be no bother. I said I'd give 'em to Giles, and if he's out I'll leave 'em in his hut.'

Giles wasn't to be found, so he spent some time writing something with a flat black pencil of the gardener's upon the piece of paper which he'd wrapped round the tools. Then he wrapped them carefully up again, put them back in their bag and left it on the work bench.

*

Back from Birmingham, not having heard from Ruskin, Claire received the bag of sharpened tools from Giles. No longer much interested in carving, she asked him to return them to his potting shed. And there the tools sat, together with Tom's writing, with its guess at the answer to the question she wished to put.

Meanwhile, giving up the subterfuge of chisels for sharpening, she hurried towards the lane and the forge. But when she got there with her question, she found just Ann, who tried to tell her by means that only her family could understand that Thomas was getting the children a bite to eat and Betty gone up town with a shilling that Will Manning had left on his last conjugal visit.

*

In fact, Betty had been in Birmingham or travelling for all of the time that Claire and Mary had spent there. And more. She had started much earlier and ended later.

It had been mid-morning when Betty parted from the carter who had given her the lift to Digbeth in the dip by the Old Crown Inn. She'd asked a street-corner paper seller for directions. He seemed friendly and harmless, so she asked more than she meant to.

'Who?' he said, 'a Mr E or B Jones, a painter-like. Never heard on him. But hang on missus, here's a chap as'll know. The usual, sir,' he said, handing him a *Gazette*.

The chap was a doorman at the Public Library whose job, despite Baker and his well-meaning committees, was to keep the likes of Betty away from the corporation's collection of books.

'Never heard on him either,' said the doorman. Betty was beginning to move away…'Hang on now, you say you want to see pictures?'

Betty nodded.

'Yes, well there's an exhibition kind of thing in Corporation Street, but you'd have to pay to get in, and besides…'(this was where

Claire and Mary had wasted their sixpences), 'you'd best not. Be a sight better off getting a tram to Aston Park. Just for the ride even. There's a big house – free to all, too. That's where that there Mr Baker has had all the paintings and that put.'

She just had to walk up the hill past the market and then up to Dale End, straightforward. She thanked them, but didn't know about going there really. She perhaps wouldn't have done, but going through the market, as she'd been told to as it was on the way, she found exactly what she wanted for her shilling or the best part of it.

And there was a big clock which told her she'd lots of time to get to Aston Park, if she dared to, and be back in time to meet the carter. She had never been in a conveyance so magnificent. So, carrying her dress in a bag like a lady, she climbed aboard with all sorts and conditions and took in the real ceiling that the vehicle had, a handsome curved ceiling. And to be drawn along on shining rails as smooth as you like by twin horses not dragged by some nag over a bumpy lane!

Her enjoyment was marred by fears that she would miss her stop. So she got off when she glimpsed a bit of green amongst all the new brick with a man who said, no this wasn't the park but he could lead her to it. He knew a short cut across this waste land which was being got ready for building.

He took her through what had once been a little wood, now all hacked into splinters, where he began talking about a man who had lately been executed for an outrage on a female, and asked if she did not think it very hard, and whether she would have the heart to swear a man's life away.

Betty, who had been looking forward to seeing some work which would uplift her, something noble, was now accosted in this base way. But the man looked a poor thing, less up to the heavy work of life than she was herself. She took comfort as they walked on, she not answering, he mumbling on about the executed criminal's bad luck, saying that if it had been him he'd've give her a shilling, which would make all the difference. He had a shilling he assured Betty and in a minute he would get it out and show her.

Three quarters of the way through what might still in parts have passed for a wood, the man made to grab her arm. Betty transferred the parcel to her left hand (he'd offered to carry it but she'd declined), stepped back free of him, and wrenched off a half-broken foot or so of stout stick, with which she promptly laid him low. It was a three-inch stem of holly with which she'd hit him, as if she'd put a fresh head on him with her big hammer.

That accomplished, with her heart pumping, she continued in the direction she had been going — rather than retracing her steps past the moaning man — and soon came to another tram route in one of the radiating roads which Joseph Chamberlain had made to the centre, and got back to Dale End without further mishap, glad of her strength. Relieved now that she'd given up on Mr E or B Jones. Yet slightly disappointed. However, luck would be on her side today.

Not only shaking no longer, not only rejoicing that her dress was safe, she walked to the Bull Ring through the market in good time to meet the carter who was to take her back again.

She saw again, and waited for it to strike the quarter then the hour, the great clock with its mechanical giants. Then she looked in the Bull Ring at the statue of Nelson and at St Martin's. Not only that, but as she did so, she caught a glimpse, without knowing who he was, of a little gentleman (a stained glass designer for Morris & Co) with a thin face and little painterly beard standing in the porch door of the refurbished St Martin's. This was Mr E or B Jones, of course. She didn't know then, but it's possible that she came to realise later when Fors drew the four women together: her and Ann, Claire and Charlotte Lavenham.

Betty noticed a haggard-looking woman make as if to approach EBJ, but think better of it as a carriage stopped to take him away.

*

Shortly after which Betty's own conveyance — driven by the expected carter — pulled up for her. He had had a good day, successfully delivering all he had brought, and having the luck to pick up a part load for the return journey, which would mean a detour in the direction of Dudley — but well worth it.

'I reckon,' he said, 'you brought me luck, Betty. And what's that you got in that there parcel?'

It was the dress of course, which Betty referred to cheerfully enough — though there was now something about the way she had nearly lost it which made her thoughtful and a little downcast about how she had come to earn it in the first place.

The journey passed without incident through a country of smoke and vapours, of canals and sidings and waste land until the Clent Hills began to pop up before them; upon which, Betty's heart lifted and she gave thanks for her safe return.

*

Claire thought Mrs Lavenham would bring her water colours with her, and if so, would probably like to try the remaining bit of thatch to the south of the town. It was a pity that Uncle Melville's house still failed to have much resemblance to a country cottage. All one could say — with its Minton tiles in the hall and conservatory; and all its eccentric bays and alcoves — was that it certainly was a change from the bleak symmetry of the Stott's residence in Bloomsbury.

It was set on the edge of town, with two or three others in large gardens on one side of a fairly long avenue of elms, with farmland on the other. When the winds were from the south west, as they were at this time of year, there was no smoke to bother anybody. The elm avenue began with self-importance, but petered out into a track which led to some grassy mounds where children played.

Claire remained curious about Ruskin; and, though disaffected with her chiselling and critical of the instruction received through *Fors*,– on the whole, respectful of what he might have to say. Accordingly, she decided to try again to educate herself from pocket editions of his works purchased from the local stationer's. Particularly those which were illustrated: after carefully looking at which, she discovered that the door and window openings of the Melville home were based upon things recorded by the Professor on his travels.

*

Most mornings, after a brisk walk to the Halt west of the town, Mr Melville caught a train to Birmingham where he was on the board of a bank. He was a gentleman banker with a progressive disposition who held regular conversations with Mr Baker whose pipedream it was to establish a municipal bank. (Mr Baker's financial acumen was considerable, for he had at an early age made a notable success as overseer of a poor persons' savings scheme.)

As bad luck would have it, Mr Melville was committed to such a meeting — a meeting postponed from the previous day — just when both Mary and the governess chanced to fall ill. Consequently, Mrs Melville had herself to take charge of little Ruth and re-organise the small domestic staff to provide comforts for two invalids. The water on this side of town was good, so, although both the young ladies were feverish, there was no undue alarm about their condition.

For these reasons, together with the fact that the day was fine, Claire made the helpful suggestion that she and Sarah should go for a good long walk into the countryside. Mrs Melville had been on the point of making such a suggestion herself, and ordered a light picnic basket for them.

Sarah skipped happily along the canal bank and Claire moved the basket from hand to hand as it was heavier than it had looked. Given the weight of it and the young girl's hearty appetite (Claire was learning to have a care how much she ate), they were happy to sit down by a lock, watch the barges and consume what they wanted.

They gave the food they did not require to the lock-keeper's children, who kindly offered to return the basket to Mr Melville's house. So they continued their walk with just a small container of water. The day was hot.

Sarah spent a little time, affectionately, tentatively, exploring the idea that Claire, as a stand-in sister, was preferable to Mary, the actual incumbent.

Claire responded adroitly, but somewhat obscurely, by reference back to Mary's quoted lines about non-traditional forenames 'You shall keep me company, as my Ethel or Beatrice,' she said to Sarah. Who looked at her, non-comprehending.

'I'm sorry,' said Claire. 'I was recollecting a remark of Mary's about family-names. It's of no importance... I'm your cousin, dear Sarah, and very glad that you're my cousin and that we know one another.'

Claire managed Sarah's next inquiry with less sureness of touch. It concerned the strange undulations in the grazing land which were an unmistakable feature of the landscape. Regular dips and rises so deep that at times some of the cattle seemed sunk up to their knees, while others were on tip toe.

'Though,' said Claire, 'I'm not sure that cows have toes.'

'No,' said Sarah the country girl, 'they have cloven hooves.'

'Yes,' said Claire, with a little shudder, knowing the expression only from the scriptures, 'I'm sure that's right. They have horns, too.'

Sarah, unwilling to think Claire did not know all there was to know, reverted to her question about the ups and downs in the land.

'Perhaps,' Claire answered, 'it's something to do with excavations which were made when the canal was cut.'

'But,' said Sarah, 'the marks lie on both sides of the canal, and they are in line with each other.'

'You are suggesting, then,' said Claire, 'that the marks on the land were made before the canal was cut?'

'Yes,' said Sarah, 'I think that's what I mean. The whole thing is like a giant's ploughed field — with great furrows up and down — with the canal as a ditch made later.'

Claire applauded the similitude, and couldn't improve on it: 'Whatever they are,' she said — and she had no idea, though she could have recited the dates of all the English monarchs and their consorts with great accuracy, 'whatever they are — they're more like molehills than mountains.'

After another half a mile they came to a little bridge over the canal with some steps up to it from the towpath. They sat beneath some convenient shade, talked about trivial matters and observed the traffic between the Severn ironworks and the Black Country workshops.

'Professor Ruskin,' said Claire after a little, 'does not approve of ironworks. Though he seems to love Iron, the colour of iron.'

Sarah asked various questions, to which Claire made answer as best she could:

'— Yes, rusty iron. He says that's where nature gets its colour — like this red soil. I liked that part. Even iron railings and so on are, I think, regarded by the Professor as well and good, if they are made individually by a smith or other craftsman. — Yes, I agree it would be difficult to make a steam engine single-handed, but Professor Ruskin seems not to approve of steam engines at all. No, Sarah, I believe it's large manufacture that he's opposed to. And so many factories, so many of them, so many. No, I can't see that he could close them all down. But he means to try! Well, because they're dirty and make things which he believes to be ugly. But it's more complicated than that — so I fear you'll have to ask someone wiser than I. It's to do I think with the way people spend their time and who makes a lot of money and how. But I don't fully follow it, so I can't really answer. Any more,' she added, in a diversionary concession, 'than I could tell how your giants' furrows came into being.'

The breeze stirred nearby leaves. Their momentary shifting gave a glimpse of old walls by a farm house which had been previously hidden. Claire and Sarah, cooler now and curious, moved to the other side of the bridge and stood peering in the distance.

A young man, evidently not a labourer was digging carefully around some stonework.

'Who is that gentleman,' said Sarah, 'in his shirt-sleeves? Do you think he's a pirate burying his treasure?'

Claire smiled:

'Well, no,' she replied, 'I think he's a school master, but what he's doing I couldn't begin to guess. Don't you recognise him? I think it's Mr Hill. You must have seen him in church.'

'Is it?' said Sarah. 'Well, yes, it may be. Perhaps I have seen him. He used to stay away. He's only started attending since you came.'

Claire accepted this as a simple observation of fact, which she found herself glad to have; but hoped that Sarah was too young to be drawing any implication from Mr Hill's increased interest in divine service. If Sarah were being other than artless, that would give an awkwardness to something she now found herself wanting to do.

But the awkwardness was dispelled by Sarah's, 'Please, cousin Claire, may we see what he is doing? I'm sure he won't mind.'

And, as if to reassure them, at that moment Mr Hill looked their way and gave a wave. It was a polite wave which had a hint of invitation, so the two crossed over the bridge and onto a footpath, which looked as if it led to the farm.

For a moment they lost sight of him behind hollows and heaps from exhausted iron-stone workings — and some associated ruined buildings (ruins were all one to Claire, in spite of Ruskin's diagrams and illustrations) — then Mr Hill appeared walking towards them, looking very neat. His jacket had been carefully put back on, but his face was warm with exercise and pleasure.

'Why Miss Stott and Miss Sarah, how good of you to step this way — or perhaps this was your intended route. We are, as it were, all out of school today. But to see the abbey, I mean.'

'No,' said Claire, 'I honestly know nothing of any abbey. Is this part of its buildings?' pointing back to the workings.

'Not exactly,' said Hill, 'though I believe the monks had some interest in the mineral deposits. If you wish, I will show you the oldest part. Though there is not much to see, so I hope you won't be disappointed.'

Claire had seen Waltham Abbey (with its Burne-Jones glass, though she had not then known his name) and, on holiday once, Whitby.

'No,' said Hill, 'I'm afraid this is not as grand as either of those.'

Claire had seen pictures of Tintern and Fountains, as she recalled, and Sarah remembered copying a drawing of cloisters, so there was plenty to say as they walked back to the abbey site.

'My father,' explained Hill, a trifle apologetically, 'was interested in such places as this. He can't get about now, so I try to report back to him.'

The remains, as he said, were slight. Nor had they ever been extensive, as he showed by measurements he had made between pier bases which had been dug clear.

There were higher walls, though, pleasingly grown over with foliage — with a fair-sized tree or two forcing the masonry apart.

'I try to keep out of the farmer's way — and seldom bring others along — but he's happy enough that I explore. And the landowner is quite enthusiastic about the researches such as they are —'

He showed Claire and Sarah the line of the cloister, with one arch still intact: pointed out how the side of the farmhouse looked different where some of the broken north wall of the church had been built in, looked inside what remained of the abbot's lodging, and, pushing firmly one bale of hay against the wall – Claire noted that, with a little whim of curiosity — pulled out another to show them, low down on the inner wall a stone, presumably not in its original place, bearing an effaced carving alongside the remnants of an inscription. It read: 'oure ladys oblacionne in the temple by thre figures of premonstracionne.'

They spelt out the words together and tried to get some idea of what was being said – were there literally three figures, or did it mean three processes? She withheld any reference – serious or self-mocking – to carving porphyry – though she envied the old hand which had cut the stone: its skill, and the longevity of its product. She congratulated Hill on his find.

'Thank you, Miss Stott. I am pleased to have been able to show you this. I sought it out for my father, remembering my childhood explorations with him of our great priory at Malvern (where he still lives, a widower). The farmer suggested that I contact the landlord, and the landlord (as it chanced) was an acquaintance of my school inspector, which emboldened me to ask for his help with this inscription.'

They put questions to him which he dealt with well enough:

...'The nub of the matter, Miss Stott, Miss Sarah,' he said, summing up what had emerged, 'is that this site — these remains — might be thought of as having been particularly holy, in that the abbey was founded, as the stone says, by premonstration — the site being chosen by prophecy of St Norbert (or by his followers, for I think he was dead by then) as the place where the white canons should live.'

The two young ladies were impressed.

'No,' said Hill, 'I'm no Professor Ruskin. I haven't got it in me to know whether work's good or bad or indifferent — 'what I do have is a reasonable idea of whether something is old or new. These tiles' — and he removed some sacking —'are old, and I guess they must be good, too, because they remind me of the famous ones at Malvern.'

He pondered the tiles turning them over gently in his hands:

Claire and Sarah were about to take their leave when Sarah remembered to ask about the giant's furrows. Claire had held back from being the inquirer, suspecting this was something she ought to know already.

Hill was very pleased to oblige.

'The first clue,' said he, 'is that this is still called Manor Farm.'

And then it all fell into place for Claire. The common land, the feudal strips, the crop rotation. She had heard all this before and blushed that she'd made no connection between some of the duller hours of her schoolroom with what was so interestingly marked upon the ground.

Claire's cheeks burnt, too, with a little crossness and humiliation that it had taken a Board School teacher to remind her of what she had forgotten, to show up her ignorance. And then she was ashamed that she had caught herself looking down on him for what he was. She made a quick resolution: not to look down on Hill nor to look up to him, but – even if it was un-lady-like – to look him straight in the eye. She did so, and – cause and effect – she saw him stumble over his own feet.

*

It was mid-afternoon. They had left Hill with his tiles and ruins some time ago. They were walking further along the canal between the yardlands, whose shadows were reappearing now on the nearside, which at midday had looked lit and flattened. They resolved to turn round the next corner and see what was there, and then return.

As they continued, the first thing they saw were some medieval strips showing red-brown soil; and then lines of green vegetation carefully pricked out. These were yardlands under cultivation!

Now they partially knew something. What it was they knew they were not sure. So they continued along the canal, which veering to the right, brought them parallel to the strips — and, first within sight of those who were working the land, and then within conversation's distance. The workers were attired in a mixture of old English smock and modern workmen's shirt sleeves. Nothing remarkable in that, then — but what were they up to?

The nearest man stopped to lean on his rake:

'Good afternoon, miss, miss. I can see you are interested in what we are doing...'

He explained that they were a colony — 'a bit like a band of monks. Oh, you've been looking at them there pieces of an abbey' — which they'd set up using the old yardlands for the old fair-dealing which had been their purpose. He pointed out how the tract of land which they worked co-operatively (with one yardland allocated within it to each individual) had been made into an island in modern times by intersections of the canal and turnpike road and the railway (out of sight in a shallow cutting). 'Nobody, least nobody they can trace, owns the land. We've put it to rights, like. You should ha' seen the state it was in when we took over. Not been grazed — let alone dug for more than fifty years — and then not as yardlands.'

Another man came over and mentioned Ruskin.

Claire could not resist telling him she had met the Professor.

'Pleased to hear that,' said the second man, 'well, if you see him again, pass on my respects. Of course, writing about giving back land to the people's one thing, doing's another.'

'Come on, George,' said the first man, 'the Professor don't put himself forward to be no political leader.'

'No more he does,' said George, 'I was just teasing. But I hear he's set up a community of workers in Sheffield and is reckoning on 'stablishing another in these parts.'

Claire answered that she understood as much.

'Well, then,' continued George, 'if you meet him tell him we've been and gone and done it. But tell him thanks. We eat properly and we have this big old house — like a grange — which had all the doors and windows hanging out. Just as he's described — *ruined*, for the pity of it "an old English cottage or mansion built somewhere in the Charles's times", in — what is it? — in his little book *The Two Paths*. And there we live. As to what got me going. It wasn't writing, though it often has been. Perhaps you wouldn't mind listening to this tale; and you could put the Professor in mind of it if you see him. He might want to print it out in that *Fors* paper of his…

'This is what happened. It was ten year ago and I was a navvy, been working on London railways. Now there was a certain landowner — a gentleman by birth though a bad lot by nature, who saw fit to erect a five-foot high iron fence across the Common. If I remember right, Professor Ruskin hates fences, especially when they're factory-made railings. So I reckon he wouldn't mind hearing this tale, ifn he hasn't heard it afore. That railing stopped up all the rights of way. So people in the neighbourhood had to walk miles and miles to get anywhere they needed to go. Now luckily there was another gentleman living nearby, a true gentleman, who had rights as a tenant on that common along with the ordinary folk. And he got a contractor to hire 120 of us — with crowbars and all the right gear for — you can guess what — dismantling.

'Course, nothing would ha' happened without his money. But a good way to spend it, if you asks me. Hired a special train for us from Euston, he did — left at midnight and by 1.30 am we were off the train and within three miles of the spot. Then things go wrong. I'm not sure I should be telling you ladies this part, but here goes. You see, the contractor and another man had been carousing like in an inn near the station and arguing about their share of the payment. They brought liquor on the train too and were in no condition to tell us where to go and what was wanted of us when we got there.

'Luckily, a stiff little gent stepped in. Not a gent really, nor yet a working man. He was secretary of — what's it? — Commons Protection Society. Had read a bit — writing by your Professor and that Mr Morris — he'd got us organised like, marched us along the road in good order, told us not to make no unnecessary damage. And before breakfast all them fences were on the ground. And some on us, young ladies, took care they never went back up again.

'So — and you could tell your Professor this bit — after a month or two more's ordinary navvying like, I decided I wanted to be — how d'you say? — on the side of the angels. So that's why I'm a digging and raking this field like they did in the old days. And we asked nobody's permission first neither. So we're free — and all the better for it!'

'That sounds splendid,' said Claire — but, not as naïve as she sometimes seemed, and a little her lawyer-father's daughter, 'Wouldn't you feel easier if you were secure? About the land, I mean. I have heard how Professor Ruskin is working to put the St George's Company on a proper footing...'

'Get mixed up with lawyers, you mean,' said George, unaware of Claire's family connection. 'Funny you should say that, miss. Because there was some chaps here only the other day as was interested in what we were doing. And, you know, they didn't quite fit. So me and him asked them if they was from the Commons Protection Society, but they wouldn't give a straight answer.'

'So,' said his companion laughing, 'we reckoned they was lawyers. No, young ladies, nothing is for ever, and we haven't the money to act as if it was.'

'Any way,' said George, 'we've got the grange, like I said, where our wives do a spot of weaving, and — land-work, too, when care of the children permits —'

' — For,' said the other, 'they have that in common. Care of the children. Like Plato, you know, in his Republic.'

'I'm afraid I don't,' said Claire, shamed by these working men, but then recalling that she was only a female and needn't apologise for her limitations; and then wondering why she should be so defeatist for her sex, 'though I really think that you should write down all this for Professor Ruskin.'

'No,' said George, 'best that you pass it on for us, if you get chance. We don't go in for writing, but we read and learn. The best of our readers take it in turn to give us all a page or two over supper —'

'Like,' said Sarah, who'd listened carefully to Hill, 'like the monks of old, come back again.'

'Yes,' he replied, 'though we are men, women and children together. Talking of which, here come some on 'em' — simply-clad worker-women coming up from the direction of the railway cutting — 'so we'd best get back to work and be seen to be working. If you come this way again, we'll show you the grange.'

*

Halfway through their journey back – getting tired now – they stopped again at their first resting place. They no longer needed its shade, though the day was still bright. There they found Hill, who had obviously lingered so as to encounter them again.

'Forgive me, Miss Stott, Miss Sarah,' he said politely, 'I was some time finishing my work at the abbey, for the owner came along and put at my discretion the use of the tiles of which we spoke.' He showed a bag containing them. 'After which I was not sure whether you had returned this way already or not. But I felt, if you had not, that a long time had elapsed and you must be growing very tired with such a lengthy walk.'

They continued it together, Hill saying (or pretending) that he was hearing for the first time of the new monastic settlement or commune which they described; while Claire learnt — Sarah apparently already knew — that the grassy mound near her house, to which the avenue of elms led, was the site of an ancient moat house. So all about them, in spite of modern industry — the canals, railways, spoil-heaps — was the old England of Friar Tuck and Robin Hood.

*

Claire's uncle, having checked the Saturday trains, was also proceeding homewards. After his work with the mayor, part of which had taken place at Bellefield, Baker had driven Mr Melville to the station in his own carriage — for he knew Miss Melville was ill and wished to get her father back home as early as possible.

Arrived at the station, the two gentlemen had been given the kind of news which would have occasioned in Ruskin (whatever the inconvenience of it) a grim smile of satisfaction: the locomotive had developed boiler trouble and there would be a severe delay. Upon which Baker had insisted that he drive Mr Melville all the way home, urging the opportunity of further conversation during the journey.

Driving the last few yards to the elm tree avenue, they were surprised and not altogether pleased to see Claire and Sarah walking with Hill, though they had a high enough regard for him as a promising young school master.

The carriage slowed to a stop and Hill stepped forward with a brief word of explanation and a little blush. Claire's uncle observed the latter, but thanked Hill warmly enough. However, as the carriage was turned around by the driver, with both men still on board, Melville murmured to Baker that it must be many years before Hill could think of marriage. Baker agreed.

Melville stepped down at his front gate, Baker stood beneath the carriage door and raised his hat to the young ladies, But, no, if they would excuse him, he wouldn't step into the house. His own youngest daughter — much of an age with Miss Sarah — was to play at a concert that evening — her first such engagement, and a small affair, but naturally as a proud father, he must be there in good time.

Claire thanked Hill, who raised his hat again, and walked away taking care not to make the backward glance which he knew would be out of order. Melville and the young ladies entered the house together to be greeted by Mrs Melville, anxious for them individually, but now flustered that they had all returned at once.

Melville said nothing further, expressing only relief that Mary had had a less fretful day and that little Ruth could soon be restored to her governess — but in the privacy of the bed-chamber confided to his wife his satisfaction that Mrs Lavenham was coming. She, he felt, would provide alternative company for Claire and a protective shield from the likes of Hill (though — unknown to everyone — not from his pupil Thomas Manning, whose unread message remained in Giles' potting shed).

8

'The publication of this book,' with these words, Ruskin's pen – the one that had belonged to Sir Walter Scott – moved across the paper. Deciding against bringing his writing implement and its former owner into the passage, Ruskin continued, straight to the point: '...has been delayed by what seemed to me vexatious incident...'

Joan Severn was bustling noisily outside his door, but he did not call to her to come in, and after a little she went away.

'The publication of this book has been delayed by what seemed to me a vexatious incident, or (on my own part), ' writing now with great rapidity, 'unaccountable slowness in work.'

That was to have been the final sentence to the Preface of *Laws of Fésole*, a new work – but he would now make it the opening one, instead. Ruskin gave himself a short respite to glance over some of his key assertions; deciding – there was no smugness in it, he frequently took himself to task severely – that, on this occasion, he was eminently in agreement with himself:

'When natural disposition exists, strong enough to render wholesome discipline endurable with patience, every well-trained youth and girl ought to be taught the elements of drawing, as of music, early, and accurately.'

He had written these words as a general proposition based upon his experience of teaching working men at the Ormond Street college. But, in re-reading them, an image of Thomas Manning's hands came into his mind; and he realised that it had been there throughout the Preface. Ruskin had paid little attention to the boy

154

at the nailer's shop — even less to the baby, though it had served as a money box — being engrossed as he had been in the face, figure and activity of the two forge women, the nail-bearing, nail-creating Fates. So he had no certainty about the look of the boy.

The drawn hands were another matter. They did display the kind of 'natural disposition' he had just written about: struck him as resembling a little Leonardo sketch much enlarged by a glass — a sketch not of hands, but of some unlikely war machine; rimless wheels, maybe, for some vehicle which progressed with a clambering action. In Fésole[1], in the old days, in the Italian city states with their regulated guilds of artists and craftsmen, there were clear openings for a capable boy in a studio, as an apprentice — in conditions sometimes no better than those of the forge where he effectively lived — but with the prospect of moving on to nobler work.

Until by the grace of St George there could be a comparable system in our own time and native land, suppose the boy Thomas were to have the benefit of present-day training in art, what good would it do him? Ruskin's next paragraph provided a pessimistic answer:

'The ordinary methods of water-colour sketching, chalk drawing and the like, now so widely taught by second-rate masters, simply prevent the pupil from ever understanding the qualities of great art, through the whole of his after life.'

He heard a small noise from one of Joan's children. They took up some of his space and some of his attention at Brantwood. Suppose he were to bring in a child of his own? Not one of his pets, because they could be contrary, but a boy under his control — a wild boy like Thomas, brought in as a rival to Joanie and Arfie's brood — a Rousseau-esque experiment.

---

[1] Fiesole

He could come as a gardener's boy, and have healthy air to breathe, good food to eat, drawing materials and access to books, and examples from the masters if he proved apt. Having thought the thought, Ruskin grew indignant at it. Why not every urchin in the land? Where would it lead? Would no one share the task with him? Wasn't that the point of St George's Guild? Besides, this boy was not among the truly wretched. He might make his own way.

Yet had any other lad in that station shown him a drawing with the same kind of rough force he had seen in unfinished work by Morland and Ward? They were only stepping stones on the way to Turner, but could such a boy take a comparable path on his own? The manner of the work suggested he might, but the times in which people had to live threw doubt upon the possibility.

Another 'yet'. Unlike those well-bred young misses whose little talents were presented to him daily through the Post Office and, not infrequently (and perilously to his own peace of mind), in person —the lad had neither sent the work himself nor had it sent for his advantage. It had been forwarded by a benefactor of St George at the proper instigation of an honest puzzler called Hill.

Ruskin suddenly felt easier. He hadn't handed over the boy to one of his disciples at tenth remove, he had put him in the care of Albert Dürer. And Thomas Manning might thereby learn, might go on to prosper. Look at George Allen, once a carpenter, now the publisher with sole rights in Ruskin's works; look at Benjamin Creswick, once a grinder, now a craftsman turning to sculpture. Were not they, whose aptitudes he had recognised and nurtured, were not they more to be envied than poor John Ruskin...?

There was a knock at the door, which he did not respond to.

Working people should be guaranteed food, clothes, housing and a minimum wage. These a priori necessities seemed still as far from achievement as they had been when he first propounded them; as far off being achieved in existing society as ever. But St George's land at Bewdley was another matter. Might not Thomas find himself an artisan craftsman there — if not as a boy, then as a young man, if not as a young man, then as an old one (if he survived) — an artisan craftsman with a reverence for great art?

Happier now with the *Fésole* Preface and its implications for the likes of Thomas Manning, he turned to his correspondence — a perpetual task: but one which he did not flinch from. He rapidly penned frank replies to several young-lady pets (including one who was about to become a former pet):

'The real reason for not pressing you to come is I don't think I shall like you half as well, now, as when you were of the tree-climbing, haycock-jumping age! And you'll be sorry! – and so shall I.'

However, with that out of the way, he found again the one letter in his present pile for which he had not been able to provide a pat answer. He re-read it carefully, a shade uneasily. It was from Claire Stott.

Autumn 1877

1

Charlotte Lavenham had some unusual luggage. She had taken up photography. Claire was relieved that she would not therefore be expected to work at her own dispiriting water colours to keep her friend company. Or to display the feeble scratches on her porphyry.

'It is quicker — that is, the act of recording is far quicker, though developing the plates can be tiresome,' said Mrs Lavenham, 'quicker and in some ways more à la mode than water-colours. Give me a hand with this one, will you?'

'This one' was a bulky framed photograph with an exotic tale to tell:

'Where do you think that was made, Claire?'

'Oh,' she replied, 'Somewhere abroad,' – guessing wildly, 'Cathay?'

Mrs Lavenham laughed heartily: 'Not quite,' she replied. 'Not Cathay. The Old Kent Road would be nearer the mark. Have you heard of a man called John "China" Thomson? – and the thing is they can be directly reproduced without the need of an engraver.'

'You bewilder me,' said Claire, ' who is he? — this Mr Thomson? And no engraver? How can he, how can you, do it?'

'Oh,' said Charlotte, 'that's easy. They are set up in a studio — my studio, in this case. He's a Scotsman — Mr Thomson, I mean. We get a stage-painter (and they come very cheap) to do a backcloth, and then we dress up the models and I pose them — which I fancy Professor Ruskin wouldn't approve, but it's fun.'

'And you have learned to use all this – this equipment?'

'I have, courtesy of the said Mr "China" – I bought a book of his. As for developing exposed plates, there may by now even be some local person here. But, if not, we shall ride into Birmingham; where the work can be done while you and I are shopping.'

'Delightful,' said Claire, 'so much more delightful than my sad attempts at cuneiforming porphyry.'

'Doing what?' cried Charlotte.

Claire had not meant to mention porphyry, but it was part of her story, so she had to touch on it, playing it down – had to say *something* about the Professor's nailer women and the two figures she had seen – half seen in the forge. And about her subterfuge to get a better look at them which Thomas had spoilt. And how her chisels were still (she supposed) in Giles' potting shed, and how – maybe – now that Mrs Lavenham had come to stay, they could both go back there confidently together. First, they'd need to break one of the mended chisel blades, and then –

'Stop, stop, my dear Claire, my mind is in a whirl, I'm afraid – '

Charlotte had been thinking about her photographic equipment at the start of Claire's muddling exposition, assuming that she'd be able to show it piece by piece to her young friend, and then involve her in some simple local photography... Instead, all this.

'I think I do recall,' she said to Claire (which indeed she now did) that Professor Ruskin would be saying something more in this month's *Fors* about handicrafts – and also, yes, someone said they had heard it was about forges in this part of the world.'

'You haven't actually read it, then, the August *Fors*,' said Claire eagerly. 'Ah, please allow me.'

Whereupon she turned to her copybook entry and then to the whole passage.

'Well, I never,' exclaimed Mrs Lavenham, '"two other Englishwomen", to be sure. And are you saying the manual workers – the two women – live in this neighbourhood?'

'Just up the road, if these are the right ones…But there's the gardener, Giles. I must…Excuse me a moment…' She caught him and had a quick word. He promised to return directly.

'I was afraid,' said Claire, 'he might have thrown them out.'

'Not the worker women – ?'

'No, 'said Claire, 'my porphyry carving stuff.'

'You were working on silhouettes perhaps?'

'Oh, no. Just cuneiform. I should have stuck to candles.'

And Claire, leaving the reference to candles unexplained…more collectedly now, explained her previous ruse to get a good look at both of the women, and how Thomas – and then she had to explain about Thomas – had forestalled her with his polite suggestion about taking her bag with the tools in. And how she hoped she and Mrs Lavenham would now be able to walk there together, carrying her little tool bag; would walk there together – when the photographic equipment had been safely set up – would visit them, identify the two nailer-women –

'And perhaps,' said Mrs Lavenham, in more business-like tones, 'I could record the interior of their forge photographically.'

But now Giles was here, bringing as directed, the bag and the chisels.

'No,' said Claire in answer to a quiet question, 'he has very properly left the poor scratched stone behind.'

She peeped into the bag because there was a slight rustle, an unfamiliar something. It was the right bag, so the contents couldn't have changed. But something else was there. Gardener's writing, or done with a gardener's pencil Something of Giles' to return. Design for a flower bed? A recipe? What was it?

A piece of paper wrapped around the tools, covered with thick black writing – bold, about eight words to the line. A few interlocking pothooks and an occasional slip of memory or with the spelling or a skid with the gardener's pencil, but essentially reading as follows:

> Yet it was not chiefly in their labour in which I pitied them, but rather in that their forge-dress did not well set off their English beauty; nay, that the beauty itself was marred by the labour; so that to most persons, who could not have looked through such a veil and shadow, they were as their Master, and had no form nor comeliness. And all the while, as I watched them, I was thinking of **two other Englishwomen**, of about the same relative ages, with whom in planning last *Fors*, I had been standing a little while before Edward Burne-Jones's picture of Venus's Mirror, and mourning in my heart for its dulness, that it, with all its Forget-me-nots, would not forget the images it bore, and take the fairer and nobler reflection of their instant life.

Claire was a quick reader, and had paused. Mrs Lavenham's eyes alighted on the right place: her hand went up to her mouth — which for a moment held her back from reading out, then declaring:

'Two other English women…. Two other English women who are no longer incognito! Who would have thought it?'

'This boy,' said Claire, '*he* thought it. A slip of a lad. Identified us — or gave us the chance to identify ourselves, if we wish to take it.'

She was disappointed that she would never now put her improved plan with the chisels into effect. Tom, the polite boy with a cough, had come up with a better one; beaten both of them to it.

There was silence for a while until the ladies singly and together reached a decision not to be precipitate in their approach, to think what they should do.

*

Still at Brantwood, Ruskin had got away from another batch of young ladies – one of whom had caught sight of him in the garden and insisted on being admitted. Another had been despatched across the Lake to old Kate; a third – but a least she was pretty – had corrected some proofs for him: timidly, uselessly.

Now there was a new letter from George Baker to deal with. Evidently, the father of the boy — Thomas, who had drawn the spoke-like hands — was making himself useful to Creswick in Sheffield. Thus, Ruskin was further relieved from any lingering sense of tutelary obligation, given the beginnings of opportunity so near at hand. (Pets were trouble enough, why add pests to them?) Baker had enclosed a letter from Joseph Hill, the schoolmaster, with a tentative suggestion that Dürer's hands might be placed alongside those drawn by Thomas and kept in the master's house at the Board School.

Ruskin exclaimed in irritation, and wrote in the margin of the letter:

'But not as a species of trophy. A comparison of the drawings may be instructive, but not if they are locked away. Such things are for use! Is the child himself in agreement? A cabinet, yes, but one which may be opened…'

Running out of space, he moved to the margin of the other letter —

— 'opened and, used — in a library or little museum. With some familiar well-wrought objects from the locality. Some lace — ' he crossed this out. 'Some — why not? — a set of nails, made by the two women I spoke with. A special commission of every nail made in the area — a single example of each. For which I will pay a shilling a dozen. And I would like three good springs or sprigs of holly to be gathered — for which I'll pay nothing. There is a reason, but I haven't time to explain. These nails are made by hand, and machinery's coming in, more's the pity. Yes, pray set this up and settle with them —'

He had been forced to take his pen to a fresh sheet:

'Dear Baker — excuse the previous poor beginnings to this letter, but I am much pressed. I have suggested you pay the women for this and send me the account. Also for the cost of the little *openable* cabinet too.

'This after all is a sparrow in the hand, while our marble halls set in your timeless grove at Bewdley is still a golden eagle in the bush.

'Moreover, though the place where they dwell is not Bewdley —why not, for a little while — for Worcestershire nailing is equally the topic of my recent *Fors* (along with your splendid acres) — why not a village museum, for the true Dürer, the Venetian item, the St George copy and the other little (but true) Ned Jones? Not forgetting the holly. I relent and will explain its import. Look up 'Oliver' in your dictionaries and you will follow my reasoning. And

I should like Betty — yes, Betty, for I shall not forget her — to be told. If you agree, get Mrs Lavenham — for I hear she's in the area to set it up. You'll know her pretty water-colours, but I believe her capable of different work. As she does herself — though, because she has an obliging husband, she's not always going to take advice as to its direction from yours truly, J Ruskin.'

*

Though there was no shop man who undertook photographic work in the town, Mr Hill knew a competent enthusiast who had all the necessary chemicals and equipment for safe developing from all kinds of originals. This gentleman gladly accepted Mrs Lavenham's exposed plates, with a token payment to help him finance his own hobby.

Soon Claire was able to see herself in sepia holding the big bounding family dog, whose head had moved into a blur.

'That, in itself does not matter,' said Charlotte, 'it might be thought to give the impression of movement. There is a danger that portraits may look too stiff and posed.'

There was a pretty one of Claire, relaxed with a curled cat in her lap.

'Yes,' said Charlotte, 'I think I must have several of these made. Certainly one for myself — for I should like to retain one print as well as the plate, one for you — and one for Professor Ruskin — in reserve, that is, for Professor Ruskin...'

Claire smiled and blushed and made a little disclaimer.

'Not until he asks,' said Charlotte, 'but ask he will and then you'll be glad that you have a spare one for him. Besides, he likes cats.'

'From what you tell me he must have a large collection of mementoes — of, what does he call them? — his pets. Not meaning cats and dogs. I'm not sure that I want to be a pet. One pet sitting on another. For don't you think a pet with a lap is much the same as a lap-dog?'

' — it's only his way,' said Charlotte, 'of coping with a great sadness in his life. But, yes —'

'So I have heard,' said Claire, 'without knowing any of the particulars of the case — but this,' pointing to the cat, about her legs now, and in the picture too, 'is the pet, not this —' herself.

'Certainly,' said Charlotte, 'and this little child, too' — a picture of a niece of the family who'd visited, 'is she not also a pet — a dear child?'

'Yes,' said Claire, 'but does Professor Ruskin collect young ladies as domestic animals or children? Is he the keeper of a menagerie or of an orphanage?'

Charlotte looked startled.

'I'm sorry — I'm not sure I shall hear from the Professor again — he brings out the pertness in me. I was sent here by my family, I can only suppose, to lose that unattractive quality — and yet, what have I done? First, broken good tools and defaced fine porphyry; secondly, conveyed to the gentleman my disenchantment with the ancient world, and the unreasonableness of his, the Master's, teaching. I have had no reply.'

'You are sure to get one. It is just that kind of teasing which he likes.'

'I'm not sure,' said Claire, 'that I am teasing. I think I am cross with him, put out by his inconsistencies. As to photographs, hasn't the Professor spoken against them? To the effect that they are pictures made by light — and hasn't God (and here he speaks fairly enough), hasn't God provided us with a whole world of pictures made by light for our every day observation without the use of chemical processes?'

'I believe the Professor has reservations about photography as an end in itself,' said Charlotte, 'but he has made extensive use of daguerreotypes. I don't know that that is inconsistent, if they were used as an aid to observation. Anyway, he'll tell you himself that you shouldn't look to him for consistency of judgement. And I find in that the fun in him. For there is fun, you know.'

'I hope so,' said Claire, 'for I could grow tired of playfulness in an old man — unless he answers my letter very soon.'

*

So Ruskin and his *Fors* and the unrealised images of those 'other women' — complementary to the 'other ladies' (themselves) — were all set aside. Now they knew as much as they did, they had an unspoken agreement to let it alone; perhaps a feeling that the story would be resumed of itself.

Charlotte turned over the photographic prints she had made: the house, a shady corner in the garden, the conservatory with the animals, Claire and Mary and Sarah, Mr and Mrs Melville, Mr and Mrs Melville and their three daughters, Mary and Sarah and baby Ruth, Mrs Lavenham with everybody (by means of a very long exposure, which left a trace of her arrival on the scene), and — the only one of its sort — a hedger and ditcher at work in a nearby lane.

'Ah,' she exclaimed, 'this one has turned out well! See. He will serve the purpose — be the first of a series which — with your help — will be of interest not only to my husband but also, I believe, to Professor Ruskin, busy as he undoubtedly is.'

This put Claire in mind of the visit she had made with Sarah to the medievalists by the canal — as she had called them in a mental heading note for Ruskin. She had gathered they were referred to as 'communards', but the term hadn't arisen in their talk.

Mrs Lavenham was interested, so the next day they set off. As the journey would have been a long one for someone carrying equipment, and it was not clear whether it would be practicable to record the scene of the men's labours, she had brought along with her no more than a small sketch book.

The ladies took the same route as previously. Arriving at the bridge where Claire had rested with Sarah, she pointed out the abbey site, and began to speak about Hill's enthusiasms in a way which caused Mrs Lavenham to look at her a little curiously. There being no sign of him, they pressed on.

The day was not so hot as on the previous excursion, and their legs were longer than Sarah's, so it seemed much sooner to Claire that they had arrived at the bend in the canal which would reveal the yardlands under cultivation as in the old days.

However, what they saw as they turned the corner, after anticipatory comments from Claire, was a poor anti-climax — though the lawyer in Claire, even in speaking to 'George', had been forearmed against such a turn of events. Most of the crops were still standing, but there was no sign of those who had looked after them: the communards had evidently been evicted.

Already beside the canal was what looked like the foundation of an extensive wharf: with men at work – and the first of many carts tipping rubble to provide a temporary hard-standing. Perhaps it was the beginnings of some scheme to transfer goods between the canal and the railway.

Claire squinted near the sun to see. She was pleased to find no 'George' amongst the workmen. So he had not been immediately driven into navvying again. She hoped that he and his fellows would re-group and try to survive on handicraft work at their 'grange', or had already gone in search of unwanted yardlands in some remoter place than this.

This pastoral thought passed; but Claire was more affected by the abandoned crops and spoilt history lesson than at first she'd thought. It left her with a dull headache — not helped by squinting into the light, and her feeling that she had given an over-eager account of what they were about to see, and wasted Mrs Lavenham's time and energy.

So, disappointed, they turned tail and set out to salvage what they could of the day by calling at the abbey ruins where Mrs Lavenham made sketches of some details. At least they had not had to struggle with the camera, camera-stand, plates and tripod all the way to the yardlands and back; and the abbey inscription would not have been susceptible to photography: too dark, too inaccessible, in too poor condition. As she came to the end of her drawing, she eyed what she had done, then laid down her paper and addressed Claire:

'Professor Ruskin,' she began, and both ladies knew that this recurrence of his name would have to do not only with what was left of the abbey, but also with Thomas's recognition of them – 'Professor Ruskin – we should ask the Professor for his view of our discovery, don't you think? '

Claire shook her head. Not at present, she thought. She dragged her shoe in the hay-dust on the floor like a little girl as she gave her little girl's laugh; laughed at herself for so doing — and then noticed from the absence of dust in an area to her left evidence that another bale had recently been moved. Nothing odd about that, save that it had been both moved and replaced — and, she now recalled — when she was with Sarah it was where Hill had stood for a moment — in what could be construed as a blocking posture.

Claire was about to point out this to Charlotte Lavenham, when she noticed that the artist and recorder had placed a piece of soft paper over the old inscription and was beginning to make a careful rubbing of it using a small block of graphite, to see whether any finer details would emerge.

Claire was interested in what her companion was doing, but also in whether anything else lay behind this other bale. She eased it forward as she had seen Mr Hill do with the first one to reveal the inscription.

From which Mrs Lavenham looked up, her task complete, but only a little wiser — there was perhaps the vestige of a broken canopy, which may, centuries ago when it was more intact, have contributed to the stone's survival. Nothing else.

Quickly she turned to what Claire had found behind the bale. Another architectural detail. Again, it was low down, displaced and skewed; well worn too, suggesting that it had once been high up and beaten about by the weather. There was something of a corbel — this was a word Claire had picked up from the pocket editions of Ruskin — something of a corbel about the two-foot carving.

'How curious,' said Claire, 'it reminds me of Humpty Dumpty as depicted by Mr Tenniel and yet, presumably, it is old —'

And then she became quiet, for it occurred to her, that the great scoop out of the creature's belly (with the little hands holding it agape) was not, as she had supposed something akin to a spooned-out breakfast egg, but the interstices of a frightening female form.

Had Claire not been with her, Mrs Lavenham would have examined the stone object more closely. She had not seen its like before, but had heard of such things on the outer wall of a church (if memory served her right) in Herefordshire.

'How strange,' was all she said, declining any further rubbing or drawing, and pushed back the bale of hay, so that the carving was hidden again.

They left the ruins, when Mrs Lavenham had a thought:

'Best,' she said, 'not to mention our find to Mr Hill. From primitive times no doubt. Sarah was with you, and so — '

— 'He did right to keep it from us,' added Claire.

Mrs Lavenham rather admired Claire for her reaction, or rather lack of one. She's young, she thought to herself, but decidedly not silly-young. While Claire, interested rather than downcast, after they'd walked a few more yards, added intuitively, and with a certain sparkle:

'And definitely not an exhibit suited to conversations with Professor Ruskin.'

(Though concordant with the nightly drawings Turner made in the whorehouse near his home. But even Charlotte Lavenham knew nothing of any of that.)

2

At Brantwood Ruskin was passing material for the Oxford Michaelmas lectures from hand to hand, and in and out of his mind; wanting slides made, commissioning very large charts — showing, for example, tiny details of bud growth, of flowerets in moss, of little whorls and sproutings of medieval stone work. He was marking passages in books, raising dust, breaking up manuscripts, writing and destroying; corresponding in friendly fashion with Miss Jean Ingelow to ask her opinion about a line of verse, quarrelling with Octavia Hill, his former ally (attacking her for discourtesy), writing affectionately to Burne-Jones to engage him against Whistler (Ned reluctantly acceding), scribbling his next *Fors* and the one after that, reading his Bible strenuously, though more and more certain that salvation lay through work done to the best of his ability, and so working all the harder for that — something which Rose (whose presence he felt in the faintness of his exhaustion), he hoped, did not dismiss as firmly as she had in life.

He was irritated to find that the galleys of *The Laws of Fésole* (the Preface had yet to be set) had been gone over so reverently by his recent young lady visitor that she had ignored several bad typographical errors, supposing them to be Ruskinian importations from Italian antiquity. To persuade her nonetheless of his gratitude and that he needed to be left to get on with his work unaided, he had made her a present of the galleys with some notes in his own hand — which she would sell to a collector — and sent her packing. The page proofs, which replaced them, he had ('of course, of course') to handle himself. However, for all his earlier designation of the task as tedious, there were things there which he was not ashamed to own, didn't mind re-reading. For instance:

'Never, if you can help it, miss seeing the sunset and the dawn. And never, if you can help it, see anything but dreams between them.'

The first of these maxims reminded him to work hard with his paint-box — and for a while he recorded all the comings and the goings of the sun, provided the sky required more from his art than a watery monochrome wash. But the second sentence — though he did not amend it — gave him pause for thought.

He woke from a dream or dreamt he woke. His glowing Turners had vanished from the walls. At first, he thought, this meant he was in his old nursery at Denmark Hill, when he was very young. But his father's little William Henry Hunt was not on the wall either. And he knew the special smell of that room — its plaster, its floorboards, a certain something under the wainscoting — and this was not it. And then he felt (in his waking dream or his dreaming awake) a twitch on the bedclothes by an unseen hand. It was not his mother or the maid in the old days getting him up for prayers. It was clear — that there was someone there in bed with him. He could not think who this could be and awoke. Dreamt and dreamt awake and awoke still dreaming and confused.

'Ah well,' he said to himself, 'I have made my bed and am lying in it with that as my only aid to understanding.'

He seemed not to be in bed in point of fact. The page proofs were still before him. He put these aside, came across Claire's last letter, which he had used as a bookmark, and took up his pen:

'Forgive me, Miss Stott, that I have not replied to you in your rural retreat. How curious that I, too, have been in Worcestershire — on the edge of the very place where your aunt lives. Forgive me also for not knowing you were there — if you were already there — or if I knew for forgetting — I am so pressed at the present time.

'Your observations about the chiselling made me wince — not so much for their fun at my earnestness about such matters, for — yes

— you have a pretty wit (nor prettiness in that alone, by the by) — but for my fear that you might well have incised not just your hard block of porphyry, but your blue-veined forearm — of which (forgive me) I caught a glimpse when you so fetchingly stood before Mr Jones's painting.

'Doing my best to weigh up what has happened (rather than doze over it!), I think that, first (as I claimed) you will have gained something — and I think you confess as much — something from your endeavours; second, I, too, have learnt something — a whole lesson: that amongst females not born to it only the plain ones should flourish an edge tool. Your role is to work upon the consciences of gentlemen, so that they remake the world in your image, as something true and good.

'Indeed, I confess that you have already begun to take on this role a little — with respect to my poor self. Have you seen the August *Fors*? There you'll see the sort of thing that I mean. Do you suppose that I would have been shocked by the women nailers that I observed had I not been struck by the contrast between the personages of your fresh young self and the splendid Mrs Lavenham and these poor things? You and she quite out-idealised the elevated images of Miss Graham which Mr Jones had so edifyingly created in his studio. If it had not been for the antithetical recollection of you both, I should hardly have seen the two workwomen as members of the fair sex — as I write the phrase it seems wrong; should have simply wondered at their craftsmanship: for their skill and concentration (though blinkered and confined) is truly admirable. And I have made a small practical gesture to ensure that it is not forgotten. I believe you will in due course be hearing something from Mrs Lavenham about it.

'I fancy,' Ruskin concluded shrewdly, 'you are a serious young lady at heart. And if we are to correspond further, I believe it should be on a basis such as that.

'Ever your affectionate JR.'

*

There were letters for both Claire Stott and Mrs Lavenham by the same post. Claire received the above, and Mrs Lavenham an approach from Mr Baker on behalf of Ruskin. Early the next day — earlier than expected — Baker called at Mr Melville's and, trusting that Ruskin would be too busy to intervene, boldly gave Mrs Lavenham a free hand.

That settled, the three of them went to the Board School, and looked over some of the material while Hill was finishing a lesson. Mrs Lavenham took the opportunity to explore in pencil Ruskin's cast of the boss from St Mark's ('like an astrolabe,' she said, 'stylised at the centre, then moving out and round' — sketching that — 'into a swirl of naturalistic leaves'. It will, I think look best mounted above the cabinet containing the smaller items').

Hill, flustered that his distinguished visitors had been kept waiting, tried to apologise. Baker, however, would have none of it. ('On the contrary, Mr Hill, you are on time. I am too soon.') He explained that an important matter concerning the proposed Shustoke Reservoir had been discussed in committee late the night before, when not everyone could be present. He was anxious that the decision should be taken by all those entitled to vote, and so members were to re-convene in — he looked at his watch — a little over four hours.

Assuring Hill that he did, indeed, mean to carry out St George's business in Worcestershire that day, and that his heart was very much in doing so, he asked the schoolmaster to bring his class in a few at a time to look at the assembled material. Just as with a council meeting, he encouraged everyone — all the children — to give their opinion. And afterwards in the big school room, he said a few un-pompous but instructive words, at Hill's urging, about what being mayor meant.

175

Hill ensured that the museum objects were safely put away for now in a locked cupboard, and Baker rounded things off by bringing in branches of holly, turning the season into Christmas, so as to demonstrate how their springiness could work a great hammer and give their name to it. That done, he left Hill some notes to retail to Betty, glanced at his watch, drove some miles down the Bewdley road for a quick meeting and rapid lunch with Benjamin Creswick and his assistant. Creswick reported progress at Beaucastle — Baker, heartened, would meet him there in two days' time — and Will Manning received his first commission there and then — a small one, but to be able to say he was making something 'for the Professor' was a step up for an ordinary working man.

*

Next day was a bad one for Betty and Ann. There was washing to do, the children were fractious and the weather was hot. First, when you were sweating, the sparks seemed to catch between your eye-lids and stick them together. This was happening to Betty, and all she could do was scrape them off with her finger nail and carry on. Then a cinder went down Ann's boot. Voiceless, she had to plunge the foot, boot and all, into the cold water 'bosh'. They were, however, working steadily enough, if glumly, when Joseph Hill arrived, very cheerful.

'Betty,' he said, 'I told you once before you were famous. First, an account of your way of working in a gentleman's paper (for all that it's addressed to workmen), and now you've got a splendid commission.'

'That's as maybe,' said Betty, working and not quite following, 'and the gentleman left sixpence with the babby — least she didn't swallow it — but that sort of thing puts ideas in your head like. I wasted half a day looking for a picture like the one he told about in his paper — should ha' known better. So I still got to do extra — I don't want Thomas to lose his schooling.'

'Ah,' said Hill, 'but let me tell you.'

He explained, while the two women worked on, that Ruskin thought the days of the hand-made nail were numbered, that the Professor's object was to employ them to turn out all the different kinds of nails of which she was capable — Betty continued working but went into a sort of mumble or chant — 'spikes these in course, dog-eared spikes — but small stuff, well there's tacks, hobs, brushes, clinkers — and, of hobs — clasp, round, patent, Welsh, square, fancy, fancy square, Albert, Victoria, star, cress, fitter — oh, and some others — and clinkers — have I said clinkers?— and battins, and clouts and clasps and brushes and brads, and tingles and tenterhooks, and sparrables and strakes, and — of course — tacks, doornails and sprigs. That's not counting the horsenails — cogs and frosts and that — 'cause women aint never been let to mek them. Daresay us could, but too late to start. So let's see — tacks, hobs, brushes, clinkers'…and she went through her list again in much the same order.

'So, Betty,' said Hill, 'how many do you reckon there are all told? How many kinds do you know about?'

Betty thought: 'Around four dozen, I'd reckon. But I couldn't just set to' — she was still working, though a shade slower — ' and make 'em like. They have to be set up for each kind. Wouldn't pay. How many he want of each?'

'This is the bit that'll surprise you: two.'

'Two hundred? — Not two dozen?

'No,' said Hill, 'neither of those. These are specimens, made specially. He wants just two of each, as I understand, to be kept for the future so that people'll know how you and Ann used to work and for why.'

'A pretty idea,' said Betty, 'Just like a gentleman and a professor. But it can't be done. I'd have to change the block, ask around from others, borrow, waste time. Best teach some young lady the job — like that one who came in here, chiselling stone she was, I understand,' she chuckled, 'or trying to.'

'Ah,' said Hill, 'but you haven't heard the Professor's terms: he'll pay a shilling a dozen.'

Betty momentarily slackened to catch what he had said, glanced swiftly across at Ann, who got the general sense of it; returned, phlegmatically to her work, saying:

'You mean he'll offer me nine shilling for the job? A week and a half's pay for that?'

'That's right,' said Hill, 'and top marks for mental arithmetic. Even with asking around, it's not going to take you an hour to set up each nail — besides, it'd pay you to buy a few in —'

' — Couldn't do that,' said Betty, 'not if the gentlemen's asking us to make em for him ourselves.'

'Well, then, you could make a few extra to sell, couldn't you? And you could get Thomas to do some of the asking around and setting up now, couldn't you? And you could do it bit by bit and not start until you'd got most of the stuff ready to hand, couldn't you?'

'Reckon I could. I'll see what our Thomas says.'

'You do that,' said Hill, 'he's got an old head on his young shoulders.'

'Reckon so.'

'And mark my words, Thomas is going to be interested in it. They're going to go in the case with that drawing of his. Does that surprise you? It'll almost be like having the hands — and we could add some of the tools — almost like having the hands that made the things together with the things that they made. These things, Professor Ruskin thinks shouldn't be forgotten by history. As for the case itself...'

And he explained that Will had the honour of making it — and a decent fee for doing so.

*

Two days later into the forge walked George Baker, who had called on the Melvilles on his way to see Creswick in Bewdley, accompanied by Charlotte Lavenham and Claire Stott.

'Good afternoon,' said Baker. 'I think Miss Stott wishes to have a word or two.'

'Yes,' said Claire uncertainly — though taking security from the presence of Baker, after discussion with whom she had learnt there could be no mistake: these were the women visited by Ruskin in the forge, just as they themselves were the women who had spoken with Ruskin in the gallery.

'It's just to say,' began Claire, 'that I've not come to sharpen my chisels. That I've given up work that I could never master, and which (if I could master it) would be much less use to anybody than a single one of your nails. I've called to say that Mrs Lavenham and I are the other people mentioned in Professor Ruskin's article, which I now realise you've read — my thanks to Thomas for his sharpening and, yes, his sharpness. Forgive me for holding back — but I was not sure, not until I got those lines from Thomas — and am only here now, as you can see, after confirming the details of Professor Ruskin's visit with Mr Baker.'

Oh, Miss,' said Betty, 'you owe us no words, no words at all, but all the same I am pleased to hear you speak 'em. It was strange that you should come here in any case — by accident like.'

'Yes, it was,' said Claire, 'thank you for listening to me' — they were bound to give a lady a hearing, but they had done more — voluntarily staying their hands for a little. Claire noticed: 'We've not come to hinder your work now — especially as it's so hot —'

'Makes no odds to us, miss,' said Betty, 'it's always pretty warm in here, like. Though it's hard on the children.'

They were playing around the maiding tub splashing and gurgling. Betty suddenly called out to them — 'Don't you get drinking that there water now. It's fever water, like I've told you.'

Claire hoped this was just hyperbole, but Baker looked concerned and had a word of his own with the children.

'Now,' said Mrs Lavenham speaking for the first time, 'we must let you get on. But we shall be back. I have something to show you— something for you to be part of if you wish.'

'I'm for letting events tek their course at present,' said Betty, 'as they seem to be bringing us better fortune like.'

*

Ruskin had finished his *Fors* for next month, but Fors itself was bringing him no news or portents. Nor had Claire Stott replied to his, admittedly tardy, letter — and he sensed that a few weeks ago she would have done so. Worst of all, there was no sign from Rose. Not even the animadversions which arose from the — oh so many traces of her in his former writings. She seemed quiescent. The world was going on without her.

He brought out and studied a small portrait he had made of her in 1860, when she was thirteen. A lively, solid girl this. Who would have thought that she could have become a deranged skeleton? Fresh-faced, with a broad, intelligent brow (and with a good back to the head). A sensibly centre-parted clutch of gold hair drawn back, a serious mouth with a little dimple of mischief — and only the uplifted eyes looking a little saintly. No, this wasn't St Ursula; no, this wasn't the infuriating opponent — but neither was it the spirit from whom gifts of dianthus came, this was the down-to-earth Rose, her pretty puppy-flesh over the good bones, lodged now in their Irish mausoleum.

*

As Ruskin had suspected, answering his letter was not something Claire Stott was immediately impelled to do, given the interesting immediacy of Charlotte Lavenham. The two ladies had walked a little way with Mr Hill — over to the abbey again with no mention of the lewd carving, and around the mounds of the moat house — close to the Melvilles' villa — with an old print showing the structure which had once stood there. Now they were back in Betty's forge, as they had promised — and — as for the Professor — they were in a sense on his business, which he could be told about when the story was more complete.

Mrs Lavenham was taking some low life photographs — in emulation of 'China' Thomson — of carters, farm-workers, nail-makers — nail-makers less frantic than usual, making specimens for Professor Ruskin's display case.

There was an element of fun about it, a serious kind of silliness in their mood: Betty and Ann posed at their anvils, Betty and Ann and Thomas outside the hovel; then, with the help of the local camera enthusiast, Betty and Ann and Claire and Mrs Lavenham all together.

'We're like a page of Professor Ruskin's writing,' said Claire.

'The four of us,' said Betty. 'Seems unlikely. As unlikely as working people reading the learned gentleman's printed letters every month with all their hard words and bits in foreign tongues as he sends to 'em regular, though some on 'em do — spell every word on it out.'

'Ah but,' said Claire, 'you should remember that that letter, the piece of writing we have all read, isn't really about us. We — Mrs Lavenham and I — we're only on its pages by accident. We — as Thomas showed he'd guessed by a message he left — are the two *other* English women.'

'Are you, Miss?' said Betty — 'Well, yes, I suppose that's what the gentleman did say — though I don't know what our Thomas had in mind — where's he got to?' — he had crept out — 'I should have thought it was me and Ann more like. I should ha' thought it was working women who was the other always. Means like outside, wouldn't you say? And you couldn't be much more outside than me and our Ann — well, we spends our lives stuck inside this here outside-place, for a start. So I reckon he got it wrong.'

*

'Two other English women,' said Ruskin into the Oxford lecture room — so crammed with listeners that many a speaker would have had to shout himself hoarse, but the Professor's legendarily audible light voice delivered not only colloquial asides but rhetorical tropes as if they were conversational intimacies: 'Two other English women…' Ruskin was working with a plethora of paper before him, though he no longer attended to any of it, and had thrown off his gown in the energy of the gestures with which he called upon a bewildered assistant to produce the appropriate professorial chart from the heap.

Strange juxtapositions of utterance and image ensured the audience's delight without, it seemed, throwing Ruskin, who had developed the ability to use whatever was displayed as a jumping off ground for whatever came into his head.

A slide of two pretty little girls by Kate Greenaway ('whose pure work I am commissioning for *Fors*') had brought him to talk about The Mirror of Venus and the four women — two of them ladies. He seemed confused about which of them had been with him in the gallery. Perhaps that was a rhetorical device. Perhaps not…

*

Betty and Ann were coming to the end of Ruskin's special nailing job, and with it the end of an unprecedented period of careful consideration and comparative leisure. Claire and Mrs Lavenham had returned with the photograph of the four of them together, and they had other things with them in a large bag.

Betty reverted to her theme of which pair of Englishwomen should best be thought of as the two 'others':

'I know what the professor said, but it's a question of — how do you say it, beyond the pale, like, aint it? That means the same as outside, don't it? — what we've been talking about — or did when I was at school — for, yes, I was sent to school when they could. And enjoyed every minute on it. But along side you two ladies, you couldn't be more outside than us two, now could you? So I still reckon the gentleman got it wrong.'

The way they grouped themselves bore out these observations. They looked like creatures of quite separate species going two by two into some Ruskinian ethnological, or botanical ark in defiance of Mr Darwin: two ladies with braided hair and simple gowns gathered at the waist (and a touch of Tudor in the shoulders and sleeves); two female nailers — with, yes, some facial resemblance to the two 'others' (as Ruskin would have it) — multiply-layered (in a parody of a matron's garb of twenty years earlier), protectively shawled, apron-ed, bibbed, over shapeless thick hangings — which hung upon them as they would upon a clothes horse or a mangle or an old bedstead.

Each pair looked quickly at the other, and then stared at the camera; each feeling 'other', to be sure, and ill at ease about it.

*

Professor Ruskin's audience was in stitches. It laughed at first at its own fear of laughing as, grotesquely flapping the sleeves of his gown to illustrate a point, he walked up and down mimicking a critical adversary. But when everyone saw that Ruskin laughed too, they felt easier about it; becoming uneasy again, when he continued laughing after they had stopped. The shorthand writers by now had lost their way and the assistant's bewilderment had an accretion of surliness about it, but Ruskin still got home some good hits.

The Professor was in the grip of what he felt needed saying. His habitual good nature and (even now) idealism were twisted by the sarcasms he discovered on his own lips into spleen and misanthropy. Likewise, his affections suffered; likewise his love, Rose. She had sent no further sign: in this, as in her unshakeable beliefs, she was guilty of disloyalty and cruelty to him personally; of being an unrelenting adversary in death as in life. Like the Furies she went by a kindly name and under friendly guises — furnished with dianthus and vervain, and with the face of a lovely English— that is to say, Irish — girl.

'You are so horrid, St C,' said the ghost of Rose, sitting in the front row. 'It is bad for you, and bad for other people that they are attracted to your horridness. Is this kind of loveless rant all that is left of what we meant to each other?'

Ruskin felt a sudden rush of energy and reassurance. He accepted something in the air, a perfume? — that he took to be Rose's regret, and diverted his resentment against her into measured outbursts against what man had made of God's world. Past unkindness helped him, put an edge on his tongue, hurt him into the eloquence of scorn.

Ruskin became aware that he was using his personal suffering, as he had his illnesses, to further his work. Thus he sent everyone home provoked and prodded; with reports of eccentric behaviour and dangerous utterances. Thereby ensuring an even greater crush to get into the next lecture in the series.

*

Ruskin had summoned Benjamin Creswick — whose work at Beaucastle was complete. He despatched him to the Oxford Museum and then chuntered about the perversion of his principles in that building.

Others might have gone on to say that words failed them, but Ruskin had an endless supply; their purpose being in the present case to commission exemplary casts of true Gothic, also several sections of fresh-cut ashlar (being the antithesis of the 'brick-bats' of which the museum building allegedly consisted); both for use in his next lecture. He intimated that he wished Creswick and Will Manning to visit the South Kensington Museum with him to select further illustrative material.

*

In the little village museum, in the master's room at the Board School, again, Mr Baker was wanting to ask Mrs Lavenham something. He delayed doing so until Hill popped out to see what had happened to Thomas who had gone some time ago to fetch Betty and Ann. Baker placed the Burne-Jones drawing of Alcestis on the table. It was now simply mounted, and protected by a fold-over fly-sheet.

'I hope,' he said, 'that Professor Ruskin will think I did right in affording the scrap of paper some little protection.'

'Yes,' smiled Charlotte Lavenham, 'but I can understand your caution. The Professor is very opinionated about the management of frames and mounts — and, of course, everything else.'

When she saw that Baker was keeping loyally silent, Charlotte began to inspect the drawing, looking closely at the face.

'Mrs Lavenham,' said George Baker, observing her, 'you, though an artist, are looking at this drawing in the same way that I found myself doing — and I have no credentials whatsoever.'

'I know what you mean,' said Charlotte, 'I think it's because I have been taking photographs — I suppose I'm looking for a likeness.'

'Exactly what I felt,' said Baker, 'when I first saw the portrait, if it is a portrait. I found myself thinking that this was a face I should recognise. Not that she's likely to be seen in Birmingham.'

Involuntarily Mrs Lavenham put in:

'Oh, but you might. Her family are from the Midlands' — and then added, 'though she's dressed up – half-dressed as Alcestis here.'

Baker was startled — he had been touched by the story of Alcestis and of the sacrifice made by her for her husband in classical times; now she seemed alive and vulnerable — as his own dead wife had been twelve years ago. He quickly came to himself:

'You do mean, I take it, the person who was the model for this figure would not now be working for Mr Jones in London?'

'I believe not,' said she, 'it would have been some years ago' — and clearly could have said more.

Whether she wished to do so was not clear, for at this point Hill returned. Thomas Manning had been delayed over some necessary arrangements for the children, but here were also Betty and Ann with some carefully-packaged specimen nails — several dozen in all.

Baker had propped up the other things that were going in the display case for the women to see. The arcane craftsmanship of the St Mark's boss was wonderful, but its rendering in plaster gave it a dead look. Mrs Lavenham was urged to display beside it her pencil version of the exhibit, which would serve to connect the look of it with Alcestis.

Meanwhile, Betty was intrigued by the Burne-Jones figure. Her initial surprise that it had clearly once been naked had been replaced by a sense of Burne-Jones' reasonableness in putting the figure's clothes on for her later — which, was his usual practice. She heard Mrs Lavenham say that.

'So,' said Betty, 'that's what I was looking for that time, is it?'

Betty was not a woman who could afford to dissipate her energy in brooding, but the Birmingham man's maudlin attack upon her had dwelt unpleasantly in her mind. At first she coped by dismissing it as the sort of thing which happened to a woman like her But two new things had happened to cheer her up.

The first was that she had learnt from Hill (who had it from Baker via Ruskin) of the connection between holly-boughs and her treadle hammer, the big Ommer, the oliver. It seemed right to her that when she had laid her assailant low it had been with the tools of her trade. And the second was this, the Burne-Jones drawing of Alcestis. It was, though not the end of her quest towards she knew not what, part way towards it:

'Say the name again,' said Betty.

For a moment Charlotte supposed Betty to be on the same tack as her conversation with Baker had taken, and almost disclosed the name of the picture's unfortunate model. But Betty meant the name of the artist:

'Edward Burne-Jones,' she supplied.

'Ar,' said Betty, ' E or B Jones. That is the same one as I was after in Brummagem – pardon me. I had it wrote on a bit of paper.'

She was looking for the first time at one of his drawings. Such a thing as this — drawn on his own piece of paper where there had once been nothing — had become special to her.

'He's begun to make her veiled, like,' Betty ventured.

'Yes,' said Claire to Betty, 'I think, he was beginning to make her sad or proud, or both. It says she's Alcestis. I'm not sure what the story behind her is.'

George Baker knew that; knew about her sacrificing herself. But, because he had connected the story with his wife's death in child-birth, and had had to look it up, he hesitated to answer the implied question.

The pause encouraged Betty:

'Forgive me for speaking out of turn,' she said, 'but what she's called don't seem to matter to me. Because it's — um — what I call a good bit of work (bar a bit of rubbing out), if not that cheerful — No fuss, like — except, maybe, the veil. A bit like our Tom's hands drawing — I like them you know, his 'hands', better than them famous German ones.'

Like Tom, she preferred working hands. Her new-forged spikes, hobs, sprigs, brads — all those she had had in her head and made with her hands — were to be set in the show-case by Mrs Lavenham after discussion with Will. She had in mind the displays of baronial weaponry blazoned in the great halls of famous manor houses.

They began to look at them together: the dog-nosed railroad spikes meant for the colonies were like tent pegs almost, while others were as small and sharp as fish bones; some had almost a look of woodlice about them, and yet others tiny, regular mushrooms. Labelling was important and matching them accurately against such descriptive lists as could be relied on.

*

At one time Ruskin liked nothing better than making lists. But it was exacting work – whether for nails or paintings. He regretted he had agreed that his collection of Turner water colours should be displayed in Bond Street. He shrank from the inevitable catalogue preparation and dreaded being deprived of them.

To see no pictures – or to see them with all their colours gone, see them leached into monochrome. This was a grey recurring dream.

The blackness of the greyness of the night closed about him. The bedclothes switched. He couldn't remember whether the woman, Effie, Euphemia, Gray — who had invalidly borne his name — was in the black or grey of the night truly called by one of those names for shades or some other no-colour.

*

Baker could not stay. He had got Mrs Lavenham to write down the name of the poor, fallen original of Alcestis in a quiet moment. The eyes of the others were on the display of nails — though there were still a few to be made — taking care not to spoil the romance of the occasion. He was going to keep an eye not just on the streets of Birmingham for that face, but also to ask some ladies who provided shelter for the destitute if they had come across anyone with her name.

Mrs Lavenham concentrated on the nails and became cheerful again:

'Swords into ploughshares, don't you think?'

The four of them were of one mind.

Photographs. For the record, here is Ann holding a parasol and Betty standing by a spiky-looking potted plant, which has about it the look of St Ursula's symbol of domestic purity, vervain — but is more likely to be one of those stiff, thin, Victorian ferns. Here is the same group again, but Betty is wearing her new frock. There had been something worrying still about her frock — she had even thought of giving it to Ann. But this first wearing of it for dressing-up with ladies turned it into the stuff of unreal fancies, associated with laughter. And if she were to have a child as a consequence of the way she'd got it — she'd avoided a rape, but had obliged her husband (who'd given her the shilling) after her day out. One of her current flock was sickly and, if it died before winter, the new little one could have the same name in spring — or near enough the same — in its memory.

Here they are, with the addition of Claire on the left and Charlotte on the right. A happy accident this, which broke up the two-by-two effect. It had come about by Mrs Lavenham's running to the wrong side. True she is only just in frame, and the picture is set lopsided as a consequence, but all the women have succeeded in prolonging their amused confusion until the camera has finished its work.

The next print is grouped in the same way, more posed but (as photographs of this era go) to relaxed effect. Claire is wearing a sack apron and Ann is holding a hat brought by Claire. ('It's all right,' Claire had said, 'to try it on' — adding, and then wondering whether she should have, 'I can have it put in the oven after.' To which Betty had replied, ' I don't reckon our Ann's got any vermin, but you'd best be safe than sorry with any of these things of yours.

And we can only put anything on — if we really must — if that's understood between us, like.')

Assured that that was the case, the last two prints record a pleasing pastoral: first, the four women hatted and cheerful; all done up as ladies and with suitably staid expressions; finally, they are all factory girls on an outing; with lit cheek bones, lit chins, hands and arms easy, un-wooden and ready to give a monochrome cheer.

After the four of them looking much as in the above description had considered the look of the quartet in the picture, Betty couldn't forbear saying: 'But I wished I'd a took more care to be tidy. Not to look like a lady, I don't mean that — ' and went to return to the forge.

As if on cue, Mrs Lavenham had popped outside and back again. And now, taking something from her bag, had spread that something across her front — Ann giggled. If anything could have made her speak, this was it. But, no, that was not possible. 'A lady's dress,' Ann wanted to say.

'I couldn't wear that,' said Betty in her turn, 'not a lady's dress. And what's that thing? — like a bird-cage; or one of them things I saw once, a what-d'y'-call-'em, lobster pot.'

But she knew what it was really.

'You could, ' said Charlotte, 'just for the camera.'

'And one for Ann,' said Claire.

'There now. Who are the two other English women? We are four Burne-Jones ladies displayed in the Grosvenor Gallery, far away in London town.'

The four of them got the knack briefly of being together. The working women pulled off their aprons and their forge dress and the ladies put them on. Betty stood sideways on to the camera to show the effect of the crinolette, with her dress all tight and straight up at the front, and swung out behind.

'We could pass for sisters,' said Claire.

'I believe so,' said Charlotte — and they were happy together for a half an hour.

*

Rose had still sent no further sign. The five stems of dianthus pictured on St Ursula's window-ledge stayed firmly within the little fence or support which kept them upright in its open-handed urn. Similarly, the sturdier vervain on the left, sprouting from its ornamental jar. Neither, for example, began mysteriously to grow, though Ruskin looked long and hard at the painstaking copy he had made.

An angel flooded in morning light continued to stand in the doorway to the room, bearing a martyr's palm in its right hand and in its left a shroud. Ursula was after all to be, in St Matthew's words, steadfastly one of those 'who marry not, nor are given in marriage, but are as the angels of God, in Heaven.'

3

This same text from St Matthew had been given to Ruskin by Rose as her ultimate response to his proposal:

'Ye do err, not knowing the scriptures, nor the power of God. For in the resurrection they neither marry, nor are given in marriage, but are as the angels of God in heaven.'

Ruskin was numbed by Rose's decision, shaken by her death-sense — affronted by her implication that he, John Ruskin, son of stern Margaret, after his years of childhood learning and recitation from the Bible — with chastisement for putting a word wrong — that he could be ignorant of the scriptures. And who was this to say so? Regardless of Rose, what kind of reporter was Matthew? A functionary, a tax-collector...

Ruskin's ripostes included a jeering added Preface[1] to the special book, he had written primarily for Rose as pleasant, constructive reading. Now it was fenced off with an outrageous, printed rebuke:

'...you, with all your pretty dresses, and dainty looks, and kindly thoughts, and saintly aspirations, are not one whit more thought of or loved by the great Maker and Master than any poor little red, black, or blue savage... and, of the two, you probably know less about God than she does...You are not yet perfectly well informed on the most abstruse of all possible subjects, and...if you care to behave with modesty or propriety, you had better be silent about it.'

He and she were united in their irreconcilability.

---

[1] *Sesame and Lilies*, Preface, 1871.

But in those days before her death when she still had her mind, and the two years after that, Ruskin and Rose had grown closer and kinder.

So now the ghost of Rose was relenting; and, when Ruskin took himself off from Oxford to town and then to Surrey by train and cab, accompanied him.

He had called to mind childhood days by the Wandle; decided to make a further sentimental visit to the river. To its source at Carshalton, already dedicated by Ruskin to his mother's memory: as a girl she had lived in Croydon, then a small country town.

'I don't doubt mama,' he said to his dead mother as he approached the site, 'that I shall have more clearing and cleaning to do here. You must see that I do it properly.'

There was a silence — a more measured silence than when he addressed Rose.

Ruskin cut himself a stick to demonstrate that he was in the country. He deviated from an irritating new road and descended an incline to the old path (which he was pleased to find not much changed) by the banks of the Wandle — only a small stream here, and one which grew less and less significant as a barrier as he walked.

He was reminded of the celebrated (and sometimes mocked) poem by his friend Jean Ingelow, about lovers on opposite banks of an ever-widening river, as they and it move towards the ocean.

'St C,' said the ghost of Rose, 'why do you not ask the authoress of *Divided* when you next meet her, why her lovers do not turn about face and come back to their starting point – as you are here?'

'Ah, my Rose,' said Ruskin in apparent independence, ' why cannot you and I meet again as easily as these two banks — though,' for he had come to a reedy stretch, 'the point at which the two become one is, I admit, not as clear as one might think.'

The stream, this branch of the Wandle, was at its beginning now in these springy reed beds; with, ahead, hints of some upland. Ruskin strode with his stick towards the spot where he had worked on the spring which fed the stream; where he had wiped clean its fair face before leaving it to look after itself. He was increasingly apprehensive for it, when he perceived in the distance new roofs near to what he judged to be the spot.

His feet left first the moss and then the downy grass behind, and began to crunch on shards of tile and broken pot. He looked ahead for a glimmer of the water, the surfacing trout he had furnished the pool with, the glint of dragonflies, the sun — for he had to admit the sun did shine that day — the sun upon the stone monument he had set like a wellhead by the side of the living pool or fountain, at a point where there would always be fresh bubbles of water.

Ruskin had expected, as he said, to have some work to do; was prepared to hire a man on the spot, as he had done before, to help with the scouring of the pond and restore the clay seal of its basin. But he began to wonder whether he'd come to the wrong place, for there was no pond, neither a pristine one nor a befouled one to be seen thereabouts.

He was about to retrace his steps and look up and about him again from the lower marshy land when he noticed that the weeds grew higher in one part of this place of coarse grass and builder's litter. He trod about there and got mud on his boots, though there had been no rain for some days.

Ruskin flailed about with his stick in some bewilderment. Probably he had misjudged the direction: the new roofs and boundary walls had altered the sky-line making it difficult to locate somewhere once so obvious. He was about to leave when his stick hit something. That something proved to be the base of a piece of fashioned stone set in the ground at the muddiest point. It was all that remained of what he had been seeking: his (a loyal son's) memorial to his mother, Margaret Ruskin.

Upon his father's tomb in Kent Ruskin's tribute to 'an entirely honest merchant' still safely stood. He had added some lines to it about his mother on her death and burial there. But her special place here in Surrey had disappeared.

Ruskin called out angrily: 'A spade, a spade!' and went in search of one.

'Oh St C,' said Rose, 'why not let it alone? Why did you put up monuments for them? Aren't you ashamed that you've lived on your father's percentages, upon the products of that same usury which is anathema to you? Shouldn't you have included in his epitaph that the family capital was shrewdly invested?'

Ruskin who had appeared to be attending only to the necessity of acquiring a spade, and certainly was not hearing in any accepted sense of the word, muttered in an unusual surly fashion, 'I gave his money away.'

'Yes,' said Rose, 'you gave it away. But by what right was it yours to give away? Anyway, St C, I liked them. They were kind to me when we met. But they were bad parents — bad, as bad for you. And I hate to try tell you this, my dear friend, but that woman you never mention — no, not even in so much as a thought with words in it; that woman chanced to be right. I mean Mrs Millais, as she is now. Effie Gray as she was. Yes, yes, she did you terrible harm (as you did her) — and to myself, another poor young thing. But she was right about the 'whole batch of Ruskins'. If they'd been good parents they'd have let you marry that nice little Adèle Domecq, and we'd never have met.'

'Ah Rosie,' said Ruskin gently, in sudden shame, but not in answer, 'I put up gilded monuments to my mother and father, and it was all vanity. Did I do as much for you? What did I do?'

'Your clock stopped,' said Rose, 'or, rather, they stopped it for you. Adèle Domecq was fourteen and they denied you her, as if she were already too grown up and experienced. With tears in his eyes and tenderness in his heart for his only son and a kind word for me, your father was still a bigot and a snob — You wanted Röslein to stay thirteen — and yet she was already a woman. I tried to kill that in me. Culpably. And so I think I'm only on the edge of heaven.'

'But,' said Ruskin, as if in answer to something — his own question: what did he do in her memory — your memory? He supplied the bitter answer: 'I wrote terrible words.'

Said Rosie: 'Yes, you wrote pure things of your mother and, more than once, terrible words of me. St Crumpet. These:

To the woman
Who bade me trust in God, and her,
And taught me
The cruelty of Religion
And the Vanity of Trust,
This — my life's most earnest work
Which — without her rough teaching,
Would have been done in ignorance of these things
Is justly dedicate.'

He thrust her words, his words, out of his head:

'I don't remember — nor do I want to remember — what it was I wrote for Rose — about Rose,' said Ruskin, 'but it was wickedly done. At least they were not cut in stone, as this was... Terrible words, and now I must dig my own grave.'

Not having found a spade, he returned to the fragment of his mother's memorial; tried to shift it with his bare hands.

'Forgive,' said Rose ambiguously.

Ruskin's mood lightened, as if he might have heard her.

'Perhaps she has forgiven me. She would insist that everything would be put to rights in heaven. Though not through marriage.'

He was unaccountably cheered. Perhaps she had relented – had perhaps listened to his argument...

Not far from where he was standing there was a recent Ruskin-Gothic gate in the tall wall of the back garden of a new villa. He opened it and went in. Straightaway he found a gardener, told him he wanted a spade and why.

The man agreed readily enough and declared himself happy to lend a hand, though he was just as new to the area as the house and could not recall any pond.

So they each took a spade and dug together – the man in silence, Ruskin with vehement commentary on each shovelful.

'Fair earth,' he said. 'It is good to dig the fair earth... But this is none such... Here is an old shoe. Can the foot which once wore it be in this sickening pit too? Here are some... large, smashed bones – all that's left of some mistreated old horse... Now we come to obscene potware. Then a substratum of cinders. But where's my mother's stone? Can the ruffians who filled in the sacred pool have carried it away?'

They dug on in this wise until they came to the end of the infilling and hit something hard.

'This may be it,' said Ruskin, 'the memorial stone.'

'Not sure about that,' said the man. 'Looks like a pipe to me, sir.'

Ruskin cried out that a sewage pipe — which it evidently was — should have been driven through his fair waters. He peered at the nasty ochre of the concave pot; stepping back, when liquid spurted and seeped, revolted.

The liquid settled. Ruskin sniffed. Settled, gurgling. And Ruskin saw with satisfaction that pure water was still flowing at a certain depth either side of the foul pipe. The place had been the right one, and the spring had proved true.

'I've seen enough,' said Ruskin. 'Let us quickly shovel back this dead self of mine, and forget my childish life by the springs of Wandle.'

'Let me, sir,' said the gardener, wondering whether the gentleman was quite right in the head.

But Ruskin insisted that they worked together. After which, he gave the man some small change, on condition that he was allowed to carry one of the spades back to the garden with his own hands.

'For,' said Ruskin, 'I have need of these daily exertions. Besides,' casting away the stick, 'my hands are free — I have no use for that now. I find I am not in the country after all, but in the town with its broken pottery and old shoes.'

They entered the gate and found the owner of the villa there inspecting his greenhouse. Ruskin introduced himself and explained the purpose of his visit to the site of the pond.

'My dear sir,' said the householder, 'you place me in some difficulty. I don't know what you'll think, but I acted for the best, as I saw it.'

'What's that?' said Ruskin, steadily.

'Well,' said the gentleman, 'they were going to break the stone up for ballast. Had already taken it off at ground level. Upon which I thought it would have better chances on the other side of my wall — pardon me for thinking so. Not far from its original place, as I thought, and not going to come to any further harm. Yes, sir, I saw your name in the inscription and meant to write to you at Coniston about what had happened. I should have done so. Yet I put off and put off, for there was an awkwardness about the whole thing. The stone is safe enough just round the corner, as you'll see.'

Ruskin saw. There it was in a rockery, a dry-land rockery, albeit with cockle shells and some creeping Ginny, with the words — no need to read the words, his own words — which the mason had carved for him:

> 'In Obedience to the Giver of Life,
> the brooks and fruits that feed it, of the
> peace that ends it, may this Well be kept
> sacred for the service of men, flocks,
> and flowers and be by kindness called
> MARGARET'S WELL. This pool was
> beautified and endowed by John Ruskin Esq, MA, LLD.'

Ruskin glanced at it, but said nothing.

It seemed better,' said the gentleman apologetically, 'than that it should be destroyed —'

'They destroyed the sweet pool,' Ruskin interjected, 'but could not staunch the source of it.'

'They certainly did their best to — their worst, that is,' the gentleman replied, not quite sure of Ruskin's meaning. 'Said they were from the council. Would you wish to have the memorial taken into your keeping?'

'Let it stay where it is,' said Ruskin, 'as high and dry as it is. I can see now that it was folly to have tried to save a little of the old England, and record that I had done so. All of that's gone beyond recall. All gone in my life time. If I had started my work fifty years earlier I might have accomplished something.'

Declining refreshment, he said goodbye civilly, and felt easier that he could be angry about the pond yet not be required to maintain it.

Rosie said, 'Oh St C, I do believe that an albatross — one of your many albatrosses — has fallen from around your neck.'

'For the time being,' said Ruskin to thin air, reflecting his mood, but about nothing in particular. 'And worse will befall those who survive,' he mused cheerily in gloomy terms: far from Morris's vision of rural England reclaiming the city, the filth at the Wandsworth end of the Wandle would soon be met by the filth from Surrey, with Morris's Merton works standing part way between, tainting the waters of Pope's 'blue transparent Wandle' and Ruskin's recollection, with vegetable dye. The badness of things was a comfort.

*

Autumn now, and Betty's sickly toddler had already died of what was perhaps the fever. For the sake of the others they hoped it was just 'something she'd ate'. Yes, Betty was with child again, but was strong and could always work throughout her time. There would be no sign of the growing replacement child beneath her swathes of protective clothes.

'You miss them more when they're the bigger ones,' said Betty calmly of the dead infant, 'though I'm not one of them as can't keep count of how many babbies they's had.'

Mrs Lavenham and Claire had kept away for a little after the news, but they returned with the cheer of harvest home — though nailing was season-less. Photographs of harvest, of stooks of corn and of a frightening corn dolly. Attired in a muslin dress, the last stook, its corn hair peering blankly, eyeless above the neck of a girl's dress (another family's 'bigger' child — the dress of a dead girl — dead certainly of the fever this one, so the dress not saved for her sisters), as if the resurrection next year of last year's barley would help the girl now harvested.

*

George Baker was presiding over the sewerage committee: deaths from fever had plummeted in the town over the last year. 17 million gallons were being supplied by the Birmingham Water Works Company — ownership of which had passed to the municipality a year ago.

Figures were being put to the meeting by an official: 'the closure of 3,000 polluted wells, the mass installation of water closets.' Another spoke of the projected new reservoir — previously approved in principle — which would hold 420 million gallons.

Baker, from the chair, was congratulatory:

'You will not mourn, gentlemen — none of us will — the passing of the insanitary back-yard pumps and the dangerous shallow wells — all very well in rural areas — but death traps for an urban populace. To live safely in this town until now — you will recall this, I believe — meant belonging to that minority who could afford the hucksters' charge of a ha'penny a bucket. A ha'penny a bucket! What price could a poor man put upon his family? How many buckets a day — a week — could he afford? How could he keep such water separate — this cheapjacks' water from good springs — how could he keep this separate from the convenient, but infected supply which he could draw at his own door? He could not, of course. Let us, therefore, commend this second report — is that in order? Anyone against? — and authorise the working group to finalise plans for the Shustoke Reservoir...'

*

Ruskin inveighed against the spoliation of Lake Katrine by Glasgow waterworks, mourned the former clarity of its shallowest waters, the canalisation of Thirlmere for the inhabitants of Manchester, the foulness which suburban builders had brought to the Wandle. Birmingham's projected reservoir in Warwickshire troubled him less: it was far from the central Jerusalem of his world map, far from Lakeland and the Scottish mountains, from Carpaccio and Rose. Rose living through him. She was calm and benign just now — but still sent no clear signal, other than interfering with his preparation, and putting mischief in his lectures.

*

Betty's husband was in London town to meet Ruskin. Claire was to go back home, Mrs Lavenham having gone before. Daringly, amazingly, Thomas was to take care of the shop and Gran the little children while Betty and Ann had a once in a lifetime chance to see the sights — Will had a relative in Stepney who would put them up. Claire insisted on knowing their address.

*

Claire's father was more than glad to see his daughter. The servant Alice had been caught in some drunkenness or dishonesty and dismissed. With her departure, all the smirch on the artistic life had gone (it was as if she had invented it — and, indeed, it seemed that she might have contrived that her tittle-tattle was overheard to do her mistress down). Mr and Mrs Stott met Mrs Lavenham and were pleased with her, and perfectly happy that Claire should attend Lady Lindsay's evening reception at the Grosvenor Gallery to see the paintings still on display. Burne-Jones was perceived by them as a pious gentleman (for they were outside the circle for whom Zambaco had been a by-word).

*

So here Burne-Jones was, in a churchly setting: the restored St Martin's in the Bull Ring, Birmingham. This was his second recent visit to the town where he had been born. He was overseeing (because Morris had to be elsewhere) the fitment of some left hand panels to a memorial window.

Moses, half the size of life and dressed in pretty Morris fabric, was in place; and, at the top, a quatrefoil angel set in blue waves of the air (which were to recur), equipped with a musical instrument and rich red wings. Otherwise, the colours were muted, the replaced ashlar helpful (unlike the hangings at the Grosvenor), the workmen quiet, the light of day revealing.

However, it was his design for the section beneath the Moses on which Burne-Jones was musing. He had received a letter that morning. The design of that little panel was a daring one, with, he knew, some autobiography to it. In the middle was an upright pole or stem, around which was coiled a snake — the Serpent, the Tempter. The Subject, though, was the Annunciation — and Mary was the New Eve. So the snake was head down; dead, diseased-looking and part decayed.

An exorcism — not that the snake's head was in her likeness — an exorcism of Maria Zambaco, the temptress; the formerly ubiquitous Maria Zambaco who had attempted suicide on his account, and nearly been the death of himself and his wife and family; and finally his reputation. He knew Ruskin was embarrassed by the traces of the Zambaco visage in the pictures at the Grosvenor Gallery. But now Maria Zambaco had gone to Paris to set up her own studio, taking with her, if no longer a piece of his heart, a pound of his flesh.

The letter, received that morning was not from Zambaco, but he had concealed it from Georgiana, his wife Georgie. It came from a favourite professional model, the outlines of whose naked limbs were (to his eye) not only definable, but clearly identifiable, beneath the draperies of the Virgin Mary in the glass.

He recalled the drawings on which the figure was based and the sessions some years ago at which he had made them. Other drawings from the same sketch book — otherwise broken up — had been kept together as relating to Love Leading Alcestis at the Oxford Drawing School.

The woman who had sat for him, whose body animated that of the Highest — the image set in glass before him — had fallen on hard times. It was her letter which he was reading. She had caught sight of him on his last visit to the church; but hadn't liked to approach when she saw the carriage come for him — because, as she said she 'no longer looked her best'. There was a bit of humour in that, but he winced at the thought of her fallen life, of what was eating her flesh away. She was now a day-patient in a low hospital. Such things did happen. He would send her something.

*

On the night of Lady Lindsay's reception, Mr and Mrs Stott (who were committed to a later function at Lincoln's Inn) were mildly surprised to see Claire and her friend departing so early for Bond Street. Their surprise would have been greater had they known that their daughter's journey would take them through Hackney. Mrs Lavenham recommended the Metropolitan from Euston to Liverpool Street and then a cab. They hoped there would be no faintheartedness.

Mrs Lavenham's forte was encouragement:

'Oh Betty,' she cried, barely through the door, 'how smart Will is!' — Will Manning dressed in his best, off to meet Benjamin Creswick, the latter having been introduced to Sir Coutts Lindsay, who would receive the menfolk in a separate room, while his wife and the ladies were gathered upstairs.

'Mr Ruskin aint able to be there himself like,' replied Will, smoothing his back hair — 'wants us to go in his place, don't he?'

Will thought of himself as a craftsman now — one who'd learned the hard way.

A frock of Claire's was a good fit for Ann, and a high-waisted one of Charlotte's still did for Betty.

Betty said something indeterminate, but Mrs Lavenham — though childless, in spite of her husband's attentions — knew what she meant but assured her that no one would notice.

'See,' said Mrs Lavenham, 'I said before we were sisters. That's not right — we're twins.'

They spun their skirts round in the parlour of the house — which was not thought so very strange, for the relative was a cab driver who carved picture frames in his spare time, and so knew the odd ways of lady and gentlemen artists — when suddenly he found himself saying 'excuse me' to Betty, his cousin.

'Blow me!' he said, 'it's our Bett.'

'There now,' said Mrs Lavenham, 'that settles it now, doesn't it?'

Settled it enough to get them as far as the door.

Betty cringed and wanted to turn back.

'It's no use,' said Betty, 'no use. I can't go through with it.'

There was much persuasion and awkward rejoinders from Betty. At last she came out with it:

'It's my hand. It shows I'm only a working woman' — that mattered more to her than the thickening of her body (a comely one for a woman of her class). 'They'll see my finger. What sort of lady has hands with a finger like that?'

'No one will know,' said Mrs Lavenham, 'you've got the gloves. Pull on your gloves. Everyone will wear gloves.'

'But it's not cold. That seems the funniest part. I didn't want to do that — pull them things on over my rough hands, they snag so. But I suppose if you say so —'

'—I do say so—'

'We both of us say so.'

'— Then I suppose I shall have to...'

*

Ruskin was in bed early in his old nursery at Herne Hill after a quiet evening. The Severns were at Brantwood to look after the grounds, and — by his orders — to permit inquirers to view the house (he insisted only on not being there himself as an exhibit).

So he was here alone, in his childhood home, except for the cook and a maid, and it was easy to believe that his mama and papa had just stepped out for some air and would soon be back.. He recalled the delight of returning home with his parents after escaping from Effie. So glad to be with mama and papa, so glad to have them again as inhibitory and admiring travel companions.

However, the sad old business was in his loins and on his mind when he awoke the next morning. Sad business — disastrously so —

because the repercussions from it had caused Rose to refuse him. He could have managed things otherwise. Could have contested the nullity suit, could — for what would Effie's assertions have been in opposition to his? — could have blackened the name of the deserting wife. He could have despatched her — metaphorically at least — to consort with derelicts beneath the arches off the Strand, as in Augustus Egg's depiction of a Fallen Wife; could have made it impossible for Millais to take her (for the good of his art not in malice against the woman).

But even as there was something about Effie that he had flinched from, there was an aspect to contesting the suit which made it incumbent on him, rather than exposing her to disgrace and ruin, to take all the blame for.

Ruskin did not, of course carry about in his head (unlike the letters from Rose, and great tracts of the King James Bible) the sworn statement he had made to his proctor twenty three years ago, with a view — later rescinded — to offering it as evidence. But the experience was with him, like a phantom declaration:

'It may be thought strange that I could abstain from a woman who to most people was so attractive. But though her face was beautiful, her person was not formed to excite passion. On the contrary there were certain circumstances in her person which completely checked it. I did not think, either, that there could be anything in my own person particularly attractive to her, but believed that she loved me as I loved her, with little mingling of desire.

'Had she treated me as a kind and devoted wife would have done, I should soon have longed to possess her, body and heart. But every day that we lived together, there was less sympathy between us, and I soon began to observe characteristics which gave me so much grief and anxiety that I wrote to her father saying they could be accounted for in no other way than by supposing that there was a slight nervous affection of the brain. It is of no use to trace the progress of alienation. Perhaps the principal cause of it — next to her resolute attempt to detach me from my parents, was her always thinking that I ought to attend to her, instead of herself attending to me. When I had drawing or writing to do instead of sitting with me as I drew or wrote, she went about on her own quests and then complained that "I left her alone."

'For the last half year, she seems to have had no other end in life than the expression of her anger against me and my parents: and having destroyed her own happiness, she has sought wildly for some method of recovering it, without humbling her pride. This it seems, she thinks she can effect by a separation from me, grounded on an accusation of impotence. Probably she now supposes this accusation a just one — and thinks I deceived her in offering consummation. This can of course be ascertained by medical examination, but after what has now passed, I cannot take her to be my wife or to bear me children. This is the point of difficulty with me. I can prove my virility at once, but I do not wish to receive back into my house the woman who has made such a charge against me.'

Prove his virility at once? Demonstrate his maleness? On 27 April 1854, the date of the document, he had no doubt that he could refute the charge of impotence.

By his own account 'another Rousseau', that is, an onanist, Ruskin had taken care in younger days to cover up any pictures which might catch him in such an act — as his father insisted they were to be covered every Sabbath day. He was glad that he had no need now to apologise to his Turners — to the noble paintings, as distinct from the copulatory painter's obscene sketches — for they had not accompanied him to London on this present short visit. He did apologise to any unseen spirit for what he was in mind to do — as he began to explore his person. Would he have needed witnesses throughout the sordid act lawyers required, or would they have been satisfied by a measurable quantity of end-product?

Carefully separating his dirtied mind, on the one hand (the sewage pipe from the pure spring), from any thought of Rose; on the other, from the erotic gynaecology, Ruskin tried to summon up a recollection of the not-beautiful actress whom he had visited, when something not very much had happened between them, during his first independent tours of Europe with the guide, Couttet.

After a minute or two, it was clear that his effort (an empirical investigation, no more) wasn't worth the candle — though there was a sort of mortification of the flesh about it that was not inapposite. Resolving to leave such display and evacuation to that baser part of his consciousness whence stemmed unworthy dreams, he intoned some cleansing morning prayers and was free to resume attempts at conversation with Rosie.

Soon he was up and about, late for him. The day went rapidly in work and one-sided dialogue with Rose. He was keeping clear of artists and galleries – he wouldn't be at the Grosvenor, for instance. Tomorrow he would be up with the lark: setting out to meet Benjamin Creswick and Will Manning at the South Kensington Museum to study certain items and with them make copies (or have them made) as illustrative material for the final Oxford lecture, which was now a week away. As they thus would have gained a thorough knowledge of the items chosen for the lecture, Ruskin proposed to install Creswick and Will as aides for his final lecture, in place of the usual college demonstrator.

This functionary, a meticulous man, had been urged by Ruskin to absent himself from his post for the final lecture of the series, and given a coin or two as an inducement to do so. He was a man who always adhered punctiliously to prior instructions, and so would presumably oblige by his absence. This characteristic was both a strength and a weakness. In Ruskin's last lecture the man had stuck rigidly to what had been arranged beforehand. Unfortunately, Ruskin was well-known for his impromptu alterations and inspirations. So, as a consequence of the poor assistant's inflexibility — together with Ruskin's fondness for parentheses and repetitions, an episcope image of Walpurgisnacht had done duty as Sunrise over the Venetian Lagoon; a steam yacht on Lake Geneva as The Fighting Téméraire; and Glasgow Corporation waterworks as the Falls at Schaffhausen. Ruskin's large specially-drawn charts (some by Benjamin Creswick) had also been misapplied, with effects which most of the audience supposed to be indicative of Ruskin's sarcastic bent.

*

The four English Women were nearly at the Grosvenor Gallery, with its intimidating — and scandal-mongering doorman — when Betty dug in her heels like a dog resisting its leash.

'Please,' she cried, 'I cannot go in that place. Do not be so cruel as to make me.'

'Cruel,' said Claire, who was enjoying the occasion, and the little element of deception — yet how crass she told herself that it had to be seen as deception —'how are we cruel?'

'Because,' said Betty, 'because I shall be found out. I've only to open my mouth and they'll guess what I am and the kind of place that I come from.'

'But,' said Mrs Lavenham, her heart sinking, 'does it matter if you are — as you say — found out?'

But she knew that it did.

'Betty,' said Claire, 'there's an easy answer.'

'What's that?'

'Why, let Ann do the talking for you!'

'But,' said Betty, 'she don't — can't — speak.'

'Exactly,' said Claire.

They went in and were thought a very fetching quartet. While most of the ladies present were engaged in small talk and sherry, the four of them inseparably scrutinised the eight Burne-Jones pictures, and really looked at little else (a peek at the Tissots, for Claire). At The Days of Creation — the gathering angel host, with the performing globe, formless at first and, saving for the last, the innocent nakedness of Adam and Eve; at the unfinished St George whose copy they knew so well; at Fides, Spes, and a Sibyl; at Temperantia (whom Mrs Lavenham knew to be Maria Zambaco), pouring water from an urn onto curls of fire or desire at her feet; at The Beguiling of Merlin (Zambaco, half-erased, ill-replaced); at The Mirror of Venus; under the eyes of Venus swathed in diaphanous robes of crystalline blue. The four women observers faced the nine russet-clad maidens of the picture, and like them looked down into the lily-padded forgetmenotted waters. There they descried again the four pictured faces (beside other visage-less maidenly fragments); all, in accordance with the laws of optics, unchangeably heads-down, decapitated, by the margin of the mere.

Claire looked at Betty. Betty smiled and seemed about to speak. But she had not forgotten. For the muteness of the visitors — or maybe they were thought to be foreigners who knew no English — had been accepted. She took out a little notebook from her borrowed bag and wrote of the inverted images — neatly, with a borrowed pencil:

'They stand on their heads because the world has turned upside down.'

*

An upside-down world where all women would wear clothes best suited to their work for that day, where the pure air of Ruskin's settlement at Bewdley would blow clear Thomas Manning's lungs, where all children would make old bones, where books and pictures in marble libraries and galleries set in ancient groves would enlighten Thomas and his kind, where without aspiring to be gentry, youths would work honourably at something fine, and be respected in a community where just laws were freely accepted; a place like Shakespeare's Arden, like Italian hill villages (as the English saw them), where there would be no exploitation of people or resources, no factories, no usury, no crime; where John Ruskin and John Ball could dream without fear of waking, where closed communities would not produce cretins, where geology would be unchanging, and landscape eternal; where water would be crystal-clear, and fever unknown; where daily lives would be surrounded by the beautiful and the useful, and those terms be interchangeable; where everyone who was able to work would work, and those who could not work would cheerfully be given and cheerfully receive — in accordance with the teaching of *Unto This Last* — benefits as full as the workers: a world where little children and chickens in forges would be free from sorrow and grime, pursuant to the teaching of Rev F D Maurice et al, and the novels of Charles Kingsley.

4

Ruskin loved children, or such versions of them as he met in his several annual visits to pantomimes; but objected to babies — seeing them as grey, unmoulded whelps, putty-flesh to be licked into shape by the mother-bear of the old bestiaries. Joan and Arthur Severn had acquired three of this kind of thing which had grown into playable-with creatures. But three was the appropriate number, enough to occupy his mineral collection, his story-telling capacity, and his fund of practical pursuits.

They had delayed telling their dear Coz until a gap in his Michaelmas lecture programme brought him to Brantwood — that an additional Severn offspring was to be expected. Arthur was cheerful about the prospect, Joan not unhappy, Ruskin dismayed.

'And you plan to lie in here at Brantwood?' Ruskin said, tentatively.

Joan correctly interpreted his observation as a strong wish that she would not do so:

'No, dear Coz, with your permission — for this will be a Christmas child — as winter comes on, we shall retire to Herne Hill.'

'Very wise,' said Ruskin, relieved, 'because should you have need of additional attendance for the birth, our Lakeland snows would be against you. Though until then it does mean — forgive my selfishness — I shall have you and Arthur to organise my visitors, and' (chuckling), 'would-be visitors, and sing me Winter songs.'

He would be spared, too, Joan's presence in the dark days after Christmas, at the turn of the year, and onto the dismal sacredness of 2nd February, the anniversary of his suit, of his wait (as with St

Ursula's husband), of his rejection; of, by 1878, his twelve years' attendance and hope of a more favourable decision. Which still would come to him through some sign from beyond the grave.

Before that there was his work. The house made other work. Ruskin had turned, and was still turning Brantwood from a rustic retreat into a sizeable residence — much as Scott had with Abbotsford, but without the martial accoutrements; and, indeed, as Arthur sometimes said out of earshot, with little taste or care for comfort. And now there was to be a further change: an addition to the Severn family to provide for.

An extra room would make no problem, as so much of the architecture was higgledy-piggledy. Ruskin set to and made some sketches. It wasn't a child's room that he had in mind, but an escape place — for himself from the new child — maybe a covered way, maybe an additional turret room, maybe an extension to the boathouse.

He engaged a local craftsman to fashion a cradle — a traditional one, he insisted — and spoke of mother-of-pearl inlays at either end. He gave Joan a sovereign to put by for the child.

But then there were worrying signs. Joan was faint and obliged to rest. Ruskin dreamt of blood on the moon. His breakfast egg was tainted. Rosie spoke to him worryingly in a dream:

'I have no calendar,' she said.

*

Ruskin was touched by this poignant encounter, but the blood worried him. So he decided it did not constitute a sign, that it referred to the past not the future. And it was, and remained, a dream: not a physical manifestation — unlike the gift of dianthus and vervain. Not projected out of dreamland into the world of every day.

And from the world of every day, back into dreamland: the same conclusion one morning when still half asleep. Nearly awake, he experienced a hallucinatory vision of the manuscript page in which he was writing his dawn-sky account for *Fors* of how dianthus and vervain had come to him from St Ursula. There the page was, before his unopened eyes, being written — his pen scratching — as *he* had written it — all he had written on it, with the crossed words reinstated, uncorrected —' of what Little Bear has thus sent me the flower from against out of the dawn in her window to put me in mind of, — the religious bearings meanings of the living mother.' Then he saw — and he twitched to see — the words he had cancelled being struck out again — 'from', 'against', 'bearings', 'living'. It did not trouble him to re-live those moments, — but, then, the whole page was being slashed. His entire work being disarticulated and cut about. He rushed to the door, half awake and alarmed.

There in the corridor, coming from the direction of Joan's room, he saw a maid with a blood-stained sheet. He hurried to Arthur.

'Has she cut herself?' was his innocent cry, quickly amended to 'has the surgeon been forced to operate?'

'No, Coz,' said Arthur turning his face away as he spoke, 'there is no occasion for surgery, but the child is lost.'

Ruskin gave Arthur's hand a commiseratory squeeze, as his heart came into his mouth. At first there was his unspoken relief and then anxiety and guilt.

'And Joanie?' said Ruskin.

'She is weak,' said Arthur.

'But she'll pull through?' asked Ruskin.

'They hope to save her,' said Arthur.

There followed ten distracting days during which Ruskin alternated between hand-holding sessions with Joan (Joanie, Doanie, Di-ma – nick-name-y, intimate, baby-talking sessions) and frantic efforts to work — with wild switching between new prefaces to old works, old prefaces for unwritten books, sketches for further utopian projects, catalogues of holdings, and correspondence.

Ruskin received news from an acquaintance whose elder daughter he had instructed in drawing, that the youngest and dearest, was seriously ill. Ruskin responded immediately with several lines of bright fancy and some drawings and a funny verse or two for young Grace and, particularly, little Flora. His letter, written in love, tipped the balance with Fors, for in ten days Joan — though not Flora — was pronounced out of danger.

*

It was known that Ruskin was again to speak extempore, so the strong possibility of his giving voice to the outrageous, including the outrageously true, ensured the Oxford Museum was packed.

Benjamin Creswick and Will Manning were in attendance, better prepared — because less specifically-briefed than the museum demonstrator had been: 'When I click my fingers, display whatever you think appropriate. There will usually be a key phrase, and each chart or plate bears an appropriate label.'

The audience numbered fully a thousand. Ruskin mounted the rostrum, a slight figure in gentleman commoner's cap and ample gown. He was taller than was generally supposed and when he stood up straight, even those at the back could catch the glint of his eyes in the gaslights he detested — and the waving of his hands when they were uplifted as they frequently would be.

Ruskin made an expansive gesture: 'Lector, si monumentum requiris circumspice: If, like Sir Christopher Wren (whose work I would undo, if I could), I were supposed to be in need of a monument, I would prefer a nameless mound of turf to this expensive necropolis. Yet I have it on my conscience that I am partly responsible for it. Fought for, supposedly on my behalf, by good friends of mine, this, The Oxford Museum, is a building whose frankness is matched only by its ugliness. No, grieved as I am to grieve my friends, I can find nothing to admire either in the conception or in the execution of it...'

Images of what he did admire — St Mark's Basilica and capitals of the sun, moon, and Adam and Eve from the ducal palace — were successfully introduced at this point.

'So,' said Ruskin, 'I am at odds with my friends, at odds with the public. Yet for fifteen years, I was the public's darling, because of my pretty prose; written not to please myself but to satisfy my father. I should never have finished Modern Painters if it had not been for his insistence.

'For the next fifteen years, I was an enemy to the public, banned from the pages of *The Cornhill*, forced to set up a publishing house under Mr Allen (who had the advantage of having done something useful with his life: that is to say, he is a carpenter by trade) in order to speak truly of the poor and of religion — and of the economic connections between the two — that is to say, of capitalism, of usury, and of the usury of religion: the false doctrine that a human soul can achieve salvation through the sweat or good life of some other being, in spite of pursuing in his own person a life of vicious indolence or heartless extortion.

'But at the present time — and I thank you for your attention today — there is a feeling abroad — I put it no higher than an uncertainty — that it is no longer self-evident that what I purpose must be unworthy of men's attention. That is because of the gradual perception that I speak on behalf of Life — unlike this place in which I stand, which has been constructed on behalf of and at the behest of Death.

'I say, if you want to paint a dog, love him, and look at him; this institution says, if you want to paint a dog, vivisect him first, and boil all the flesh off his bones afterwards.

'I say, if you want to see beauty in a woman, ensure that she is virtuous (and, if possible, learned); they say, kill a bird, stuff it and stick it in her hat...'

The delicate hands and tapering fingers paused and gestured to his assistants: to convey the mischievous character and mistaken preoccupation of the university museum's collections in particular and of men of science in general: bones and bits of bird were at this point displayed, together with drawings illustrative of how a living swallow flew.

Ruskin spoke in pity and horror of the sin of killing a bird in flight, against the manufacture of arms, against the Turkish War; against the oppression of the Irish ('the true purpose of the army being to protect the person of the sovereign') — and moved on to the essential conditions for art in Great Britain: the most pressing of which was the demolition of every ugly building in Manchester and Glasgow —and therefore of those cities in their entirety.

The life of art was in religion, the humility of art was the poverty of the artist's life, the food of art was the passionate study of nature — by which was meant the ocular study of nature, by the naked eye, not by means of contraptions and claptrap: the human, the humane study of nature — of things as they are — was the nub of the matter. To illustrate which, images of Ruskin's own minute studies of moss, which stood up to enlargement, were displayed.

'In practice,' he said, 'an artist should receive a fair wage, but no more — as Turner did: £28 . 7s for three drawings of Florence is what he got for his work — each of which would carry a price tag of £500 to £800 nowadays from profiteering dealers.'

He gave examples of great art in Florence and Venice — and, a favourite theme — described how a school of landscape art had burst out organically in the eighteenth century, at the very point when medieval evocations of Nature had given way to classical banalities. So, farewell Nature, echoing groves, seasonal growth...

He inveighed against contemporary affronts to nature, humanity, and taste too: 'In Ealing Cemetery I hear a bell-tolling machine has been set up at the cost of £80, and the sexton, turns on the lamentation.' Will Manning presented a picture of this machine — or something very like — which was greeted with applause.

Ruskin was stumbling across dead sheep 'lying there in the midst of the children at their play', on the bare beds of former rivers – rivers whose waters had been carried away to serve the needs of the mechanised manufacture of unnecessary objects. With such injuries inflicted and incurred in this world there could no longer be joy in any other. Neither nature nor religion could any longer provide a basis for Art. In fact, they precluded it.

'Consider whether, even supposing it guiltless, luxury would be desired by any of us; if we saw clearly at our sides the suffering which accompanies it in the world. ...the cruellest man living could not sit at his feast, unless he sat blindfold. Raise the veil boldly; face the light; go forth weeping, bearing precious seed, until the time come, and the kingdom, when Christ's gift of bread, and bequest of peace, shall be "Unto this last as unto thee"...'

Unto This Last, where the only Wealth is Life. It was above all, Ruskin's insistence on accepting Christ's teaching in His parable of workers in the vineyard which lost Ruskin his respectable English readership (gaining him Gandhi's later). A readership well lost, with this parable of social justice the key to his life and thought.

So far his audience had followed him well enough to know that they often disagreed, and to admire his eccentric handling of ideas;

also the panache with which Will Manning (who seemed to have come into his own) was managing the visual examples.

Ruskin had set out vigorously his reasons why there could be no great art in his own country in their own time, enlisting in his argument, on the one hand, again, the example of St Ursula, 'a pure Venetian maid'; on the other, 'the principalities and powers of Satan' (a frisson here from his listeners). He enjoined them to seek to know Christ only through the simple act of low church communion. He paused impressively, and seemed to have the power not merely to hold the audience in the palm of his hand, but to lower the flame of the gas-lights.

'If you choose to do otherwise,' he resumed, 'your service of Christ will become a mockery of Him whom you seek to serve. Your faces — all your faces — will be turned from the light, turned to the wall; your worldly knowledge, your precious objects, drift into the stuff of drear and dangerous darkness.'

He gestured to his helpers.

Smoke and the smell of sulphur drifted into the museum:

'Every day your virtues will be used by the Powers of Darkness,' he called over the sound of drawn-back chairs and coughs, 'to conceal, or to make respectable, national crime. Every day, your felicities will become baits for others; your ideals, wreckers' beacons to betray worthy vessels — driving them onto the breakers of despair. And — amid the darkness — every false meteor of knowledge will flash' (coughing himself now, overcome by smoke and alliteration) 'and every perishing pleasure will glow, to lure you – the un-living and the un-dead – into the gulf of your graves.'

5

After their triumph at the Grosvenor Gallery and hearing from Will Manning and Benjamin Creswick of the excitements of Ruskin's address and its reception, Claire Stott had written to the Professor from Mr and Mrs Lavenham's seaside house suggesting, quite delicately, that his precept and their example in taking Betty Manning and her sister to the Grosvenor Gallery were complementary. She was not sure that she liked his reference to her 'blue-veined forearm' in his previous letter, and so had set her London anecdote into a consciously serious discourse — on the subject of poor people and the duties of her class to them, accompanied by a photograph of the four of them standing before The Mirror of Venus.

She had not expected the swift response which she got. That was both the fact of the matter and the subject of the letter — how he sought to make himself less busy by the rapidity with which he disposed of his business. Yet, therefore, he became even busier and, therefore, could not let Claire's letter stand until she was back home. If he did — she couldn't quite follow this — his failure to have dealt with it would leave him more preoccupied than the act of preoccupation which had given rise to his reply. For all the warmth and hurry of it, it was the warmth of hurry rather than the hurry of warmth. Ruskin's writing was hot, its content cool. He was very busy. The lack of Autumn daylight was the worst he had ever known. He wondered whether the best interests of Betty Manning were served by the kind of charade she had described — apparently for his approbation.

He asked Claire whether she thought expenditure of capital on luxurious dress tended to make a nation rich, conveying in a parenthesis his horror of cast clouts — of, in particular, handed-down finery. He touched on his notion of simple, but distinctive modes of dress in accordance with class or trade.

He appeared to Claire to have lost his sense of fun and was thereby diminished — and she hurt and rebuffed. He inquired whether she, and all other well-to-do ladies, should not be as he was, very busy. Since business should not negate reflection, he asked whether her mother knew what she had been up to — all of which (for he stressed that the friendship of Miss Stott was important to him), he wrapped up in an elaborately affectionate final paragraph or two, containing particularities of advice.

'Professor Ruskin,' said Claire to Mrs Lavenham,' treats me like a child, which I believe I'm growing out of.'

'He treats all of us as children,' said Mrs Lavenham, 'sees us as in his care.'

'Isn't that presumptuous of him?' asked Claire.

'For an ordinary man, yes,' said Mrs Lavenham, 'but this is how Professor Ruskin is — he feels responsible for us.'

'For us all?'

'For us all.'

'How can that be? What has led him to this pass? '

'He has a secret sorrow,' said Mrs Lavenham.

'But since I — even I — have heard of this (a hint of it, even before we met), it can't be a secret as far as most people are concerned. Has it become a public private sorrow, like Lord Byron's?'

'Nothing so discreditable,' said Mrs Lavenham, 'you are suddenly hard on the gentleman.'

'I am. For, as I say, I am not a child — certainly not his child. Why did he not get himself a family of his own and confine his attentions to them?'

'Because,' said Mrs Lavenham, 'he feels — and there is evidence in his favour — that someone who has no ties of blood may be more level-headed than someone who has.'

'And yet is he? Is he level-headed — practical? If so, on which topics? Carving porphyry? — I feel not. The nature of women? — I am doubtful. And the inferiority — for I'm sure he feels it — of the work of Mr Tissot. And the insults he offers to — to the likes of Mr Whistler?'

'Some of what he says is designed to make us think for ourselves, but — I agree — that there is a body of teaching which is meant — or is often seen as — paternal advice. You say you don't feel that at all?'

'No, not any more — he has written me a most provoking letter. He advises me to read my Bible and expresses his certainty that I have a coquettish ivory-covered prayer book, which should be replaced.'

'And have you?'

'Well, yes — But it was a present — and I believe my business — a present from my father, my true father; and I do not intend to solicit its replacement from the hands of the Professor, if that is his intention.'

'I understand your point of view,' said Mrs Lavenham, 'but you're something of an exception to the rule —'

'And all the better for that!'

— 'Professor Ruskin's young lady correspondents, I am told (and perhaps I was once one of those myself), sometimes like to be provoked, and they do quite often — or so I understand — find themselves pleased to accept a keepsake or two...'

'He further implies,' said Claire, not listening, 'that if I've either grown out of fairy stories or feel disinclined to write one for him — as indeed I do — then we are likely to be a disappointment to each other.'

'And doesn't he speak true?'

'He may well have done, but he has miscalculated my years both for my own esteem and for his doubtless fatherly purposes. Besides, as I say, I still have a father of my own.'

*

Claire was mistaken in the above assumption. Her mother had welcomed the opportunity for her daughter to stay for the weekend with Mr and Mrs Lavenham to get some sea breezes into her lungs even so late in the year, particularly in view of what seemed to be trifling illness in their area of the city.

Claire was called home urgently, but by the time she arrived her father's heart had given way under the sudden onset of influenza. His family received some consolation from religion — Claire covering her white prayer book in black velvet, but steadfast in her use of it — and the reassurance of more than adequate provision in worldly terms made by the late husband, father and lawyer.

Unable to face the Bloomsbury house, Claire returned sadly to Worcestershire — a convenience for Mrs Lavenham who felt a certain constraint in being the guest of even so respectable a widower as Mr Baker: she was wanted there to finalise the arrangement of the Ruskin and local material as the beginnings of the village museum and forerunner of the ambitions for the St George settlement at Bewdley. So both ladies were once more guests of Mr and Mrs Melville.

Claire Stott had forgiven Ruskin a little, and acknowledged that it was Mrs Lavenham, and not Ruskin himself, who had referred to him as in loco parentis. Mrs Lavenham recollected the conversation they had had and much regretted her remarks to Claire seeing them now as not only unfortunate but 'tempting Fate' — prompting Fors? Or, *Fors*.

They turned to the work in hand. Will Manning had a flair for display and had achieved with Creswick some expertise in woodworking. His exhibition cabinet was competently enough made, but what made it unusually suited to its particular purposes was the set of small recesses and grooves which he had fashioned in the backboard to fit exactly (without the need of securing bands) each of the small items — a nailer's old hand-hammer and pincers, for instance, as well as the assemblage of nails, arranged by Mrs Lavenham fan-wise.

Joseph Hill brought on extended loan to the museum the medieval tiles he had unearthed, together with the coloured drawings of them which Thomas had made. Good judges — including Baker's son-in-law Joseph Southall — declared that on the strength of this work — the sure symmetry of the drawing, the taste of the colouring — Thomas Manning might well go on to earn an art school place, with even part of the cost of his education being borne by the public funds. Though Ruskin might have disapproved of such a course of training for the boy, Joseph Hill's initiative was generally commended.

Hill's standing was further enhanced — with Mr Melville, at least — when he was seen, as that gentleman privately put it, 'to have lowered his sights'; observed walking out with Missy Governess. Claire, naturally, was a little dashed at this news — which confirmed her intention to make up — partly make up — with Professor Ruskin; older men being preferable companions on the whole.

Claire's widowed mother travelled to Worcestershire to see the dedication of the cabinet to St George's purposes, at which Mr Baker presided with some words written by Ruskin, who pleaded that he was unwell (and, indeed, was unwell, though intermittently). Betty and Ann and Thomas and Will were there, too; Mr Baker insisting that they be paid not only for their artefacts on behalf of Professor Ruskin (as already agreed), but also — and out of his own pocket — for their attendance at the little ceremony, calculated at so many nails per half hour per head.

Mr Baker exchanged a word or two with Mrs Lavenham, on the whole a reassuring word about 'Alcestis'. The faces of Burne-Jones's society sitters had been grafted, for a number of years, onto this favourite nude model's artisan body. The head of Alcestis, therefore, would probably have been outside the requirements of his commissioned work, and indicative of some affection by the artist for the sitter. A good lady of Baker's acquaintance had found her, found her fortunately coherent, taught her resignation, but brought her some comfort. She died soon after.

'Better to be a nailer,' said Charlotte Lavenham, 'than a model. Yet the life to many seems an easy one, full of light and sparkle.'

'Probably,' said Baker, who was not sure, 'but I should tell you — because the Burne-Jones drawing has become special to us — that the woman, who was Alcestis, did not blame Ned, as she called him. Said he wasn't like the rest. Sent her money, when he had no obligation to do so.'

'I'm pleased to hear that,' said Mrs Lavenham. ' We did right then, to honour him, didn't we — whether we were four working girls for the day, or four ladies — to stand before his Mirror of Venus?'

Mr Baker did not share Ruskin's reservations about their coup. He replied warmly:

'I believe you did. No, I'm sure you did.'

Baker and Mrs Lavenham joined the Melville household and their Stott guests for tea. He was sensitive in his attentions to Mrs and Miss Stott in their bereavement. 'Forgive me in speaking of the sad event so soon after its occurrence, but I have to say that I do understand.'

He paused as meaning to say no more. But as nobody else took up the conversation, continued:

'My own dear wife was taken from me suddenly twelve years ago. It leaves loose ends... Your Book of Prayer enjoins us to beware of sudden death, I'm sure, Mrs Stott, your worthy late husband — whom I had the honour of knowing slightly through Mr Melville — was prepared in his own self, his own soul... but the family — though the suffering is shorter in the first instance — cannot easily have made their peace with events. Forgive me,' he concluded — 'for I am, of course, speaking only about my own experience of loss. Others may have managed things better than I was able to do.'

Mrs Stott felt that no one could have been kinder than Mr Baker: they proved a comfort to each other. He in his journeying from Birmingham to Bewdley began to call quite often. There was an unspoken thought in the mind of Mrs Melville that her widowed sister and the widower mayor might in the course of time come to share each other's lives.

But this was not to be. Mrs Stott returned to London, leaving Claire, who was now adept at managing both Sarah and Ruth Melville; the elder of whom even took up cuneiform carving, though confining herself to Ruskin's prefatory media of wax and wood.

*

Partly because of the furore at his final lecture, Ruskin had departed Oxford with a certain glee. Partly, too, because he was escaping from the city and the banks of industrial fog and sulphurous clouds which he anticipated would descend upon it as soon as the wind veered to the north. Even in Coniston, he would see industrial haze bring workaday Barrow to his doorstep when winds were in the west, and — worse — that from the cotton towns, when they were in the east.

But often there was no wind and the clouds sat heavy and sullen on Coniston Old Man and Yewdale — until something would set them whirling, whereupon they would pour into the Coniston Water, like that great conglomeration of stones and pebbles which would ultimately bury his boathouse, blank out his study window, submerge the topmost turret of Brantwood.

Inside, the house was dark. Outside, the skies were dark, darkening, darkling. Ruskin had yet to receive any sign from Rose, but Little Flora to whom his frisky letter had been principally addressed seemed on the mend, if not yet out of danger. Her father hoped she would be strong enough to reply to Ruskin soon. He had had no response still from Claire Stott to his letter about the pastoral interlude with Betty and Ann. He feared she'd found what he had to say churlish, whereas he'd meant to do the young lady the compliment of rational discourse. Perhaps he'd made this intention too obvious. Perhaps Miss Stott was outgrowing his image of her. At least their fallings out were over trifles, rather than because of the eternal verities — or lasting lies — of sectarian theology.

The heart of Ruskin still fluttered from time to time in some sort of harmony with those of living ladies; still very young, but old enough to have graduated from pet-dom. Collectively, they did something to compensate him for his loss.

But the dead Rose was his constant, the irreplaceable. His summum bonum.

He came across a drawing of her which he had made in 1874 near the end of her short life. She dwelt in the shadow of the valley of death — in remission from raving and decay. He looked at the swan-like creature and thought of the solid thirteen year old.(He'd had his drawing of her as she was then in his hand not long ago. It was somewhere — papers and effects increasingly disordered — somewhere in the room.)

Now, she was dressed, he saw, in grave goods; her hair in a snood, ears hidden, nun-like. Her coronet was of lilies of the valley, her profile Leonardo-esque and eyebrow-less, the eye socket sunken, the eye half-closed; the chin, nose, lip, contradictorily sensual.

'I never liked it,' said the ghost of Rose. 'It's morbid, don't you think? — has no spontaneity about it. No more than I had myself at that time, I dare say. But I still can't care for it, nor should you.'

Ruskin grunted slightly, as if into the other's pause.

'I'd rather have the strange one that you daren't look at. The one with my hair spread like a party hat or a paper boat. That was more honest. You must have it somewhere?'

He didn't answer. She conceded a point:

'I agree: yes, I could have eaten up my other-people's dinners on Sundays and quietly kept my biblical Sabbaths for Saturday…'

Ruskin pouted his lip in emulation of Rose in the drawing. He could attend, but not listen.

'It was a strange illness. I would not eat my food or my words. I thought and spoke contrarieties. Rather like your own less popular publications, St C, those, my unheard words? I can't make you smile, but perhaps you could lay aside that drawing of me? Stick to St Ursula, instead. Carpaccio made sure she kept her prettiness.'

Ruskin flinched as he looked over the careful, funerary image — dead as its white paper. He put it away and turned, as if obediently, to St Ursula.

*

The fringes on his bedclothes at night oppressed him. His Turners switched from dark to light and back again.. The days grew shorter. The low clouds broke, at best, into strange tattered fronds — Fell-tops bore mist caps, like locomotives standing idly, sinisterly steaming. He saw shapes in the mountain mist of cloudy dragons (the strangest things Turner ever drew), like articulated and armoured insect-forms, or prophecies of mechanised warfare.

When there was still an old English sunset, he would get it down, as a rare specimen, on paper very well — as may still be seen in the village museum at Coniston. It sickened him, as he worked, that it was the distant haze of sulphurous fumes which refracted the colours into brilliance. This, the only brightness in the blackness of the year — besides the glimmer of hope of help from Rosie — was chemical, explosive. He had not yet got to the point of stuffing his hands in his ears to shut out the sound of heavy ordnance, but what was taking place between the Russians and Turks filled him with horror at the arms manufacturers' profit — with pity for the peasant armies fattened up for slaughter by their landlords.

*

Mr Baker continued his visits and told Miss Stott of his early experiences as a voluntary teacher at a Poor School in the centre of Birmingham. They spoke too of the Professor and of his travels. Mr Baker's own public life had been too busy to permit him to take the path of Ruskin into Picardy and Savoy and Switzerland and Tuscany and Venice, but he had travelled on business — and, it transpired, for Claire led him on, by no means for trivial purposes or in well-trodden places.

'I'm sorry, Miss Stott,' he said after one such conversation, 'I seem always to talk about myself. I do not mean to do so; I begin — correct me if I am wrong — by conveying a real — and I trust not impertinent — concern for your present circumstances.'

'Indeed, you do, Mr Baker,' said Claire, 'and if the two kinds of interest seem to converge that may be because of a sympathy between your family and my own.'

Mr Baker had travelled in the Baltic — the information was given diffidently — Claire drew it out of him — on behalf of the Society of Friends. Though only a young man at the time, he had had the joint responsibility of overseeing a Quaker Fund for the relief of distress in Finland after the Crimean War. This country, a hapless ally of Russia, had been severely punished for the association, and Baker had controversially spoken out against bombardment of the Finnish Baltic coast by a British cruiser.

'Oh dear, Miss Scott,' said Baker, 'I trust you do not think me a blowhard or merely an old man who would be young and posturing again.'

Claire replied to the effect that she did not see Mr Baker in either of these lights, and that he should be less reluctant to speak of such matters than he seemed to be.

'Thank you, Miss Stott,' said Baker, 'though you can understand my guardedness about these old tales, whose purpose might seem to be to show myself in a "good" light — twenty years ago there was no such problem; for many thought what I had to say showed me in a bad one — it may just be that I recall my dear wife's response to me at that time. She had a sympathy with Finland from some connection in trade on the part of her family, and liked to think — and hear — of my involvement with its citizens.'

'And so,' Claire replied:
'"She lov'd me for the dangers I had pass'd

And I lov'd her that she did pity them.'"

'Oh, yes, thank you,' said Baker, after a moment. 'But, no, I can't say it was anything like being together in danger. I think it was the interest — some shared interests. Unlike Othello and Ophelia — Desdemona, I mean — we were happily man and wife for fifteen years — since which time, I fear I have been too busy — perhaps foolishly conjoined with the offices I have held — or which have taken me over — to form attachments other than to my family.'

Mr Baker's children were adult now, all but twelve year old Lilian. Baker and Claire were silent together. He looked at her and thought with approval of a lesson — some Shakespeare readings with that other twelve year old, Sarah Melville — which he had first quietly observed and then begged to take part in. He had played Bottom, they Titania and Oberon. Both Claire and he had felt themselves back in happier days — Claire undertook the reading for old time's sake — as, for that matter, did Sarah. Although there was only six or seven years between pupil and teacher, the latter (or so thought Baker) already displayed a competence — not a governess-y competence — very like that of a young mother.

George Baker, given the disparity in their ages, hardly knew what to think. Claire Stott, however, who had rescued herself from being a Ruskin pet, did wonder whether when she became of age, Mr Baker might still call on her in London — when he went there on business — and wish to talk to her again about his family.

*

Baker was twenty five years her senior, as Ruskin had been thirty years older than Rose — but Claire was easy in his company, as Charlotte Lavenham was with a husband of her father's generation. His good, practical manner gave security when — just at that time — class and income seemed no longer quite so unambiguously determinant of relationships. Claire found it easier to visit Betty at the forge with Mr Baker at her side. She was not the kind of heartless rich girl who would cut and run without a word to the artisans who had crossed her path, but it was not easy to return to what suddenly seemed innocent days. Baker's presence there kept things very pleasant, but less fairy-tale than hitherto — within the scope of what was judged possible. As with his public works, so his personal dealings.

She began to be less angry with Ruskin's reaction to the Grosvenor Gallery episode, realising that the momentary transformation was no more than that — save that it was an indication for Betty and her family that things were less bad for them than they had been, and a glimpse of a perhaps more equitable society in the distant future. Their present prospects, as they were, were poor. There would be little call for further 'individual-specimen' orders. There was no solution to their problems or any prospect for their craft, Baker had told her, except through giving over to machinery what they were doing — becoming museum pieces. As nailers, they could neither compete nor survive.

Claire asked a question, to which Baker responded:

'In Ruskinland? Perhaps. We can only hope so.'

*

However, the evening before she was to return to London Claire dropped in at the forge on her own.

'Yes, miss,' said Betty, 'I shan't forget you and the times we had. See there ' — and Betty peered through the smoke. On a board against the back wall was the same photograph of the four of them which Claire had sent to Ruskin.

'I keeps it in here,' said Betty, 'so the place feels transformed like into the Forge of Venus, though I don't suppose that Mr Jones would want to come a-painting here. No, I knows there's no future in nails no more, but Will's doing a bit better like, and we shall make do.'

Claire wanted to put her arms round Betty, but didn't know how to. Instead she patted her on the shoulder, caught Ann's eye and smiled, said what a clever boy Thomas was and how she'd watch out for him when he had made his name. And then it only remained — for she had the same idea as Ruskin had had — to give the baby a trifle. She picked up the bundle of clothes with the little girl inside, and hugged it in seeming clumsiness. But only because she was looking for a safe place to hide her bit of gold.

Into Winter 1878

1

In the early hours of one special day he dreamt Rose said Yes. Thereafter, Ruskin was in unusual spirits — uplifted, too, by news that the steam yacht 'Gondola' had broken down. He gazed onto the Lake and spoke quite loudly of the quietness of Coniston.

'As quiet,' he said, 'as a dog.'

Joan Severn knew Cousin John was referring to his special, well-behaved Brantwood dog, Maude. However, as the remark seemed a little odd, she instructed her husband to keep an eye on him.

So, later in the day, Arthur went for a smoke in the garden, then joined Ruskin in his study for some banter.

'Do you remember, Papa Coz, when we all fell in the lily pond at Matlock Bath? Not you yourself, of course, Coz —'

'No,' said Ruskin, 'I was ill in bed, as usual — missing the fun —'

— 'as well as missing falling in the pond,' said Arfie. 'Don't forget that, Coz. One of our party came trudging up the stairs, wet through, to show you what a state he was in — water weed and all.'

'Yes,' said Ruskin, 'But do you recall here at Brantwood ordering me off my own tennis court, because you said I was interfering?'

And they went over the silly story together — Ruskin re-airing several bon mots about the futility of lawn tennis and reciting a piece of his own impromptu verse on the same theme.

The pair of them laughed a lot at this, at the comical images, first of players distracted by the professorial eye, then (rather less so) at the sage's withdrawal from a place unsuited to his sagacity.

Whereupon — with the usual eccentric fluttering — a late cabbage-white entered the room and also became the subject of their mirth.

'You know,' said Ruskin jocularly to Arthur, 'I believe this little flying fellow was sent by that show-off Whistler to spy on us.'

'Eh,' said Arthur, fearing at first that the Coz was about to have one of his turns. 'Oh, Professor, you mean the fellow's signature,' he continued, relieved. 'The aesthetic affectation. He should write his name like an honest Christian.'

'But if he wasn't a butterfly, he wouldn't be here. We'd have missed the pleasure of the chase. See Tootles is joining in.'

Ruskin was soon across the room to join the cat, wafting papers:

'There was a woman, who called herself a medium. Claimed to be able to tame wild creatures, in the manner of St Francis,' Ruskin recollected, as he flapped the air. 'Used to have a cloud of butterflies about her. What's our best next move with this one?'

'Hm,' said Arthur, 'I think Tootles has taken care of that.'

Tootles having no further interest in the lifeless petal-thing; stretched and sat down gracefully, giving her tail a lick as she did so.

'Yes,' said Ruskin, 'but we could ask the Whistler chap if any of his spare signatures have escaped, as our cat has found one.'

They continued until bed time, making facetious comparisons between Whistler's pictures and cabbages; butterflies and signatures. They chose not to dwell on a slightly earlier Tootles' experience — a nasty encounter with a Whistler-esque wasp.

*

The next day things were different, though not as bad as Joan had feared. Ruskin was once more riffling through his precious Rose papers, because everything else that he might have turned his attention to was dark. The treasure trove of letters dazzled: gold as his Turner water-colours against the sombre hangings of his life.

Ruskin had been asked to wait until Rose was twenty one. Eleven years later, going on twelve, he was today more impatient than ever — unreasonably so, as she was dead and buried...

'St C,' said the ghost of Rose, 'don't go on so. I've told you before not to blame mama — my mama, not yours. I think you're becoming good friends with her again now.'

Ruskin looked up.

'I wish you could ask me how I was,' said Rose, 'because putting thoughts into words no longer hurts me. If you were able to set me the right questions, I might manage better answers to myself. As it is, I feel like some creature in — I don't know — some Irish folk tale, whose story I can't follow. I don't understand my part — here, on the edge of Heaven where (as I've said before) I think I am.'

Ruskin went back to brooding. Of Effie, his sham-wife, he had kept no relics, no mementos. Nothing; save (somewhere) a single pencil portrait he'd made of her — a cold skilful drawing at the time of their engagement, and a similarly cool poem.

'She was afraid,' said Rose. 'Your wife — well, not your wife — that Effie. If you were able to marry me — *able* to do so — after she'd left you, there would have been no grounds for her not remaining married to you. She thought her children would be impugned.'

'Marry me,' said Ruskin to the air. 'I was entitled to get rid of her. Marry me. You must marry me. They don't marry in Heaven? Then we must marry in my life time, if not in yours. You see St Matthew is on my side, after all. Set aside what you and I said before. Forgive me. But I must have your bond. Send a sign that you'll marry me.'

'I'll send you a sign,' said Rose.

'I think you'll send me a sign soon,' said Ruskin, 'a sign as clear as having my two most special letters to hold in my very ordinary hand. This first is the letter, this of all your letters, the only one which I kept back, the only one which you did not require me to return when we first parted. And this other, my 'star' letter, was restored to me at Broadlands after your blessed intervention.'

'I think so,' said Rose, 'It wasn't the medium. I think it was as you describe it, dear Crumpet.'

She, at ten years of age, had satirically canonised him as St Chrysostom, father of the church and founder of its litany — like some parody of his father's expectations that he would become a bishop. He caught himself smiling, even though the train of thought was so familiar, then recalled Leonardo's observation, that the image of a man who smiles is indistinguishable from the grimace of the same man under torture.

He twitched and sighed instead; was pleased to be brought to himself by the cat:

'Down, Tootles,' said Ruskin. 'You're not to make your bed in my precious papers. Not in my precious ones ' — Then, reading aloud the most precious of them, the first letter from his young charmer:

'DEAREST ST. CRUMPET — I am so sorry — I couldn't write before, there wasn't one bit of time — I am so sorry you were di/sap/Pointed — and I only got yr letter yesterday (Sunday), & we only got to Nice late on Saturday afternoon — So I have got up so early this morning to try & get a clear hour before breakfast to write to you, which you see I'm doing — So you thought of us, dear St. Crumpet, & we too thought so much of you...'

Once more, Ruskin felt himself both lifted up and affectionately made small and young, as he re-read it for the thousandth time.

Tears of joy came to his eyes, as he looked outward from what was supposed to be his work table out over the — arguably, sympathetic — now wet and grey prospect towards Coniston Old Man.

'No,' he said, to the abstract concept rather than to his tears or to the hills and their dismal weather, 'I do not believe in you. Nature does not have moods. You are an instance of the infamous pathetic fallacy which I have described — defined, defied — in Modern Painters Book 3, Section 5, page 201 et seq.'

He laughed an immoderate laugh, and began to call out, 'Et seq, etseq, etseq, etseq,' and to throw some of his papers — but not Rosie's letters — into the twilight, the twilit corners of the room.

That was where Tootles had gone, sensing an intervention, the possible consequence of which might be that she would be put out for the night.

Yes, there was a quiet tap. It was Joanie: 'Did you call, dear Coz?' she asked softly.

'Perhaps I did,' said Ruskin, 'perhaps I did. I know,' suddenly cheerful, 'I should like some tea and scones and very much that you would join me in consuming them. Also, I have a serious question.'

Joan looked at him and, guessing correctly, replied in one breath:

'Why, yes. There is still some strawberry jam in the larder.'

2

At times he despaired of his work, at times he was unable to get on with his work, at times he was inseparable from his work, at times he was indistinguishable from his work; and so through to the end of the year, with the weather marching down upon him, like the Russian army.

But he sometimes dodged out from under his personal storm cloud, temporarily abandoned his papers. He visited Matthew Arnold and was disappointed; he visited Gladstone and was reassured. He roused himself into initiative: commissioning engravings, purchasing mineral specimens, corresponding with Jean Ingelow, rebuffing pets, considering how to respond to Claire Stott, annotating margins, raging against pollution.

Much of his daily life continued into his sleeping consciousness, and gave him tedious work to do when he should have rested. There were increasingly vivid dreams, which he managed to get down into his journal. He read again the early letters from Rosie — strange child born to the real marriage of the La Touches just as his own sham marriage was beginning — he looked for shafts of golden light; he dreamt coded menstruation dreams, and more openly masturbatory ones, in which he showed his serpent to Joanie (tempting her in the Garden of Eden), and (as in his unused statement to the Proctor) 'proved his virility at once'.

In More's Utopia couples were obliged to see one another naked before marriage. Prudish Ruskin (for all his admiration of Byron and Fielding) would have shrunk from the idea, but had this rite been a social requirement between the Ruskins and the Grays, he would have carried it out. In which case either he and Effie would have fled from each other; or grown, she into the prelapsarian helpmeet he'd envisaged, he into the fashionable escort she would have preferred.

She should have been the same colour all over, like a statue. The auburn hair of her head, her stateliness (when clothed), the high colour of her face were well enough. But the dead pallor of her body, the blackness of its creases and interstices, the darkness of her curls, of her nether curls; and her blood in a chamber pot. These things were against her.

A hint of spun gold between the thighs would have been another matter, a fine dusting of faëry pollen, a delicate bloom like the fluff on a leaf or a stem, or the glowing vistas through distanced landscape forms of Turner's noblest water colours, or of the delicate limestone crevices (with fronds and mosses) of his own skilled depicting. What had seemed to him the Cave of Grendel (or Grendel's mother) might in another female form have been a treasure; a message for him alone, preserved between — as it were — plates of gold.

*

It was Christmas Day and he had separated himself from the family jollities of Joan and Arthur — with which he had been enjoyably much involved, until it all suddenly became insufferable.

Back in his room, the ghost of Rose spoke again:

'It's two years to the day since you got back that girlish letter — the one you call 'the star', St C. You thought it was Fors that managed that for you? If it was, you may know what that means, I'm sure I don't — do you? Well, maybe it was Fors. Maybe Fors — whoever or whatever that is — had a word in mama's ear. You know, St Crumpet — I don't think you heard me when I told you before — the spiritualists who said they'd seen me sitting next to you — are, what? — don't the Americans say "bunk"? But it was they who touched mama's heart.'

Ruskin looked up, saw nothing, read from a returned Rosie letter as a Christmas treat, as follows:

'So our thoughts are crossing I suppose St C, and I thought particularly the day before Xmas, and Xmas day evening, is it not curious? I was sitting on my table opposite to the window where I looked straight at the dark night, and one star Venus glowing straight in front. When I leant my head a little I could see the long line of lamplights with a sort of bright haze over them getting smaller in the distance, but Venus was the brightest light of all. I did not see Orion, or any other star, only her. And then I was thinking of you; it made me think of the guide of the wise men, His Star in the East, only this shone in the West. She looked down so brightly over the gaslights as if it was intended we should see how much purer and brighter, though at such — such — a distance, is the Heavenly light if we would only look for it, than our own rows of yellow gaslights that we think so much of. Yes, we have a strange Peace on earth...'

Moved, he could read no further.

'I believe I could manage to write to you just once more,' said Rose.

He wiped his eyes.

Refreshed by the tears, he changed his mind about solitary reflection at Christmas, put his letter back in its golden shrine, returned to the parlour games, and thoroughly enjoyed himself.

3

Into the new year with the Russians at the gates of Constantinople: Ruskin awaited his sign. What was happening in the Balkans was portentous, but it could not be to him what dianthus and vervain and the 'star' letter were.

Rosie's thoughts and his no longer seemed to cross. However, the father of young Grace and little Flora wrote again, in sadness:

'I think you will be pleased to know that your letters addressed to Grace and Flora gave my darling in her pain a bright smile! The smile lingered and the pain did ease a little towards the end. The dear child occupied herself in composing a letter to you in her best moments. My last letter, I know, expressed my earnest wish that she would survive to complete it. I thank you again for what you did for her, giving her her last smile and a little occupation. Alas, she had not the strength or time to carry out her intention, but as earnest of her wish to do so and a keepsake of a child who loved you, too, I enclose the envelope which she addressed to you — the most she was able to accomplish.'

When Ruskin had written to the child he had himself been worried to distraction by Joan's miscarriage. Joan was now well, for which he gave thanks. But the death of yet another child – but no, he shouldn't look at it that way – would be a sad exchange for that. For the letter itself was a beautiful thing, though it spoke of death.

When, however, he looked at the keepsake-envelope from the little girl, he was astounded and overjoyed. He became incoherent. Joan overhearing, forced him to take a draught of something and got him to bed where he slept a stupefied sleep.

Next morning he was calm and asked to see the envelope. Joan promised to get it him if he stayed in bed. Ruskin could not wait. He leapt downstairs in his night-shirt, and exclaimed to Joan:

'There — see there — my waiting is at an end. Rosie has written to me. I believe St Ursula sent it from the Galleria dell' Accademia.'

Joan looked at Arthur and Arthur looked at Joan.

'See,' said Ruskin,' the writing on the envelope is in Rosie's hand.'

'It is,' said the ghost of Rose.

'Yes,' agreed Joan, 'it is very like. But, Coz, I believe this is the cover from a letter written in the dear girl's lifetime. Your papers, Coz, are in disorder. You should let me take care of them.'

Ruskin, exasperated, produced poor Flora's father's letter and showed her the date.

'Yes,' said Joan, 'as I say it is very like the hand of Rose.'

'It is. I did — as I said I would — find a way to do it,' said Rose. 'This is important.'

Ruskin grabbed the letter, the envelope and some other papers and carried them angrily off to his room. He could see that Joan believed he had confused the envelope addressed by Flora with one of the many written by Rose over the years. (Little by little the old correspondence had been released to him by Mrs La Touche.) He ran up and downstairs collecting other envelopes so as to compare them — sure that this was a certain sign, if not the ultimate sign, from Rose.

He re-scrutinised Flora's envelope, holding it close to his still keen eyes. He knew Rose's writing better than anyone else; and eventually thought he could distinguish a difference in Flora's 'John

Ruskin' from the way in which Rosie used to write his name. The differences were very slight and uncertain save for the capital J. 'It looks as if,' said Ruskin to himself, 'little Flora's spirit had at first enough left of herself to make her own mark, but then — failing — Rose took over from her.'

Nevertheless, by the end of the day he had decided that, though he was right and Joan was wrong, there was still another sign to come.

*

The message from Flora-Rose, together with the surety of the dianthus and the vervain continued to sustain him in the preliminary scurries of the coming war. He spoke wildly of the role of women in Armageddon. As they had not restrained their menfolk, every one of them must be garbed in black. He abused the monarchs who no longer led their troops into battle, he condemned the churches for 'moral organisation of massacre.' He inveighed against particularities of religion; he condemned to their own hell fire all exclusive brethren: 'It doesn't matter a burnt stick's end from the altar,' he wrote in *Fors* for Rose, 'in Heaven's sight, whether you are Catholic or Protestant, Eastern, Western, Byzantine, or Norman, but only whether you are true.'

'How I'd answer you back,' said Rose, 'if I had my earthly strength! True, St C? True? True to Beëlzebub? True to anthropophagism? You, my dear mentor, are a good and faithful servant — of yourself! You serve the poor and wretched because their sufferings impinge upon the severities of your pleasure.'

Ruskin was far from thinking on these lines: took no more notice of her than did the snoozing cat in the corner of the room. So Rosie showed her face to Tootles, who jumped onto Ruskin's desk in alarm.

'Did you have a bad dream, then, my puss?' asked Ruskin, stroking her gently, 'puss-puss, Rosie-Puss'.

4

During January spirit messages laid themselves like bookmarks upon the catalogue of his Turners which he was trying to complete. It was suddenly a bright snowy day — and he felt better — but the messages were so ephemeral and confused he could make nothing of them. Dreamland and work sought his attention. A little sketch he was making of St Ursula's curls became three iron hooks, twisted and forged by an armourer or a Worcestershire nailer.

The Devil — the Prince of Pain — was in his gut: a gothic pinnacle and bracket resembled an erected gibbet. Or he was stricken with fear of rigor mortis from touching himself — and the maternal whipping which was consequent on that kind of partial death.

With my body I'd thee worship, Rose. He was Chrysostom. He was St John Goldenmouth. He was St C, he was well-buttered Crumpet held aloft in mockery of the host, he was the ghost at his son's wedding. But he had no son, so whose wedding was this? And who was the ghost? Ruskin's father had not attended the wedding. But this was a drawing and that was a ghost.

Effie, in bridal gown and coronal, recoiling into the arms of three attendants. The groom, that same John Ruskin of Glenfinlas, but swivelled to the right a little, with the same high wing collar, the same trouser legs (breaking over his shoes at the same angle), the same delicately measuring hands, but swung upwards from their position in the Glenfinlas picture into a semaphore of surprise at Effie's reaction. Someone had re-worked, lampooned and extended the portrait. Question: Who could that be? Answer: John Everett Millais, the same artist who had made the original.

He has imagined and drawn someone or something to stand beside the Ruskin-groom, perceptible only to the dismayed figure of Effie. The ghost. The ghost at the wedding.

It was a wraith, taller than mortal men, hovering translucently above the congregation, dominating his son. Stemming like a genie from cloudy draperies. Hands clasped hypocritically to left pap, eying Effie severely through optics.

The substance of the vision fixed itself in Ruskin's consciousness, became a series of lines, like smoke in the air, like shapes drawn with a smouldering stick against the night sky — which contracted into a pencil drawing.

Before him now was his father, living then, but as a ghost from the lampoon he could never have clapped his literal eyes on — Millais' sketch, which, though made for Effie's amusement and vindication, seems to find the groom innocent. The wraith bore horns upon its cadaverous cranium. And for the tossing, turning recipient of this vision, an ascription had been added, 'John James Ruskin, 1785-1864.'

If this, his father's ghost, was a false ghost? Ruskin, unlike the Prince of Denmark had no uncle that had slept with his mother. But his loving father had played the very devil with him, and also with Effie.

*

Ruskin got up and went through some devotional exercises; acts of exorcism, to rid the Devil of his father's face. He rubbed his eyes to clear them and the ensuing great purple blotches and after-image lights were like a meretricious painting, probably by Whistler.

'Beauty is in the eye of the beholder,' snarled his adversary.

Ruskin replied with a non sequitur for the ears of Rose, 'I could, I'm sure, fulfil my vows.'

But his bed stayed cold as the grave, if not as private — for its coverings were being switched away from him during the night and flung about his ears.

Tootles appeared before him, a household familiar. Her purposes were inscrutable. Withdrawing, she found a corner of the right size, and was hidden.

Rose appeared before him like Helen of Troy in *Doctor Faustus*.

Ruskin asked the arms manufacturers what he was required to barter, not for this animated dust, but the living Rose.

'Twenty years' silence,' said their delegate, the Devil.

'Far too much,' said Ruskin, aware of his own loquacity, 'I could not keep quiet for a half of that. Nor do I believe in you. Though, I'm afraid my bride does,' he continued, proudly, apologetically, 'So I might, after all, have to settle on those lines.'

The Devil did not answer. Ruskin felt a loss of empowerment; had seemingly not held the Fiend's attention. He spoke boldly again:

'Ten years, then. I speak also for Rose, my bride.'

The feigning Devil was quickly upon him:

'Eleven,' said the Devil, who like the Bishop of Manchester, seemed to be good at figures.

'If,' said Ruskin, 'there is to be so much silence, it has to be conditional: I must have an equal amount of active time — to work,' said Ruskin firmly.

'Work at what?' said the Devil, 'you didn't please your father and become a bishop. And you were rude to a clerical friend of mine.'

'That was why I didn't want to become a bishop,' said Ruskin, who was gaining strength from the consciousness that he was holding his own.

'Bishops are fair game,' said the Devil, 'Eleven years' work and eleven years' silence?'

'You can do better than that,' said Ruskin.

'No, I can't,' countered the Devil.

'Very well, if that is the best offer available to me,' said Ruskin.

'It is. So let's settle on 1889 to 1900.'

'For the silence. And then, finally, I'd die?'

'Absolutely,' said the Devil.

'In that case,' said Ruskin, 'I — we — accept.'

'Done,' said the Devil.

*

February had been the pagan feast of purification. It was the first of that month in the year 1878, and tomorrow would be Lady Day. Ruskin called out loud:

'Tomorrow it is Lady-day, when it will be twelve years, since you bade me wait for three. Rosie, my Rose, I am tired of waiting.'

*

In the afternoon of the next day, while Joan was out, Rose — tall but slight — Rose kept the promise which she had made, and made the promise which she had never made. She came to him as a bride in a white dress — there was a congregation with some recognisable faces, none of them hostile — she answered him; answered him in her physical presence. And, paradisaically, he matched her presence with his. His limbs became as weak as water; to flow as water, water as pure as water once was. Ruskin saw again the wild roses, sacred to Demeter, running in a cleft of Derbyshire limestone (as drawn by him obsessively); lost himself in her, in the vistas of Turner's Gates of the Hills. They were Adam and Eve in paradise, Hero and Leander before the parodies, Heloise and Abelard before the emasculation. So the signs had been true ones — dianthus and vervain from St Ursula, and Rose's handwriting from Flora. He had interpreted them correctly. His happiness was intense, his knowledge of it fierce.

It was now evening. A cold evening. He had retired to his room early, with a fight on his hands to keep Rose and defend her, to keep and defend himself, to safeguard his generative parts with their new importance. Not against those who'd attacked him or with whom he'd quarrelled and wrangled. Not against Effie Gray or Rose's mother or erring disciples such as Octavia Hill; not the Whistler-crew, the capitalists, the clergymen, the deserving poor.

No, it was the unreasonable and, even, the ludicrous with which he was threatened. The cats and monkeys of O' Shea's Oxford carvings had no more menace about them than Edward Lear's limerick drawings. Or, rather, they had just as much — stood layered, head to head, tail to tail at the edges of his mind. Orders of angels and devils in some great tympanum of the Last Judgement became Turner's drawn whores, displaying themselves again shockingly, tempting him to enter their stony genitalia, in a mockery of what was sacred to Rose and to Demeter. His Turners — brilliant — flashed before his eye or his mind's eye, then dipped their colours.

He was in the Rosslyn Chapel again, amongst its green men, its serpents, its masonic symbols; then caught up with the O' Shea travesty of it; terrified by the absurdity of gothic fictions — with their thunder claps and vaults, their gibbering and their skulls, their passé Jacobean legerdemain and simulacra. Nonetheless, terrified he was; and the temple of his reason was rent — as were the flagstones (floorboards?) beneath him: through which the smoke and smell of sulphur from diabolic trickery drifted upwards.

That it should be the dark powers he had invoked, the stage effects he had used, at the dénouement of his last Oxford lecture was not unexpected. (The clouds of his visible breath froze before his eyes.) Nor was a tinkling of bells and shifting furniture from the Broadlands séances. But that both Queen Victoria and Queen Gertrude (his real mother, Margaret, having been turned into a standing stone) should be of the Devil's party was — he laughed loud and long at it — amusingly based upon the proposition that he was Prince Hamlet (a Prince of Suburbia, who had spent his middle years in Denmark Hill) and that Rose (Ophelia) had got herself to a nunnery. He continued to laugh, until the Devil caught him by the belly and doubled him up.

Afflicted with stomach cramps, farting sulphur, choking with gun-smoke — for fear that he had — after all, after all — not succeeded in saving Rose from her half-life behind Christ beyond the frost flowers on his window — he struggled ignorantly, like Hamlet with Laertes (breaking away every so often, to make strange entries — revealing, inscrutable — in his diary, even now).

Earnestly, reasonably requesting Concordance, that Hamlet be given another Act so that he himself might live, or that Hamlet have fewer Acts, so that Rose should not die, he began to babble nonsense in his everyday cultured voice with a touch of Scots. Impelled to do so by the harsh calls of a peacock, which in his vanity he had introduced to the garden of Brantwood.

Georgiana Burne-Jones was a pure bastion against the principalities and powers of Satan; though, for a while, he could not remember who Rose was or where Rose was. Why was she not by his side? Where was her frozen breath? He recalled with sudden joy that they were now one flesh — there could no longer be talk of their separation. It was wonderful that she, being indistinguishable from himself, was unable to stand forth. Such was the consequence of the solemn compact made by them, each to each — on Lady Day and in St Ursula's sight.

As he had expected, he now shared Rose's belief in the Devil — and had to confront Satan alone because Rose was no longer separable.

Fortunate that her spirit was within him — her body even — not just her spirit-body. He felt his strength, his power to withstand, rising within his breast — beside the irregular beat of perhaps two hearts lodged there side by side — rising with the devoutness and exclusivity of his own upbringing and the narrow, steely vision of Rose's religion.

So Satan would be upon the both-of-them, the two in one, the duality. But their match would be a match for any devil. Everything irrelevant, irreverent must be excluded.

Ruskin had previously locked his bedroom door, he now barred it. He stripped himself naked — tearing his clothes as he did so — in the fireless room (fireless by his order) and awaited the Miltonic adversary, who — horned like his father in the lampoon — had the same smothering expectations and choking love as in reality, and would come propounding usury, like the Bishop of Manchester, whom he had put down in a recent number of *Fors*.

*

In the freezing February night, he paced the floor. His breath was frozen into his side-hair. Uncovered, all the soft parts of his body; nor any weapon against the Fiend, save a still strong arm. His hands could make a tight but not secure grip: they were chilled and becoming numb. He did his best to get some life back into them. There was a poker in the grate, but he wanted no weapon, no artificer's advantage. This was to be a fight of body to body.

And when he was victorious — as he would be, if there was no treachery from cousin Joan-Dragon — New Jerusalem would arise, without the miseries of book-keeping and accounts, the resignation of trustees, the bickering of acolytes. (He was improvising consequences, elaborating the deal with the Devil.) Then would St George's banner be raised high above Worcestershire. And then would flow 'a pure river of water of life, clear as crystal, proceeding out of the throne of God and of the Lamb.'

And there and then (This from the book of Revelation, got for ever by heart as a child — and so on, much more):

'In the midst of the street of it, and on either side of the river, was there the tree of life, which bare twelve manner of fruits, and yielded her fruit every month: and the leaves of the tree were for the healing of the nations.'

He was comforted by this thought; that sterility could become fertility, that broken bones could mend and wounds could heal — the wounds of the world and those he was about to receive from the visitation of Satan.

The Fiend suddenly sent minor spirits in a great pother of business. Ruskin ducked and wheeled away from hordes of owl and batty creatures. The poor forked hominid, John Ruskin, becoming accustomed to terror, grew stronger from the experience of it. Whereupon Satan despatched grotesque temptations; but Ruskin, strong in Rose, and Rose strong in him, stood impervious.

After which Satan changed his tactics: made nothing happen and no time pass. The shivers of John Ruskin were uncountable and uncalibrated.

All night long — and, it seemed, for many dayless nights he waited, until what appeared to be the first faint sign of dawn — a greyness, a grizzling — entering the room. Ruskin moved towards the window to scrape away some of the thick frost from the pane, to try to determine whether it was a true dawn, or some diabolical lure. His assumption was that if blackness had fled, Satan had elected to postpone the final encounter.

The frost was so thick as he tried to scrape it away, that his nails were ripped and broken with the effort. Using the last of the sense which remained in his dead hands, he clumsily lifted the sash to peer out. Upon which — in the way that an approaching steam-engine might seem to materialise out of its own steam — a presence manifested itself in the early morning moonlight which leapt upon Ruskin, and in one person, Rose. It had come from behind a cheval glass in the corner, and materialised in a sniff of outside air. Sharp.

Satan's nails — claws — lacerated their flesh. Ruskin fought back, his frozen hands — cold and inflexible as iron — trying for a mortal grip on the muscled throat to force Satan out of the animal carcase he had entered. Obscene china was broken; glass smashed.

Afterwards exhaustion. The naked and clawed, scourged man threw himself upon his bed — assailed still by demons and imps; and by leering witches, sprung from his bedposts (whose hideous visages Ruskin would later reproduce in a carefully-worked drawing).

The room grew quiet, though shrills and gruffs that set his chattering teeth on edge, were audible outside it.

At first Ruskin believed that his defeat of the Prince of Darkness in his animal manifestation, his slaying of that beast, had routed his other enemies. On the contrary: the Fiend had recalled them, added reinforcements.

Unrecognised and unrecognisable voices grew louder; until the guns sounded at the Gates of Constantinople. Whereupon, his door smashing down, John Ruskin was revealed naked and gibbering — alone but for broken remnants of Tootles.

He tried to communicate with those who struggled with him, to say, that though Joan and Arthur Dragon and the servants were pouring poison into his ear and manhandling him into the night of his coffin, the Turners which hung all about it, his princely blazons, had become more beautiful than ever before; radiantly, transcendentally beautiful. The Devil had given Ruskin back his eyes, before delivering him into the hands of the Dragon.

He struggled for a while, accusing his relations and servants of killing him to get his property, then, when he and St George had tried and failed to pierce Joan Severn's side (he could see all the Carpaccio lances repelled harmlessly by her scales), he allowed her to screw down the coffin-lid and lower him into the vault.

*

In the last hours before his encounter with Satan, Ruskin had written many excitable letters, some unsealed: as the warmth — for all the cold — and the commingling grew. The golden glow... He knew the communion of proven virility, sweetly accepted.

*

For a month he was insane, for two months weak. When he sat once again at his desk, a stubborn mortal returned to his work, he found a letter, he'd written, ready for sending. It began:

'We've got married — after all after all — but such a surprise!'

End Note

Ruskin was not well enough to appear personally in November 1878 to answer the libel suit. The action however went ahead; the verdict of the court being that, while his opinions on Whistler were well-founded, he should not have published them. Upon which Ruskin resigned his Oxford chair on the grounds that the office was 'a farce if it has no right to condemn as well as to praise.'

Between 1881 and 1887 Ruskin suffered five further attacks of 'brain fever' ; during which, 'through purgatorial fires the ineffable tenderness of the real man emerg[ed], with his passionate appeal to justice and baffled desire for truth'[1], and from each of which he recovered to be back hard at work again in a month or two, entirely, if often oddly, lucid. A passage from Ruskin's own account of his 1879 encounter with the Devil is on page 261 below.

Following a final attack in 1889 — after separation from another young lady, Kathleen Olander, who earnestly wished to marry him and who remained single during his life time — he was left able to do little more than write his name. And even that capability only at the beginning of his eleven years' silence; though he could smile and utter monosyllables.

He remained quietly at Brantwood under the care of Joan Severn, until his death eleven years later in 1900. He was then succeeded as Master of the Guild of St George by George Baker.

The facts of Baker's life, including the visit made to him by Ruskin in 1877, during which the professor observed two unknown female nailers in Worcestershire, are in line with the account given in the above narrative, though the personality traits attributed to him are conjectural.

---

[1] W G Collingwood, cited Ruskin *Works*, vol XXXV, page xxviii.

The real Baker became mayor of Bewdley, and went on to marry a young wife and start a second family. However, Claire Stott and her household, as well as the Melvilles and the Lavenhams (though the latter have some things in common with the real Allinghams), the Mannings and Hill, are fictitious; as are Ruskin's dealings with them. Other artists, models, writers, patrons, relatives, and Ruskin's cat have been referred to by their real names.

Where a printed source is given or implied, the Ruskin text is authentic, as are the letters of Rose and Effie. Millais' 'Ghost at the Wedding' is in the V&A, Turner's erotic drawing in the Tate. The Oxford lectures in the book represent Ruskin's views at the end of the 'seventies, and are based on press reports.

Though the Bewdley Museum was never built, the collection of the Guild of St George at Sheffield is substantially intact. From 1976, it was housed in a handsomely-converted wine lodge in Norfolk Street — appropriately so, given the origin of Ruskin's father's fortune in sherry. Unfortunately, when Sheffield's Millennium Gallery and Winter Gardens opened, the Ruskin Gallery was incorporated; a down-sized 'interpretative' version which displays very little of the collection. Those who wish to see Ruskin's work would now be better advised to visit the Ruskin Museum in Coniston village and Brantwood itself, or the Ruskin Library and Gallery on the Lancaster University Campus.

*

When John Ruskin died on Saturday 20th January 1900, *The British Medical Journal* immediately made public for the first time Ruskin's description of how he had fought with 'the Evil One' more than twenty years earlier. It appeared as a report headed 'Mr Ruskin's Illness Described by Himself' by 'H'. This initial is believed to signify Dr Harley, who was on friendly terms with Ruskin. A slightly fuller version than that reproduced opposite was tucked away (also in small print) by Cooke and Wedderburn in *Works* XXXVIII, p172.

Mr Ruskin's Illness Described by Himself

I became powerfully impressed with the idea that the Devil was about to seize me, and I felt convinced that the only way to meet him was to remain awake, waiting for him all through the night, and combat him in a naked condition, I therefore threw off all my clothing, though it was a bitterly cold February night, and there awaited the Evil One. Of course, all this now seems absurd and comical enough, but I cannot express to you the anguish and torture of mind that I then sustained. I walked up and down my room, to which I had retired about eleven o' clock, in a state of great agitation, entirely resolute as to the approaching struggle. Thus I marched about my little room, growing every moment into a state of greater and greater exaltation; and so it went on until the dawn was about to break, which, at that time of year, was rather late, about half past seven o' clock. It seemed to me very strange that that, of which I had such a terrible and irresistible conviction, had not come to pass.

    I walked across towards the window in order to make sure that the feeble blue light was really the heralding of the grey dawn, wondering at the non-appearance of my expected visitor. As I put forth my hand towards the window a large black cat sprang forth from behind the mirror! Persuaded that the foul fiend was here at last in his own person, though in so insignificant a form, I darted at it, as the best thing to do under the critical circumstances, and grappled with it with both my hands, and gathering all the strength that was in me, I flung it with all my might and main against the floor...

    A dull thud – nothing more. No malignant spectre arose which I pantingly looked for – nothing happened. I had triumphed! Then, worn out with bodily fatigue, with walking and waiting and watching, my mind wracked with ecstasy and anguish, my body benumbed with the freezing cold of a February night, I threw myself upon the bed, all unconscious, and there I was found later on in the morning... bereft of my senses...

    I lay like that for a fortnight, during which I was in a state of wild delirium, and when at last I began to regain consciousness, the most fearful thoughts took possession of me. Demons appeared to me constantly, coming out of the darkness and forming themselves into corporeal shapes, almost too horrible to think of. But even worse and more torturing than these were the fantastic, malignant, and awful imps and devils and witches that formed themselves out of various articles in the room. The knob on top of one of the bedposts... was continually turning into a leering, gibbering witch...

Principal Sources

1 Complete Works
The Library Edition, *The Works of John Ruskin*, ed E T Cooke and A Wedderburn, 39 vols, 1903-12. Particularly *Fors Clavigera* ('Letters to the Workmen and Labourers of Great Britain' 1871-1884, vols XXVII, XXVIII, XXIX); *The Guild and Museum of St George* (vol XXX); *The Ruskin Art Collection at Oxford* (vol XXI), and *Praeterita* (Ruskin's unfinished autobiography, vol XXXV).

2 Archives
Educational Trust (Whitehouse) collection, formerly at Bembridge, now at The Ruskin Library, Lancaster University.
Ruskin drawings and Water colours in the Ashmolean print room.
Guild of St George collection, Ruskin Gallery Sheffield.
City of Birmingham Central Library.

3 Exhibitions
Black Country Museum, Dudley.
Bobbin Mill, Newby Bridge.
Bath, The Museum of Costumes.
Birmingham CMAG, *The Birmingham School*, exhibition and book/catalogue, ed S Wildman, 1990.
Cheltenham Art Gallery Touring Exhibition,
Simply Stunning: The Pre-Raphaelite Art of Dressing, exhibition and book/catalogue, 1997.
National Library of Scotland, *Captured Shadows*: The Photographs of John Thomson, 1996.
Newcastle, *The Grosvenor Gallery*:
touring exhibition from Yale Center for British Art, 1996: book/catalogue, eds S Casteras, P Denney.
Ruskin Gallery, Sheffield, from Ashmolean, *Ruskin and Oxford*, ed R Hewison, 1996.

4 Diaries and Letters
Burd, V A (ed) *John Ruskin and Rose La Touche...diaries*, 1979.
Evans, J and Whitehouse, J H *The Diaries of John Ruskin*, 1956-59.
Viljoen, H J (ed) *The Brantwood Diary of John Ruskin*, 1971.
Bradley, J L (ed) *The Letters of John Ruskin to Lord & Lady Mount-Temple*, 1964.
Lutyens, M (ed) *Effie in Venice*, 1965.
Spence, M (ed) *Dearest Mama Talbot*, 1966.
Unwin, R (ed) *The Gulf of Years:* (R. to Kathleen Olander), 1953.

5 Biography
Barnes, J *Ruskin in Sheffield*, 1985.
Burd, V A *Lady Mount-Temple and the Spiritualists*, 1982.
Burne-Jones, Lady G *Memorials of Edward Burne-Jones*, 1904.
Dearden, J S *John Ruskin: A Life in Pictures*, 1999.
Dearden, J S *Ruskin's Dogs*, 2003.
Evans, J *John Ruskin*, 1954 (reproduces Millais' 'The Ghost').
Fitzgerald, P *Edward Burne-Jones*, 1997.
Hilton, T *John Ruskin*, 2 vols, 1985-2000.
James, Sir W *The Order of Release*, 1946.
Measham, D *Ruskin: The Last Chapter*, 1989.
Rooke, T ed M Lago *Burne-Jones Talking*, 1981.
Rousseau, J J *Confessions*, 1781.
Severn, A ed J S Dearden *The Professor*, 1967.
Thirlwell, A *William and Lucy: The Other Rossettis*, 2003.
Warrell, I 'Ruskin and the Problem of Turner's Erotica', *British Art Journal*, Spring 2003.
Whistler, J *The Gentle Art of Making Enemies*, 1982.
Whitehouse, J H *Vindication of Ruskin*, 1960.

6 Industry and the Pastoral Impulse
Beach, I *The Ancient Manor of Sedgeley* (Black Country Dialect), 2008.
Dodsley, R *A Description of the Leasowes*, 1778.
Kings, B and Cooper, M *Glory Gone* (Nailing in Bromsgrove), 1989.
Marsh, J *Back to the Land*, 1982.
Shepherd, R H *The White Slaves of England*, 1896.
Williams, N *Black Country Folk at Werk*, 1989.

Credits

Joan, my wife, was intrigued by the Pre-Raphaelites and introduced me to their work in 1950. We saw our first Ruskin water colour then, too — where it has been since 1904: *Cascade de la Folie*, in Birmingham Art Gallery. Without her, this book would not have existed. Jon Measham, our son, has again provided comprehensive technical support. I am also much indebted to Bill Berrett for the covers and overall design; and for enabling me to reconsider some technological anachronisms in the story; to my brother John for help with 'nailing'; and to Maureen Bell for copyrights research.

I have had the benefit of encouragement, reassurance, and reservations from other friends and former colleagues, including Shirley Duncombe, Janet Ede, Sid Madge, Hety Varty, Kenneth Varty, and Bob Windsor. It was appropriate, too, that the book should be tried out on Ruskin specialists. I am delighted that, with all the other demands on their time, James Dearden, Clive Wilmer and Janet Barnes were able to take this on. Dearden and Wilmer are the present and successor Masters of Ruskin's Guild of St George, and Janet CEO of the York Museums Trust.

Dr Dearden was formerly curator of the Ruskin Gallery at Bembridge; and Janet Barnes, keeper of the Ruskin Gallery in Sheffield. Thanks to Janet, I, too, was for a while able to learn about Ruskin in a practical context: given access to the Guild's collection to devise and guest-curate 'Ruskin: The Last Chapter' — a 1989 exhibition marking the centenary of Ruskin's final book, *Praeterita*, and the end of his working life.

Donald Measham was born in Birmingham in 1932, but has lived, taught, edited, and written in Derbyshire for many years. His publications include: *English Now and Then*, and *Fourteen* (both Cambridge); *Leaving*, (Hutchinson); *Lawrence and the Real England*, (Staple); *Ruskin: the Last Chapter*, (Sheffield Arts); *Twenty Years of Twentieth Century Poetry*, ed with Bob Windsor, (Staple); *Jane Austen out of the blue; Jane Austen and the Polite Puzzle; Fourteen Revisited* (all Lulu).